PROTECTING THE BOUNDARY

LA WOLVES DEFENSE
BOOK 4

CADENCE KEYS

Copyright © 2024 by Cadence Keys

All rights reserved.

No part of this book may be reproduced in any form or by any electronic or mechanical means, including information storage and retrieval systems, without written permission from the author, except for the use of brief quotations in a book review.

This book is a work of fiction. Names, characters, places, and incidents are a product of the author's imagination. Locales and public names are sometimes used for atmospheric purposes. Any resemblances to actual people, living or dead, businesses, companies, events, institutions, or locales are entirely coincidental. Any trademarks, service marks, product names, or named features are assumed to be the property of their respective owners and are used only for reference.

Editors: Happily Editing Anns

Manchest cover design: Kate Farlow, Y'all that Graphic

Illustrated cover design: Lily Bear Design Co

To every reader who has found me through my LA Wolves players. It's bittersweet to say goodbye to these boys.

LA Wolves Football Forever <3

PLAYLIST

"Close To You"—Gracie Abrams
"Something In The Water"—Lawrence
"Vortex"—Lizzy McAlpine
"Hero"—Charlie Puth
"Anything"—Griff
"Somewhere In Between"—Bazzi
"Be Someone"—Benson Boone
"Paradise"—Bazzi
"Free Now"—Gracie Abrams
"The Mountain is You"—Chance Peña
"Labyrinth"—Taylor Swift
"Death Wish Love"—Benson Boone

Listen now on Spotify!

ONE

Romel

There is nothing in this world that I love more than my daughter—not even football.

That fact is driven home as I watch my sweet, tiny three-year-old curl up on the couch, a small tear falling silently from her face as she stares at the television playing one of her favorite cartoons.

"She'll be fine," my mother-in-law says from behind me.

Reluctantly, I break my gaze from my daughter and focus on my mother-in-law. Larissa Brooks is one of the finest women I know, and I'm grateful she was able to move to Los Angeles after Sydney died to help me take care of Kaylee. My parents wanted to move as well, but I encouraged them to stay put in Washington. They're close enough that Kay and I can visit them, but not so close that I'd feel smothered by parents when I needed to learn how to be a parent myself.

Larissa somehow found the line between parenting me, helping me with Kay, and sorting through her own grief at losing her only child.

But even with her help, I still feel guilty every time I

leave Kay, especially now that she's old enough to be aware of how often I'm gone during the season.

I must not be hiding my feelings of guilt very well because Larissa steps forward and wraps me in a hug. "It's okay, Romel. She knows you love her, but you have to go to work. She'll be fine while you're gone."

I wish her words would soothe me, but they don't. Especially not when Kay comes first. Football has given me the ability to give her a better life than I could've ever dreamed of, but it's also the one thing that keeps me away from her more often than I would like.

Larissa steers me toward the door, keeping her hand on my back as she presses me forward. I could stop her if I wanted, but I wouldn't dare disrespect her that way.

"I was hoping I could run something by you," she says. "Kay is getting bigger and more active, as you know." I nod. "While I'm loathe to admit it, I'm not as spry as I used to be. I can't always keep up with her, which is why I was thinking maybe it would be better to get a nanny. I'll still help out every so often, but the nanny would be able to keep up with her better than I can on a daily basis, especially during the season when you need more help."

"A nanny?" I don't love the idea of a stranger in my house, alone with my daughter. What if something happens?

"There's a very reputable agency I've found. Full background checks—even going so far as to check fingerprints. They serve elite clients in the LA area, so you know they're going to cover their b-u-t-t-s to make sure that their clients don't end up suing them for all they've got."

Now new doubts fill me. "So all these nannies know they're working for rich clients?"

The last thing I need is some woman walking in here

thinking she can be a nanny for the rich and famous when really she's looking for a sugar daddy. That's never going to happen.

As if reading my mind, Larissa frowns. "Romel, please keep an open mind. This would be a professional, not some woman looking for her future husband."

"Good, because she wouldn't get one."

Sadness fills her light brown eyes—the same shade Sydney had, the same shade my daughter has. "The nanny thing aside, I don't think Syd would've wanted you to be alone for the rest of your life."

My chest tightens. "I'm not alone. I've got Kay. Plus, you and Jimmy are nearby, and I've got my brothers." They aren't brothers by blood, but they're my brothers all the same.

I don't know how I would've survived the loss of my wife if it weren't for Gabe Romero, Dom Smith, and Ty Russell—the other three members of what LA Wolves fans have dubbed The Fierce Four. They kept me afloat when grief left me hollow. They are the reason I'm able to be the dad Kay needs.

Which is why the thought of retiring at the end of this season fills me with so much guilt. It would be the end of an era, the end of the Fierce Four and the LA Wolves as we know it.

"Romel."

Oh, I know that tone.

"You know what I meant," she says, sighing heavily and shaking her head. But instead of doubling down on me not being alone, she gets back on the topic at hand. "About the nanny—"

"I don't know, Larissa."

"What if I did all the work? I'll hold the interviews and

make sure we get someone good. You know I love Kaylee more than life itself and would never put her with someone who might harm her."

That's true. If there's anyone I trust to make sure Kay is always safe, it's her grandmother.

"Alright." I give in. It's only for one more season anyway —not that I've told anyone that. "If you can find someone highly qualified and not psycho or money hungry or boy crazy or—"

She pats me on the back with a smile. "I've got it covered."

Then she pushes me out the door for my preseason meeting with the team.

Dom grips my shoulders from behind me and leans over my right side. "Who's ready to kick some ass this season?" With a squeeze he releases his hold on me and moves to do the same to Gabe, who's sitting next to me. Ty comes in after him and sits in the empty chair on my right, while Dom sits in the empty chair to Gabe's left.

"You look exhausted," I whisper to Ty as more guys on the team filter into the room for the meeting.

"Lana's sick, which means none of us are sleeping well right now."

He's got bags under his eyes, but he still looks happier than I've ever seen him. He pulls out his phone and shows me the latest picture of his girls—his wife, Lexi, and their baby girl, Lana. He stares at the picture with nothing but love in his eyes and my chest tightens. I never got that moment with Sydney and Kaylee. Sydney was so sick after

Kaylee was born, she could barely hold her without my help.

"I can't believe how big she's getting already. Time fucking flies, man," he says, still not looking away from the picture on his phone.

"Yeah, just wait until she's a threenager," I say, thinking about the attitude Kaylee got the other night that nearly left me shocked stupid. She's never talked back before, and I didn't know how to handle it.

He slips his phone in his pocket and shoots me another love-drunk smile. "Can't wait. Hopefully, Lexi will be pregnant again by then."

I shake my head and fight a small smile. "Have you cleared that with her yet?"

"She knows I'm obsessed with how hot she is when she's pregnant. She said I have a breeding kink and then smacked my chest." He still has that dopey grin on his face, and I can't even bring myself to hate him a little bit. He deserves the happiness he's found with Lexi.

I'll never admit to him how jealous I am. He gets the love of his life *and* his child. He gets to imagine a future with her where they'll have more children.

I always wanted a big family. Sydney was on the fence. We were both only children and knew we never wanted just one child, but where I would've been happy with three or four, she didn't want more than two. She said it wasn't good to outnumber the adults, and I couldn't argue with her on that.

Now, none of our plans matter because Kay will grow up as an only child anyway.

"Anything new going on with you?" Ty asks.

"My mother-in-law wants me to hire a nanny."

Gabe and Dom's conversation stops as they overhear my statement.

"A nanny—like a stranger?" Dom asks, immediately protective of his honorary niece.

"Yeah, she said there's an agency that would do all the background checks and stuff."

"I was prepared to scare the shit out of her future boyfriends, but I suppose we could intimidate a nanny so she doesn't do anything stupid with our Kay," Dom adds and I'm already shaking my head.

"We're not intimidating anyone."

"Not even future boyfriends?" Gabe asks and all three pairs of eyes are on me, waiting for my answer.

"Okay to the future boyfriends, but not nannies. Larissa would never put Kay in danger."

They all nod and murmur their agreement. Talking it out with them, even briefly, makes me feel oddly better about the whole thing.

Our coaches walk into the room, and I put aside my worry about Kay to focus on the meeting—and try to ignore the guilt eating me up that I still haven't told the three closest people to me that this is my last year playing professional football.

Meredith

I'm pretty sure I have gum stuck to the bottom of my shoe. It's not really what I should be thinking about, especially at this very moment, considering my boyfriend of nearly two years is breaking up with me in spectacularly awkward, yet diplomatic fashion. But each time I try to move my foot, the bottom of my shoe sticks to the pavement, and it's got me convinced I must've stepped in gum.

Who does that? What kind of psycho takes gum out of their mouth and just drops it on the ground like a heathen? It's gross. They couldn't wait until they found a trash can? There are millions of them in this city.

"Are you listening to me?" Cameron asks with that indignant look on his face that I used to find so cute. When did I stop finding it cute? Was it a year ago when he started making subtle digs about my body? Or was it around the same time I started questioning if I even wanted to pursue the postgrad degree necessary for the career path I'd chosen?

When did I start coasting through my life? I know a lot

of people get senioritis, but this level of apathy feels so much worse than what I've seen my friends go through.

"Meredith."

"Sorry. I got distracted."

He rolls his blue eyes at me. "Of course you did. That's part of why this isn't working. I feel like you've checked out."

I *have* checked out. I don't know when exactly it happened, but he's right. I don't want to be in this relationship anymore, and I suspect I haven't for a long time.

When I first met Cameron at the end of sophomore year at UCLA, he seemed charming and funny. He was focused on his studies like I was, but also liked to go out and have fun on the weekends. Everyone thought we were a perfect fit. Hell, most of our friends have been asking when we're going to get engaged. But staring at him now, I feel the same apathy I feel about getting my degree.

I should feel guilt or remorse or *something*. But I don't really feel anything.

"I'm sorry," I say because I have to say something and I'm pretty sure this is what he wants. He wants me to apologize for checking out. He wants me to take responsibility for our relationship falling apart so he can feel confident about ending it.

But why hasn't he ever asked me *why* I've checked out? For the first time in weeks, a surge of something bubbles through my veins. Instantly, I don't feel numb or frozen or like I'm just going through the motions. The blood under my skin heats as anger spreads, the faintest pinprick of sensation much like the tickle you feel on your leg before looking down to find a bug crawling on you.

"You know what?" I say, taking over this conversation, because fuck him. He doesn't get to make me feel bad when he's been as disconnected from this relationship as I have. "You're right. This isn't working. We should break up."

His eyes widen for a second before he schools his expression. His throat bobs as he swallows and nods, looking down at his empty plate. "I'm glad we could be civil about this."

Sure he is. He almost looks disappointed. I can't help wondering if he's disappointed I didn't fight him on it, or disappointed he didn't get to be the one that actually ended it. He's always loved having the power in our relationship, and for way too long, I didn't bother to fight him on it.

I think I settled with him because so many of my friends thought he was the right guy for me, but he's not. This conversation should've happened a long time ago.

He sets down enough money to pay the bill. "I've got to get going. I wish you the best, Meredith."

"You too, Cameron," I respond, not moving from my chair.

He stands up and hesitates before seeming to make up his mind and walking out. I lean back in my chair and let out a heavy breath I didn't even realize I was holding. After almost two years, I should feel sad, but as tension fades from my shoulders, all I feel is relieved. After not feeling much of anything over the last six months, I'll take it.

The drive home only reinforces the feeling of relief. The farther away I get from the café, the lighter I feel.

"Dad?" I call out when I get home.

After I graduated a few months ago, I moved back home with my dad. My college roommates were all moving for jobs or getting their own apartments with partners, and it didn't make sense for me to get my own lease when I didn't have a job—or any postgrad plans for that matter—lined up.

I got a degree in kinesiology because I've wanted to be a

physical therapist since I got a knee injury playing soccer in high school and became fascinated with the power of helping others heal. But then, when it was time to apply for grad programs, I froze. I questioned if this was really what I wanted to do for the rest of my life. What if there was something out there that I'd be better at, or that might pay more, or would be more fulfilling? I was filled with what-ifs and self-doubt that became debilitating.

I started going through the motions and sticking with what felt familiar because it was safe, and compared to the scary unknown of my life after college, safe seemed pretty good.

But now I'm wondering if maybe it's time to figure out what's next, as scary as that is.

I could take a gap year, try doing something else for work in the meantime, and figure out if I can find the love and passion for physical therapy that I had before. I'm basically doing that anyway, except for the finding a job part.

Bolstered by the thought of finally having a plan, I head into the kitchen on the hunt for my dad.

"Dad!" I shout.

Still no response, which means only one thing. If he's not in the kitchen, he's usually in the garage. I head out the back door and down the stone walkway my dad put in when I was fourteen. The garage door is cracked open, and inside I hear a muttered curse and the clanking of tools. Biting back a laugh, a smile pulls at my lips for the first time all day. Pushing the door open all the way, I find my dad bent over the front of an old convertible he's been "restoring" for at least a decade, if not longer. He's always been a tinkerer, and cars are his passion, with food a close second.

I have to dodge some car parts before I finally reach

him, and then rest my elbows on the side as I duck my head under the hood to see what he's looking at.

"Hey, Princess, how's Cameron?" he asks, never taking his eyes off the bolt he's trying to tighten.

"We broke up."

He pauses, his whole body freezing slightly before he glances at me. Before he can ask, I reassure him. "I'm okay, Dad. That relationship ran its course anyway."

He stares at me for a beat longer, assessing if I'm telling the truth. When he's sure I am, he resumes his work. "I never liked him anyway."

I smile, even as my heart twinges a bit. "Sure, Dad."

"I mean it. He was always so focused on himself and his own successes."

He was, but at the beginning I liked that about him. His drive was attractive to me.

Changing the subject, I ask, "What do you want for dinner? I was thinking fajitas."

"Sounds good to me."

I push away from the car and head back inside to start cooking. As I stand in the kitchen I grew up in, I get a familiar, small pang in my chest. It's moments like this—days like this—when I wish my mom was still alive. Would she have been glad I broke up with Cameron? Would she have tried to talk me out of dating him in the first place?

I love my dad. He's my best friend and always has been because it was always just the two of us. But he wasn't great with heavy emotion, and I wonder how different I'd be if I'd had a mom growing up. If my own hadn't died due to complications in childbirth, or even if my dad had been able to move on and find someone else to fill that role for me. Would I feel as lost as I do now?

I push that thought aside and get to work making dinner

because I can't change the past, but I can make sure my dad eats. Whenever he's tinkering, he gets so focused, he could spend a whole day out there and not realize he's starving until he's shaking and about to pass out.

While I prep the ingredients, I think about what jobs I could do over the next year until I figure out my long-term plans. Most of my experience in high school was babysitting. In college, I worked in a café, but I'd rather not do customer service again. As I'm getting the peppers in the skillet, I remember my friend Amanda took an au pair job in France. She argued she was using her French minor so it was worthwhile. The idea of going abroad doesn't hold a lot of appeal. I stayed in state for college because I like being close to my dad. I'm all he has and want to make sure I can still see him regularly no matter what job I choose. But I think she used an agency, and maybe that'll be the fastest way to get my foot in the door for a steady job.

As the peppers cook, I send a quick DM to Amanda on social media.

> Hey, hope you're enjoying France!
> Question, did you say you worked with an agency to get your job?

I don't expect her to respond right away, but then my phone vibrates with a message from her.

AMANDA

> Bonjour! Ya, I worked with Lacey Wilde at the Wilde Child Care Agency.

> Do they only find au pairs? I'm looking for a nanny job, but would still like to stay in LA.

AMANDA

Def reach out. I'll email her and let her know I referred you. They work with elite clients in the LA area and internationally, so I bet they could find you a nanny job in a heartbeat.

We chat back and forth a little longer about her experience with her family in Paris and my recent breakup with Cameron while I finish cooking. But once the food is done and I holler out to my dad, I grab my laptop and get to work researching nanny gigs and emailing Lacey Wilde.

For the first time in months, excitement courses through my veins. I have a goal in mind and a potential job opportunity that I'll actually enjoy while I sort myself out.

It's amazing how much can change in a day.

THREE

Romel

"And then the princess lived happily ever after."

I hold open the last page of the latest fairy tale Kay's obsessed with because I know she loves looking at the picture. She's snuggled under her lavender comforter with daisies on it, her eyelids getting heavy with sleep. I brush her hair away from her face even as a pang stabs my heart.

She looks so much like Sydney. She has the same light brown skin tone and the same corkscrew curls. If it weren't for Larissa teaching me how to do Kaylee's hair, it would've been a disaster.

Some days I'm grateful she looks so much like her mother and will always have that connection to her. Other days it feels like being stabbed in the gut repeatedly. Not that I know what that actually feels like, but I imagine it's about as painful as grief.

She gets a little furrow between her brows like she always gets when she's got something on her mind. "What are you thinking about, Sweetie?"

"Are you going to be gone a lot again?"

Now my heart hurts for a completely different reason.

"I'll be gone about the same as last season, but you know I'll always rush home to be with you, and Grammy's already said she'll bring you to a game if you want."

She hasn't been to many, but she always loves getting to watch my games, and she enjoys them more the older she gets.

Her face shutters and she burrows deeper under her covers. "Okay," she whispers.

For all that she looks like her mother, she acts just like me. I shut down instead of facing hard feelings, and I wonder how much I'm screwing her up already, even when I try to do my best by her.

"You know I love you, right?"

"Yeah, Daddy." Her voice is quiet and I know it's not just from being tired, but I don't know how to make it better.

"Good night, Kay," I say, dropping a kiss to her forehead.

"Night, Daddy," she murmurs before closing her eyes and rolling over.

I make sure her night-light is on before I turn off the lamp on her nightstand and leave the room. I close the door and then walk to my room at the end of the hall, turning off the hallway light on my way.

Instead of getting ready to go to sleep, I sit heavily on the edge of my bed and stare at my hands. My mind races as that feeling of helplessness settles on my shoulders. I want to be the best father I can be for Kay, but every day I feel like I've failed her in some way.

If Syd were here, she'd know what to do.

I lift my head and grab the picture that's been on my nightstand since she put it there when we first moved into this house. In it, Sydney's laughing, her gorgeous smile wide, her eyes bright. She radiated happiness. It was the first thing about her that drew me in when we met in college.

A tear I would never let escape in front of anyone else slides silently down my face before I brush it away. "I miss you, Sydney," I whisper, my voice hoarse with the emotions I try to keep buried during the day. "We were supposed to do this together. I don't know how to be everything she needs. I don't know what I'm doing."

I don't know how many times I've had this conversation with this picture, wishing with everything in my soul that I could hear Sydney just one more time. Just to give me an answer. To tell me how to do this single parent thing so I don't screw up our daughter. So I could tell her I love her.

I'll always love her.

Sydney and I met our freshman year of college at the University of Washington. We had the same biology seminar, and out of hundreds of students in that room, she sat down in front of me. I think I fell for her the first time I saw her, and I was a goner for her from that moment on. I asked her out after that first lecture, and by some miracle, she said yes.

We were inseparable after that. She was at every home game and some of my away ones. She was sitting next to me when I was drafted to the NFL, and then when I was traded to the Wolves. We got married right out of college and found out she was pregnant with Kay about a year after we'd moved to LA. She was so excited to hold Kay and show her the room she designed for her—the mural she'd painted of a meadow with daisies on one side and a forest with hidden fairies on the other. She stocked the room full of her favorite books growing up, and we had names for a boy and a girl picked out before our first anatomy scan.

And then about two weeks after that scan, she started not feeling well. She was worried about the baby so she went to go get checked out. Her doctor was concerned about her bloodwork from the lab and sent her to get more tests. And then we got the news that rocked the very foundation of my life.

She had cancer.

Then it got worse when they gave her two choices—terminate the pregnancy and start an aggressive approach to try to fight the fast-spreading cancer, or carry out the pregnancy and risk that the cancer would advance too far for them to save her.

It was our first real fight. I wanted her to pick herself and she refused. I tried to rationalize with her that we could maybe have another baby, but there would never be another her. She didn't talk to me for a full day before I caved—if my time with her was limited, I couldn't justify wasting a second.

What was supposed to be a joyous time in our lives became somber and filled with uncertainty. She was in more pain as the pregnancy progressed, and we had to do a C-section because she didn't have enough strength to push.

I'll never forget the moment I placed Kaylee in her arms—the love that filled her eyes before the tears. "She's perfect," she whispered.

Then she looked at me. "Look what we made, Romel."

I'm ashamed to admit I struggled to look at Kay for those first few days, especially when Syd deteriorated so quickly after the birth. She only lasted a week before her body gave up on her and she was taken from me—from us.

I was left with a tiny baby and a shattered heart. It felt like being caught in a current under the sea and not knowing which way was up.

And then I looked at Kay—really looked at her for the first time—and it was like she was the light illuminating my suddenly bleak world. She was my purpose, and she was all I had left of Sydney. It was in that moment I understood the fierce and protective love that Sydney felt for her because right then I would've done anything for Kaylee.

My parents and Syd's parents rallied around me. Then Gabe, Dom, and Ty were there. We'd been close before then—the way teammates usually are—but it was when they got me through the darkest days of my grief that solidified our brotherhood.

But grief, I've learned, is a fickle thing. It's not something you go through once and make it out the other side. Like the cancer that killed my wife, it poisons every moment with a bittersweet tang. Nothing is as bright anymore. There is always the sense that someone is missing, that I'm not quite whole anymore and never will be. That every memory made would look different if she was still here.

I've learned how to harness my emotions over the years and use them to push myself to be the best on the field. I lay it all out there and then come home to Kay slightly lighter than when I left, even if I always feel it creeping in the background.

Which is why the decision to retire has never been an easy one.

Do I want to spend more time with Kay? One thousand percent yes.

But then where will my grief go? What will help me expel all the loss, anger, and loneliness that cling to my bones and only diminish when I'm on the field?

And who will I become then?

FOUR

Meredith

Double-checking the address from the nanny agency on my phone, I stop in front of a large iron gate with a security guard booth next to it. The road beyond the gate swerves to the right and out of sight, hiding the house—or houses—beyond it. No wonder Lacey Wilde had been so thorough with her initial interviews and background checks. I thought maybe it was a little much for a nanny job, but Amanda reminded me that she serves an elite clientele only and wouldn't even pass my name on to interview with individual clients until I'd passed her rigorous vetting process.

"Driver's license," the gate guard says, holding out his hand. I grab my purse from the passenger seat, and after pulling it out of my wallet, I hand over the identification.

He goes into the booth behind him and makes a phone call. Who are these people? Maybe I'm in over my head. Am I interviewing for a family where I have to be constantly monitored by a bodyguard while watching the kids? This is a lot more than I expected.

The guard comes back out of the booth and hands me

my license. "You're cleared. Once the gate opens, follow the road in and it'll be the fifth house on the right."

So, it's a very high-end gated community and not an individual house. Okay, that makes a little more sense and makes me feel slightly less intimidated.

What he should've explained was that even from the gate, it's another seven minutes before I get to the house because of how spread out all of the homes are. I follow his directions and pull into the fifth driveway. The house has a modern black painted exterior with lush greenery surrounding it. The yard is well maintained, and I don't expect any less for this neighborhood. I get out of my car and walk to the front door, trying to calm the erratic beating of my heart. I'm much more nervous than I thought I'd be for a nanny job.

I ring the doorbell and wait. Laughter—the kind that only comes from happy little kids—filters through the closed door and brings a smile to my face. When the mahogany wood door swings open, a woman answers. The wrinkles around her eyes are prominent as she smiles at me. There's gray in her shoulder-length black hair, which is the only other sign of her age. Immediately, I feel at ease with her.

"Hi, I'm Meredith Gable. I'm here for the nanny interview."

"Of course. I'm Larissa Brooks." A child's giggle comes from behind her and her smile widens. "And this little nugget is my granddaughter, Kaylee."

A little girl who can't be much older than three or four looks around her grandmother's legs, most of her body still hidden. Her light brown eyes almost sparkle as she watches me with curiosity. Her curly hair is up in two pigtails, and she's got a smudge of what appears to be jelly on her cheek.

I squat down. "Hey, Kaylee. I'm Meredith. It's so nice to

meet you." I can't help smiling at her because she's absolutely adorable.

She glances up at her grandma and then back at me, and her lips tilt up in the shyest smile I've ever seen. "Hi," she whispers.

"Why don't you come on in and we'll get started on the interview," Mrs. Brooks says.

I stand and follow them through the house which is so much warmer on the inside than it appears on the outside. Everything is in the same mahogany wood as the door, or bright white. It feels cozy and welcoming, while the outside felt dark and imposing.

Mrs. Brooks leads me to the living room, and I take a seat on a dark green couch. It's the only pop of color in the room, and I must stare at it too long because Mrs. Brooks says, "My daughter loved having random colorful furniture to break up the wood and white."

It's the use of past tense that catches my attention and my stomach clenches.

Her eyes turn down and her hand runs over the top of Kaylee's head. "She passed away shortly after Kay was born."

I swallow thickly and look at Kaylee. She's probably still too young to fully grasp the loss, but she'll understand it soon. I was five when I first truly felt the loss of my mother. I'd been in kindergarten and a boy had asked why my family drawing only had me and my dad in it. I'd never thought all that hard about it before I started school.

I want to ask more, but I know how personal that kind of loss can be. So, instead, I say, "I'm so sorry. I lost my mother when I was born."

Mrs. Brooks's eyes widen in surprise and her mouth parts. "You did?"

I nod.

"I'm so sorry for your loss." She says it the way people do when they've also experienced great loss and know those words won't offer much comfort, but it's the least you can say. She glances down at Kaylee before sitting down across from me and pulling her into her lap.

"So, Meredith, why don't you tell us a little bit about yourself."

"Well, I'm a southern California native and just graduated from UCLA with a degree in kinesiology. I babysat kids ranging from two to ten throughout high school and occasionally during college. I've got my First Aid and CPR certification. In my free time, I love being active—hiking, playing sports, going to the beach, things like that."

"Do you also watch sports?" Mrs. Brooks asks, and there's a weight to the question like my answer will either work in my favor or against me.

"I do occasionally with my dad. He's a big baseball and football fan."

"An LA Wolves fan?"

I smile fondly and nod. "Pretty much any local team has my dad's die-hard support."

"And if you met a football player? How would you react?"

I think I get why she's asking. Houses like this one are usually reserved for celebrities, and in LA that can definitely include athletes. "I'm not as big of a football fan as I am baseball, so I would probably react like I'm meeting anyone else. Now if I met a Dodgers player, I might get a little fangirly."

Her shoulders relax and she carries on asking questions. The interview lasts for another hour, and by the end of it, I'm not even sure she's interviewing me anymore because we're talking about all kinds of things that don't seem to have to do with the job, like my last hike or my favorite bookstore that's a hole in the wall in one of the many strip malls around Los Angeles.

"Well, Meredith, I think you've answered all of my questions. Do you have any questions for me?"

"Actually, I have a question for Kaylee, if that's okay?"

Kaylee has been sitting quietly on her grandmother's lap the entire time, watching me with keen eyes that I suspect see a lot more than the adults around her think. But unlike most children I've met her age, she hasn't squirmed or shown any desire to get down and play. She watched and listened like a small adult.

But at my statement, she perks up.

"What's your favorite thing to do?"

"Color," she says, her voice still soft although she's no longer whispering.

"What's your favorite thing to color?"

She hops down and runs over to a small kids' table in the corner of the room. She grabs a piece of paper and comes running back. It's a picture of a very popular Blue Heeler cartoon.

My smile grows. "Can I tell you a secret?"

She nods slowly and leans forward when I do.

"I love this show."

Her face lights up with a huge smile, and I swear my heart melts into a puddle on the floor. I smile wide at her and spend the next few minutes talking about the show with her. I'm sure Mrs. Brooks is watching, but my attention is focused solely on the sweet little girl who I know without a doubt I'll fall in love with if I get this job. It would be impossible not to.

She also reminds me a bit of myself when I was little. Quiet and reserved, but very observant and curious.

When our conversation reaches a natural lull, Mrs. Brooks says, "I wanted to make sure you understand this would be a live-in nanny position. My son-in-law has to go out of town for work fairly often, and it'd be best to have someone living here to make things easier on Kaylee."

"I understand, and living here wouldn't be a problem. I'm living back at home with my dad now."

She smiles. "Great. We have a few more interviews this afternoon, but we'll make a decision by the end of the week and give you a call either way."

I love how she includes Kaylee in the process. "Sounds great. It was so wonderful to meet you both."

"You too," she says as she walks with me to the door.

I turn back and squat down again. "It was nice to meet you, Miss Kaylee."

Her smile is the widest I've seen it yet, and it makes me feel ten feet tall because I get the sense she doesn't smile this big for just anyone.

"Bye, Miss Mere."

I laugh softly at the shortened version of my name. To be fair, Meredith is probably hard for a three-year-old to say. Then I walk out and leave, hoping it won't be the last time I get to see that sweet little girl.

Romel

On my way home from practice, I swing by the store to pick up more eggs so I can make Kay breakfast tomorrow morning. While I'm there, I decide to detour down the cookie aisle to grab her favorites, knowing how her face will light up when she sees them.

My stomach's been in knots all day knowing that Larissa was running nanny interviews. I'm still not one hundred percent sure about having a stranger live with us—even if they'll be in the guesthouse and not in the main house. I've kept the circle of people I trust with Kaylee relatively small, and opening it up to anyone else is uncomfortable. But it's just for this season—that's what I keep telling myself. At the end of the season, I can fire the nanny and we can go back to how it's always been.

I turn the corner and stop in my tracks when another person collides into me. A feminine "oomph" catches my attention before I hear the clatter of her items falling onto the ground. Fortunately, my eggs are unharmed.

"Oh my gosh, I'm so sorry," she says, ducking down

before I can see her face. Her black hair falls in soft waves around her.

I find myself squatting down to help her. "It's okay. I should've been paying attention to where I was going. Here," I say, handing her the box of tampons she dropped. Pink instantly floods her cheeks, and then she bursts into laughter and sits back on her heels, finally looking up at me for the first time.

My breath gets stuck in my chest as her dark brown eyes meet mine. They sparkle with a lightness that draws me in. Her flushed cheeks stand out on her smooth, fair complexion, and I lose my train of thought when she laughs and shakes her head at the situation.

"Sorry," she says, trying to compose herself. "This is just something that would totally happen to me."

"Literally running into someone at the grocery store?" I ask, composing myself. I don't know what the hell that just was, but it was weird.

Her eyes shine happily. "Yeah," she says. "And that a hot guy would hand me my box of tampons."

Her eyes go wide at her slip, and her cheeks flush a deeper pink.

I ignore her "hot guy" comment. "Tampons don't scare me. You're all good."

I used to buy Syd her tampons all the time when she needed them. "Do you need a hand getting up?"

I don't wait for her to answer before I extend my hand, and she takes it with a grateful smile. Once she's back on her feet, she says, "Thanks. Sorry again for bumping into you."

I shrug, uncomfortable with how I responded to her just now. I don't react to women anymore, and I can't figure out why this stranger had such an instant effect on me, but I'd rather brush it off and get on with my shopping so I can get home to Kay. "I think we're both at fault. Have a good one." I walk down the aisle and snag Kay's favorite cookies before heading to check out.

The whole drive home, I can't stop thinking about the woman. I don't know why. It wasn't like we interacted that long, but for some reason I keep seeing flashes of her flushed cheeks and those deep brown eyes that seemed filled with such happiness, even when she was laughing at herself.

When was the last time my eyes had that kind of shine?

When I get home, I hurry inside and smile when I hear my daughter's feet slapping against the hardwood floors. "Daddy!" she squeals, launching herself straight into my waiting arms.

I hug her tight. "Hey, baby girl. How was your day with Grammy?"

She pulls back with that smile on her face that always makes my day better. "Good."

Larissa walks up, her own smile filling her face. "I think I found the perfect nanny."

"Did you get a lot of people to interview?"

"We had five that were cleared through the agency. Three of them were terrible. They didn't engage with Kay at all and didn't answer any of my questions well."

"So out of the two that did, you thought one would be a good fit for Kay?"

Larissa looks almost as excited as Kaylee. "I did. I'll show you all her info and tell you about her. Kay, why don't you go wash your hands so you can help your daddy make dinner?"

"Okay," she says, her little body squirming with excitement to get down. She rushes off to the downstairs bathroom that has her step stool and the foaming soap she loves while Larissa and I go to the kitchen.

After putting away the eggs and cookies I bought, I move to the kitchen sink, washing my hands while Larissa pulls out the fixings for pita pizza. It's been Kay's favorite lately. Based on her history, she'll probably love it for another week before she refuses to eat it for at least a month. Just when I think I know her favorite food, she decides she doesn't like it anymore and we have to find something else.

Toddlers are weird little creatures.

"Meredith Gable is the one I think you should hire. She was fantastic with Kaylee. She's more than qualified and I don't think she'll fangirl over you."

I huff. "That's a relief." But I'll believe it when I see it.

She chews on her lip, staring off in space.

"What?" I ask.

When she looks at me, I brace myself for something awful. "She lost her mother as a baby."

That's not at all what I was expecting. I grab the towel, drying my hands as I stare toward where Kaylee ran off to. "Do you think she'd be able to help Kay come out of her shell?"

It's been my biggest worry—among the many that come when you're solely responsible for the well-being of a tiny child. Kay's never been very outgoing, but sometimes, she seems to fold in on herself and I worry it's because she doesn't have her mom. Larissa does her best, but she can't be here all the time. And as hard as I try, I'm man enough to admit that I struggle to play both mom and dad.

"Kay gave her the biggest smile I've ever seen her give a stranger."

I sag back against the countertop. Kay rarely smiles for

strangers, so that's a very big deal. "Alright. We'll go with your pick."

I toss the towel behind me on the counter and cross my arms. "I'm going to retire at the end of the season."

Larissa's eyes go wide with shock. It's the first time I've said it out loud as a fact instead of a question on whether or not I should. Instead of feeling anxious or panicked about the idea of ending my career, I feel oddly settled about the whole thing.

"Are you sure?" she asks me.

"It's time. Kay comes first. I'll have enough saved and in investments that we'll be covered for the rest of her life. Hell, I've got enough that she'll have more money than she needs for three lifetimes. My contract is up at the end of this season, and I don't want to keep being away from Kay. Every season gets harder on her the older she gets. I don't want to put her through that anymore."

She steps forward and gives me a hug that I easily return. "You're an incredible dad, Romel," she whispers, her voice choked as she tightens her arms around me. "Sydney chose well."

Tears burn my eyes, but I walk to the stove and brush them away once she releases me. It wouldn't be the first time she's seen me cry, but I still try to keep it as private as I can. And Kay running into the kitchen gives me another reason to be glad I turned away. She's too dang perceptive for a kid her age, and the last thing I want her to worry about is why her daddy is crying.

"Alright, Kay, want some pita pizza for dinner?"

"Yeah!" she squeals. Larissa gives us both hugs and then leaves for the night, and I spend the rest of the night making pizzas with my daughter, dancing in the kitchen to kids' songs, and then ending the night with a couple of episodes of her favorite cartoon.

SIX

Meredith

The house is just as imposing as it was the first time I was here, but I know the truth of it now. As daunting as it is on the outside, the inside is warm and inviting and there's a little girl in there I can't wait to see again. I grab the coloring book I bought when I saw it at the store and head toward the front door.

I ring the doorbell and hear the thud of shoes before the door swings open and Kaylee stands there with a wide smile on her adorable face. I squat down and smile back just as I hear a voice that's filled with a mix of panic and frustration. "Kaylee Mae, what have I told you about answering the door without Daddy?"

A man walks around the corner and my smile falls.

No effing way.

This cannot be happening to me.

The hot guy I bumped into at the store—the one who had his large hands on my box of tampons—is the single dad I'll be nannying for. I silently pray that he won't recognize me, but my hopes are dashed when he stops in his tracks and recognition fills his dark eyes.

"You."

Fuck my life.

I stand and give him an awkward wave. "Uh, hi. I'm Meredith, your new nanny."

He steps forward, closing the short distance between us and wraps his hand around his daughter's shoulder, pulling her closer to his body.

"*You're* the nanny?"

"Miss Mere," Kay says helpfully and bless her because she totally breaks the tension.

"That's right," I say, smiling at her. "I brought you something."

"What?" Romel asks gruffly, a scowl on his face.

Oh boy. A scowl should not be sexy.

I pull out the coloring book with her favorite cartoon printed on the front from where I've had it hidden behind my back, and Kaylee lets out a squeal of joy as she reaches for it.

I squat back down. Her dad can be a scowly grump all he wants; I'm not here for him. "Want to color it with me?"

She nods.

"Do you have stuff?" he asks, his voice deep and gruff.

I arch a brow at him and he goes on. "Like boxes or anything. Since you'll be living here."

I gesture with my thumb to my car. "I've got a few suitcases in my car."

"Let's get you moved into the guesthouse before you guys play."

I stand up. "Actually, we should probably do formal introductions. It's useful to know someone's name before you live with them." I thrust my hand out. "I'm Meredith Gable."

He stares at my hand like it's going to bite him, and then

with distrust in his gaze, he grasps my hand in his. "Romel Watson."

My brows furrow. "Romel Watson...why does that name sound familia—oh. Ohhh!" It finally hits me who he is, and my hunch about why Mrs. Brooks was asking if I was really into football gets confirmed. "You play for the Wolves."

He nods.

"Cool. Well, nice to officially meet you."

He seems surprised that I'm not fangirling over him, but I wasn't lying to Mrs. Brooks in my interview. Football isn't my favorite sport.

"I'll help you with your suitcases," he says to me before he addresses Kaylee. "Why don't you go hang out in the living room while I help Meredith."

"Miss Mere," she says, and it definitely comes off like she's correcting him this time. I bite back a laugh.

Then my heart stutters when I watch this man completely transform as his expression softens and he smiles down at his daughter with so much love.

He brushes his hand over her hair, which is up in pigtails again, except this time one is higher than the other. "Miss Mere," he acquiesces.

If I thought he was hot in the grocery store, it's nothing compared to how attractive he is when he turns into a giant softy for his daughter.

"I help too," she says, her voice soft again.

The struggle on Romel's expression tells me he hates telling her no, and I can't blame him. She's too cute for words with her round cheeks and big, light brown eyes. Her complexion is lighter than his dark brown skin. I wonder how much she looks like her mother, and if that's hard for him.

Everyone used to tell me how much I looked like a perfect mix of my parents, and I think that often made it easier on my dad that I wasn't the spitting image of my mom.

"I've got a little suitcase with wheels if you want to show off your muscles and push it for me," I tell Kaylee. It's hard to deny her when it's clear how badly she wants to be helpful.

She turns to me, that big smile back on her face, and I swear it's contagious because I feel my cheeks pull up in an answering grin. When I glance at her dad, he's staring at me like I'm some kind of witch with magic he doesn't understand.

"Shall we get started?" I ask him, arching my brow.

I open my hand for Kaylee and she eagerly grabs it, and then I turn without bothering to wait for her dad. The smallest suitcase has 360-degree rolling wheels, so I give her the handle and show her how it works. Then I grab the other two and shut the door.

Romel frowns. "That's it? That's all you brought?"

I look down at my three suitcases which I thought was almost too much. "Most of my stuff is still in boxes from when I moved back to my dad's house after I graduated. I just packed a bunch of clothes and the essentials. I figure I can buy anything else I might need."

He scratches at his chest, and it draws my gaze to the way his T-shirt fits across his broad, fit body. God, why did the hot guy from the store have to be her dad? I look away, focusing on Kaylee.

"Ready, KayBear?"

She giggles. "KayBear?"

"Yup. You got to give me a nickname, so now I get to give you one."

She beams up at me and nods her head. "Okay!"

"Lead the way," I tell her.

She practically bounces as she walks and pushes my small suitcase into her house. Romel steps forward and grabs the handle of my largest suitcase. There's a moment where our gazes connect, and my heart rate picks up the same way it did when I looked up at him in the store. I thought he was the sexiest man I'd ever seen in person, and I hate the way butterflies flutter in my stomach as his gaze seems to warm me from the inside out. All too quickly, he looks away, focusing on the suitcase in his hand and then to a path that wraps around the house.

"There's also a way to get to the guesthouse without having to walk through the main house. That path circles around the house and into the backyard. You just have to undo the latch at the top of the gate. It's high so Kay can't reach it and get out without supervision."

"Okay," I say.

He won't look at me now, and I nibble my lip, wondering if he might feel the little bit of spark that I just felt. Then I remember how gruff he's been and shake off the thought. Of course he doesn't feel anything. It doesn't seem like he wants me here at all.

The rest of the short walk to the guesthouse is silent, but I'm hyperaware of his presence behind me as we make our way there. The backyard is just as gorgeous as the front yard, but also has a pool with a thick netting over it. Romel catches me looking at it.

"It's a safety net. If Kay were to fall in, she wouldn't go underwater. She knows how to swim, but I keep this net over the pool whenever I'm not out here to watch her."

"Okay, I'll keep that in mind so I always remember to put it back if we go swimming."

"I appreciate it."

"Of course. Her safety's important to me."

It's the truth, and not just because it's my job to watch her. Kaylee has already made a place for herself in my heart, and I'd be devastated if she got hurt, *especially* if I was watching her when it happened.

A hand wrapping around my upper arm stops me in my tracks, and I watch Kaylee open the door to the guesthouse and run inside before I spin around to face Romel.

His expression is serious, but there's fear in the depths of his eyes. "My daughter is my whole world. Her safety is paramount, do you understand?"

I swallow thickly. "I promise I wasn't being flippant. I know I haven't known her for long, but I can assure you her safety is of the utmost importance to me as well. I will never put her in harm's way."

His grip relaxes and then he rips his hand away as if he just now noticed he was touching me. My arm is warm where he touched me, but I try to ignore the sensation.

"Miss Mere! Come here!" Kaylee's voice breaks the weird, intense stare off we're having and I take advantage of it, grabbing my suitcase from him and going straight into the guesthouse. Romel doesn't follow. He stands frozen like a statue on the walkway just outside the guesthouse front door, and I'm grateful for the reprieve of having him in my space, even if it's only temporary. As thrilling as it is to finally feel something, it is so, so, *so* bad that it has to be for my new boss.

Kaylee is sitting on the bed when I roll my suitcases in the bedroom. "You like it?" she asks, her voice quiet. I'm used to loud kids who seem like they have so much energy it's practically exploding out of them. Kaylee is much more restrained.

I sit down on the bed next to her and bump her shoulder with mine. "It's great. But how about I unpack later, and we go color for a while, or we could do something else if you want."

She turns her cute little face to me, her lips pinched and her brows furrowed. I bite back a smile at such a small child wearing such a serious expression. "But Daddy's home."

I part my lips to reply, but she jumps off the bed and screams. "Daddy!"

Shoving off the bed, I run after her. "Kaylee?"

Romel's already through the front door and holding her, her little arms wrapped so tight around his neck, I wonder if he can even breathe. He turns a stern glare to me.

"What did you say to her?" he practically growls.

I shake my head, completely at a loss. "I asked her if she wanted to color or play and she just jumped off the bed screaming for you."

Muffled sobs come from her and my heart breaks. "I don't know what happened," I say hoarsely, unable to look away from Kaylee.

Romel's eyes close with a slight wince, and the muscles of his arms bunch as he hugs Kaylee tighter. "It's not your fault," he says with a heavy sigh.

"What did I say?"

When he opens his eyes, there's that pain again. "She thought I was leaving." But that's all the attention he gives me before he brushes past me to sit on the small love seat in the living room that's about as big as the one I had in the apartment I shared with my roommate in college.

He rubs Kaylee's back in gentle circles, murmuring so softly to her, I can't pick up any of the words, but they must be soothing to her because she stops crying and sits back to stare at him. Tears fill my eyes at the depth of sadness in her gaze when she looks at her dad. "You're not leaving?"

"Not today. I'm here all day, okay? You know I always tell you when I'm going to leave."

She looks down, her little brain processing that information before she nods.

"Do you want to color with Miss Mere?" he asks, his tone soft and gentle.

She looks up at him, her mouth in a pout. "You color too?"

Oh boy. I don't know how he could possibly say no to her when she looks at him like that, so I'm not at all surprised when he nods.

Her face breaks out in a giant smile—bigger than any she's ever given me—and she wipes her eyes before she slides off his lap and runs past me toward the main house. "Be right back!"

I laugh and try to wrap my head around the whiplash I just got. How is it that little kids can bounce back from such big emotions so quickly?

Romel stands, gripping his neck. "Sorry about that. She's got a lot of separation anxiety when it comes to me. It's gotten worse as she's gotten older."

I shake my head. "The apology isn't necessary. I get it. My dad said I was the same way when I was little. I don't remember it as much."

He stares at me like he's seeing me for the first time. "Larissa said you lost your mom when you were a baby?"

"Yeah, she died from complications with her delivery."

His gaze moves to where his daughter went. "Did you miss her?"

I chew my lip and lean back against the wall. "It's hard to miss someone you've never met. I missed the idea of her, if that makes sense. My dad showed me pictures and videos of her all the time growing up. It felt a lot like she was a relative I knew about but had never seen in person. So I cared about her, but not in the same way I cared about people I saw regularly."

"That makes sense."

Since I'm so close with my dad, I know what he's really worried about—it's the same fear my dad voiced more than once when I was growing up. "You're a great dad, Romel. I've only spent a little time with you and yet that's clear as day. She's not lacking for love just because she doesn't have a mom."

He looks down at the floor and I know I was right. How can he even doubt what a great dad he is when his daughter so clearly loves him? When he's the one person she seeks for comfort?

It seems my duties—whether he knows it or not—are to not only take care of Kaylee, but to help Romel see that he's not failing her.

SEVEN

Romel

My alarm goes off at five a.m. so I can be up before Kaylee wakes up at five thirty. I get out of bed and head downstairs to get my first cup of coffee so I can be somewhat functional by the time Kay is awake. It's unfair that kids can wake up before the sun has even risen with enough energy to power a whole city, while the rest of us struggle just to function.

Taking a sip of my coffee, I stare out the kitchen window to the backyard and notice the net over the pool is off.

My brows furrow. *What the hell?*

Panic hits me that Kaylee might've woken up before me and gone outside. I rush out the door only to stop two feet from the pool when I see long, tanned arms slicing through the water.

Meredith's body glides effortlessly, like she's been swimming every day of her life. I try to steady my erratic heart rate from the panic of worrying Kay got into the pool without supervision, but the longer I watch her, the more chaotic my heartbeat seems to get.

My jaw clenches as she stops at the edge of the pool to

catch her breath. She turns her head in my direction and jerks.

"Shi—" she catches herself before the curse word fully leaves her lips. "You scared me."

I scowl at her. "What are you doing?"

Her eyes go wide at my question—or maybe it's because I delivered it like an accusation. "I wanted to get a workout in before Kaylee woke up. I'm sorry. I should've asked."

"Yes, you should've." My jaw clenches tight at the slightly wounded expression in her gaze. I don't know why I'm being such an asshole. I scrub my face and let out a breath. It doesn't do anything to calm my heart rate, but it does clear my head a little. "Sorry. Of course you can use the pool. I just thought Kay had gotten out here on her own."

Understanding dawns on her face. "I'm so sorry. I can text you next time to give you a heads-up."

"Sure," I acquiesce. If I say anything else, I'll come off as an even bigger asshole. "Listen, Kay will be up soon if you want to dry off and come to the main house for breakfast."

She nods, but still looks at me like she's not sure what to expect from me. Frustrated with myself, I spin around and head back toward the patio door. When I hear water sloshing, I glance behind me and watch her grip the edge of the pool and push herself up out of the water. She's wearing a conservative black one-piece bathing suit, but it's still the most naked I've seen a woman since my wife died. My gaze is glued to her lithe form as she stands on the edge and wrings water out of her dark hair before grabbing a white towel that she must've placed on the lounge chair before she started swimming.

I stand transfixed, frozen to the spot. And then before I even have a chance to remind her—before she even goes inside to get changed—she walks around the pool putting the safety net back in place. My chest feels tight, and before she can catch me watching her, I duck back inside and head straight for the stove to make breakfast.

I pull out a skillet, but I barely see it. All I can see is Meredith lifting herself out of my pool, the way the water ran down her skin, her toned arms gripping the edge of the pool, and then how she took the time to secure the net before worrying about herself.

I grip the edge of the counter and tuck my chin to my chest, trying to pull myself together. I owe her an apology for my behavior—a sincere one, not the gruff, half-assed one I gave her outside when I realized I was acting like a grumbly jerk. I'm not usually a giant asshole, but I keep scolding her like she's done something wrong when she hasn't.

So why does she bring out that side of me?

I've never been that guy. I'm the nice guy. I've always been polite, respectful, even-tempered. Then Meredith shows up and suddenly I can't stop questioning everything she does and frowning at her all the damn time.

What the hell is wrong with me?

I try to figure it out, but when I hear a door open upstairs, I know my time for self-reflection is over. It's time to focus on being everything my daughter needs, especially since I have to remind her this morning that I have practice today. I'm bracing myself for the silent tears she's given more often than not lately. It makes it harder to leave her because she's not normally so emotional. She's always been close to me, but this last year, she's become more aware of me being away. It's as if she thinks if I leave, I'll never come back.

Which may be a valid fear for a kid who's already lost one parent.

She walks into the kitchen wearing her pink unicorn pajamas and holding her favorite wolf stuffy that my mom bought her the last time she was in town. She smiles wide and runs around the island to my open arms as I squat down to pick her up.

"Morning, Daddy," she says, squeezing her arms around me, her voice still groggy from sleep.

This little girl has no idea what I would do for her, or how much her simple "Morning, Daddy" always makes my day. As angry as I was at Sydney for not fighting, for letting the cancer progress because she wasn't willing to risk her pregnancy, I understand her decision whenever I look at our daughter. I didn't have the same connection Syd did with our daughter—not at the time—but I do now and I would never trade Kay for anyone or anything. While I wish I could've had them both, I'm thankful every day that Sydney and I made this beautiful, brave, and brilliant little girl.

"What would you say to pancakes for breakfast?"

"Unicorn Pancakes!" she shouts before bursting into a fit of giggles that bring a smile to my face.

"Anything for you, baby girl." I set her down. "Go grab the step stool and you can help, okay?"

"Okay," she says before running to the hall closet where we keep the step stool for when she wants to help with cooking.

The back door opens and Meredith steps through, her posture more timid and reserved than it was yesterday, and it only reminds me again about what a giant asshole I've been to her.

"Hey," she says with a weak wave. "Is Kay up yet?"

"Miss Mere!" my daughter shouts as she comes back

into the room with the step stool in her hands. She holds it a bit awkwardly, but I know how important it is for her sense of independence to do it on her own. "We're making unicorn pancakes!"

Meredith's face lights up with a smile as she gives all her attention to Kay. The room seems to get noticeably colder with her ignoring my presence. "Unicorn pancakes? I don't think I've ever had those before."

Kay looks at her, stunned, and then stands next to me and hands me the stool to open for her. "Daddy makes them."

Meredith doesn't look at me, but stays focused on Kay, and I can't blame her. "That's so nice of him."

"Yeah," Kay says and then steps up onto the top step of the stool. "I help, Daddy?"

I drop a kiss to the top of her head. "Of course. I can't make unicorn pancakes without my helper."

Needing to thaw the ice that has formed between Meredith and me, I try to offer an olive branch. "You're welcome to help yourself to some coffee, if you'd like. We've got half and half in the fridge, sugar right over there," I say, gesturing to the sugar tin. "Or some coffee creamer that I buy for when Larissa comes over to watch Kay."

She takes a seat at one of the island stools and folds her arms before resting her forearms on the counter. "I'm okay. Thanks." She still doesn't look at me, her gaze set on watching Kaylee's every movement.

Well, shoot. So much for an olive branch.

EIGHT

Meredith

Larissa already warned me that Kay had two reactions when Romel left for practice or work. She would either shut down and fold in on herself, or she would have a total and complete meltdown.

I was thankful that Larissa shared this information with me since Romel did not.

I'm not sure if it's because of our awkward interaction this morning or what, but he walks out the door after breakfast with barely a glance in my direction—simply a hug and a kiss to Kaylee, and then he's gone.

As soon as the door clicks shut, I see what Larissa meant about Kaylee shutting down.

Her tiny little shoulders droop and her face goes blank, her eyes filling with a kind of despondency that doesn't seem normal for a three-year-old.

"Hey, KayBear," I say. "What do you want to do today while your dad's at work?"

A shrug is her only response.

I haven't spent a lot of time with Kaylee, but I've spent enough time to know that this is not the little girl I'm used to. It seems like as soon as Romel walked out the door, all of the bright, vibrant color she carries in her little body walked out the door with him.

I get down on my knees and sit back on my heels so I can be eye level with her. "What's going on in that little head of yours, Kay?"

Another shrug.

"Do you want to color?"

She shakes her head.

"Do you want to play with your dolls?"

Another head shake.

I look around the room for some ideas of what to do. My gaze catches on the TV. Romel didn't say anything about screen time limitations, so I figure it's worth a shot.

"We could watch a movie or a show?" I offer.

A shrug.

Quickly running out of ideas, I see a small pink football in the corner. "Do you want to toss the ball around?" Before she can shake her head or give me another shrug, I add, "I bet that's what your daddy's going to do at work today."

Her eyes flick up at mine. There she is.

It's not a verbal yes, but it's not a shrug or a head shake, so I'm going to take it as one.

I crawl over and grab the squishy football, turning back to face her. "Okay, Kay," I say. "Hold your hands up. I'm going to toss it to you, okay?"

She looks unsure, but she puts her hands up slowly, and I take that as another positive.

So with a gentle underhand toss, I throw it her way. The small football bounces off her chest and onto the floor. But I catch the way her lips tilt up in the faintest smile.

She ducks down to pick it up and immediately throws it back at me, with an impressive arm for a three-year-old.

I catch it with a smile. "Great job, KayBear."

The corners of her lips lift just a little bit more. She holds her hands up and I toss it again.

More often than not, she doesn't catch the ball and it bounces off her chest. But her smile grows with each toss and that feels like a victory in itself. Her shoulders are no longer droopy, and her eyes aren't forlorn.

After about the sixth or seventh toss, she suddenly gets very excited about throwing the ball.

A bit too excited.

And in that excitement, she throws the ball harder and higher than I'm expecting. It passes by my fingertips, barely grazing them, but it's just enough to change the angle so that the ball veers off to the side, right toward a shelf with some ceramic figurines, including one shaped like a teddy bear with a red and white bow tie.

I watch in slow motion as the ball knocks over the small ceramic teddy bear just hard enough that the fall causes one of the ears to break off.

Kay sucks in a sharp breath. "Oh no," she cries. Tears instantly fill her eyes as she starts sobbing.

I'm guessing from her reaction that the figurines are special, but I'm less concerned about the broken bear than I am about Kaylee's well-being. I wrap my arms around her, shushing her and soothing her until she eventually settles down.

To distract her, I pull up a movie, and we watch that until she falls asleep for her nap.

While she's sleeping, I examine the figurine. It looks old, but well taken care of, and I wonder how upset Romel will be that it's now chipped and broken. The good news is it's not beyond repair. I'm sure some superglue will fix it, but it won't be exactly the same. There will always be a slight crack along where the ear connects to the head, even after it's fixed.

Considering the rest of the house is childproof, I'm kind of surprised Romel has something so breakable out in the room. It seems like a weird oversight.

Romel comes home from practice while Kaylee is still napping, and I'm grateful we can have this conversation without her overhearing, considering how distraught she was when it broke in the first place.

When he walks in, his face is guarded like it's been every time he looks at me.

"Hey."

Short and to the point. Not friendly, but not exactly cold either. I let out a sigh because I am not looking forward to sharing bad news with someone who already can't seem to decide whether he wants me here or not.

"Hi," I say back, the room already filling with awkward tension. "I'm glad you're here before Kay woke up because we had a bit of an incident today."

He stiffens, and then his gaze turns sharp. "What kind of incident?"

I walk over to where the figurines are and hold up the bear in one hand and the piece of its ear in the other. "Kay accidentally hit it with her soft little football—the pink one," I added as if this man doesn't know what toys his own daughter has. I nearly roll my eyes at myself. "The ear broke off," I say, despite it being obvious since I'm holding the ear up.

A slew of emotions I can't quite understand crosses his face. Then his gaze shutters once more, and when he turns to me, it's cold as ice.

"Those belonged to her mother, my wife."

I swallow thickly as my heart drops into my stomach.

Oh, shit.

"I'm sorry, it happened so quickly," I start to ramble. "I think it can be fixed with superglue—" He stops me by holding a hand up. I swallow any other words that want to come stumbling out.

"Just go," he says, his gaze now back on the bear. "We don't need you for the rest of the day. I have practice again tomorrow, same time. So we'll see you in the morning."

I stare at him, completely speechless and stunned.

I have never been so dismissed.

"Fine. I'll see you tomorrow," I say, as calmly and professionally as I can, and then I walk out the door.

I thought nannying would be a good option while I sort myself out and figure out my life.

But now I'm questioning if this is such a good idea after all, if this is how it's going to be, no matter how much I'm enjoying my time with Kaylee.

NINE

Romel

Usually, I can admit when I'm being a giant jackass, especially since it's so rare that I am one. Apparently, this is not a skill set I have where Meredith is concerned.

Two days ago, I had every intention of coming home and trying to clear the air after the rough incident with the pool net and me being a gruff bastard.

But then I saw the broken bear in Meredith's hand—the bear that Sydney had cherished because it was a gift from her grandmother.

And all my good intentions went out the window.

I'd left the figurines out despite childproofing the entire house because they were up on a high shelf, so I figured Kaylee would never be able to get them. Plus, it made me feel closer to Sydney knowing something she cherished was still present in our space.

Sometimes Kaylee and I would look at the figurines while I held her in my arms. I'd always been very clear with her that they were special and were not to be played with. She knew that they were her mommy's but that someday they'd be hers.

In hindsight, I know it's partially my fault they were out and that accidents happen. But that doesn't change the fact that seeing Meredith holding it broken—the bear that had been Sydney's personal favorite—made something in me shut down.

And instead of clearing the air, I once again became an asshole which isn't something I'm proud of.

As I drive home from another day of practice, I'm determined to make things better this time.

Because this isn't me. I'm not this guy—the one who's rude and cold to someone, especially when they don't deserve it. And if Meredith is feeling the tension half as much as I am, then one of us is bound to break sooner or later.

Despite my misgivings about having a nanny in the first place, I can't deny that she and Kaylee have been good together. Kay is always sharing stories with me at dinner about what she and Meredith did during the day. And while I can't understand half of what she's saying, she's happy and that's the most important part.

So, I need to learn how to not be an asshole to Meredith, which shouldn't be hard since I've prided myself on being a good guy for my entire life.

I pull into the driveway, park the car, and take a breath while staring at the front door of my house.

I love coming home, but I don't like conflict. And there's a knot in my gut at the thought that this conversation with Meredith might get fumbled up once more, because apparently I can't get myself straight when it comes to her.

I play through different starting lines for how to get the conversation going on the right foot. When I've settled on one or two strong starters and feel confident that I can walk in the door and have a conversation appropriately and calmly, I finally get out and head inside.

I close the door behind me and set my duffle bag down on the ground.

"Meredith," I call out.

"Daddy!" Kaylee squeals from the living room, and then the pitter-patter of my sweet girl's little feet as she comes racing toward me fills the entryway.

My lips curve into a smile that only my daughter can bring to my face as I lift her into my arms.

"Hey, Sweetie, how was your—what is *this*?" I stare at my daughter's cheek where a red, angry scratch is, and then I shoot daggers at Meredith as she walks in behind her.

Meredith's smile falls, but I don't have a chance to reel myself back as worry and anger consume me.

"What the hell happened?" I ask through gritted teeth.

"Daddy say bad word," Kay says.

I clench my jaw and stare Meredith down. "Why is my daughter's face scratched?"

Meredith stares back at me, and whatever warmth was on her face when she first saw Kaylee and me together has vanished. "We were playing hide and seek," she says. "And Kaylee decided to hide in a bush. She got so excited when I came up behind her and yelled, 'Surprise!' that she dashed out and scratched her face on one of the branches."

I turn to my daughter with my frown still on my face. "Is that what happened?" I ask her.

She nods with a big smile on her face. "It's so fun! Play hide and seek, Daddy."

I swallow thickly as my anger starts to fade, and with shame coursing through me, I sneak a glance at Meredith. But her gaze is locked on the ground.

Will I ever get it right with this woman?

Why do I always go to the worst-case scenario with her instead of trusting that she's looking after my daughter and it's an innocent mistake? It's not like this is the first scratch Kay's ever had before.

I open my mouth to apologize, but before any words come out, Meredith speaks. "If there's anything else you need, I'll be in the guesthouse. Otherwise, I'll be back tomorrow morning for breakfast, like usual."

She doesn't look at me as she says it, and then without waiting for me to confirm or deny that there's more I need from her, she waves, says good night to Kay, and then walks out the door.

Shit.

TEN

Meredith

Four days and I still can't keep up with Romel's mood swings. He's worse than the toddler currently helping him make unicorn pancakes for the fourth day in a row.

Focusing on the whole reason I'm here, I watch Kaylee awkwardly stir the pancake mix. Her tongue sticks out as her tiny eyebrows furrow with intense concentration. In my periphery, I catch Romel shooting glances my way. A part of me hopes he feels like an asshole for how he basically growled at me out by the pool on my first day here and makes me feel like a giant inconvenience—or worse, how I can't seem to do anything right where his daughter's concerned. He's only said a few words to me each day before he leaves for practice, but every so often I catch him glancing at me like he wants to say more. And yet, he never does. Instead, he mainly only speaks to me about Kaylee's day.

The frustration and anger simmer before it hits me that I'm feeling it so strongly. I glance at Romel who's now helping Kay pour the batter. His voice is low and soft as he talks to her, gentle, but firm when he tells her to watch herself so she doesn't get burned. What is it about this man that brings up so many conflicting emotions that I haven't felt in months?

Why, of all people, is he the man that seems to be thawing the numbness that's been inside me since my senior year of college? It's infuriating and thrilling and confusing. It's jarring to go from feeling apathetic for so long to feeling so many of the clashing emotions that he brings to life inside me.

But with the realization that he makes me *feel*, I start to wonder if maybe I'm doing the same to him. It's clear he's got a routine with Kay, and having someone new in the house is likely throwing that routine out of whack.

Maybe he deserves a little more grace than I've given him. It's only been four days, so maybe it's time to call a truce and ask for a clean slate.

I stay relatively silent while he and Kay make breakfast, but I don't shy away from him when he glances back at me every so often. Something passes between us each time our gazes connect, like a gentle understanding that we both haven't been our best selves.

Kay fills the silence as we eat, talking about a story her Grammy read to her a week ago. Some of what she says isn't quite clear—in that way that toddlers talk and you swear they've made up half the words they've used—but it's the most I've heard her talk since I met her.

I glance at Romel, and my gut tightens at the pure love on his face for his daughter. His lips are slightly lifted in the smallest smile, and his eyes shine more than I've seen them so far. He nods at all the right places in her story and asks her follow-up questions as if he understands every word she's said. It's endearing and softens me further toward him.

"Kay, why don't you run upstairs and pick out some clothes for today, okay?" he says.

She nods and leaves the table, running out of the room with an energy that makes me envious.

"We need to talk," I say, using the opportunity of Kay out of the room to address the issue that's been bothering me for a long time. My skin heats as adrenaline races through my bloodstream. I hate confrontation, but I'll call him out on his crap if that's what it takes for us to find our footing because this isn't sustainable.

He crosses his arms. "Is everything okay with Kay?"

Of course he thinks this is about Kay. I actually love that she's always his first priority. It's another attractive trait of his, but my attraction to him is the least of my concerns right now. "Everything with Kay is fine, but everything with you and me is not. I'm trying really hard not to overstep since the pool incident, and then the ceramic bear, but I feel like I'm walking on eggshells and I can't do anything right as far as you're concerned." His brows furrow and he opens his mouth to speak, but I barrel on. "I want to do my job. I want to be here for Kay. She's amazing and I love hanging out with her when you have to work, but it's hard when you're so important to her and we don't get along very well. Hard on her, and on me," I admit.

He blinks several times like he's slowly processing everything I said. He uncrosses his arms, his face the picture of sincerity. "I'm sorry. I haven't handled our interactions appropriately, and I'll admit I haven't known how to address it with you. But you're right. I got us started off on the wrong foot." He looks toward the stairs, and I know he's thinking about Kay.

"It's been just me and Kay for so long. Even with Larissa's help, it wasn't the same as having someone here full-time like you are. I guess it's been harder on me than I thought it would be to let go of some of the responsibility. When you're forced to do it all, you forget what it's like to *not* have to do it all. I don't want you to be uncomfortable here, and I promise I'm going to try to do better from here on out."

It's the most he's ever said to me in one sitting.

"I don't want to step on your toes."

He's already shaking his head before I've finished my sentence. "You're not. I appreciate everything you've done already in the short amount of time you've been here. I've never seen Kay so open. Even with her aunts and uncles, she's a bit reserved, but every time she spends the day with you, I come home and she chats my ear off telling me everything you did all day."

I can't help smiling. "She's such a great kid, Romel. You've done an amazing job with her."

He looks down like he can't quite take the compliment. "Thanks. I'm sorry, Meredith. I'm sorry I've been so... difficult."

"I should've talked to you about how I was feeling sooner."

"Moving forward, just tell me if I'm being..."

"Grumpy?" I suggest with a smile.

"I was going to say overbearing, but I guess grumpy works."

I release my breath, feeling loads lighter now that we've cleared the air.

"Apology accepted. To be honest, I haven't been my best self either. I know your situation better than most probably do. It's clear you've had set routines with Kaylee, and I can't imagine it's easy to invite someone new into your life, especially with her."

He looks at the table. "No, it's not." He picks at a dried piece of food with his thumbnail. "But that doesn't excuse my behavior."

I lean forward, my elbows on the table. "Maybe we should start with a blank slate."

He glances up at me, almost like he's hesitant to believe this conversation is going so well. "I'd like that. I swear I'm not this big of an asshole usually."

My smile grows. "I believe you."

He mirrors my smile and I have to remind myself to breathe. It's the first time he's smiled directly at me, and even if it's small, it makes me feel like I just performed a miracle.

"What made you want to become a nanny?"

He's looking at me in a way that makes me feel like he can see to the very heart of me. "I went to school to become a physical therapist, but I don't know. Senior year rolled around and nothing seemed to bring me much joy anymore. I didn't apply to any grad schools and opted to take a year off. But I got sick of just hanging around the house, especially with all my other friends starting their new adult lives. Plus, boredom doesn't appeal to me. I babysat in high school and a little bit in college, so I figured nannying made the most sense for a temporary job. So now I'm a nanny."

"I'm glad you are," he says, his voice soft and catching my attention.

My eyes lock on his. "You are?"

He nods and swallows, the motion making his Adam's apple bob in his throat. "Maybe you are exactly what Kay needed."

What Kay needed.

Why does that statement feel so unsatisfactory? And why is there a piece of me that wishes I was what he needed too?

ELEVEN

Romel

The next night, I'm struggling to sleep. It's not uncommon for me—not since Sydney died. I'd gotten so used to sleeping next to her that even three years later, I still miss the comfort of going to sleep with her beside me—the feeling of having her body next to me where I could easily reach out and touch her.

A part of me has been frozen since she died—set in my ways in some weak attempt to preserve things exactly as she left them. It's not always easy to do with Kaylee. Having a kid in general uproots every system you ever had in place. But our room is relatively the same as it was when Sydney was alive.

Larissa thinks it's morbid—that it shows I'm unwilling to let Sydney go and move on with my life. She's mostly right since there's a big part of me that can't let go of Sydney. I don't have any reason to. She was the love of my life. I'd vowed to love her for as long as I live, and even if she's not here anymore, I plan to uphold my vows with every breath in my body.

I debate taking some melatonin, but it doesn't always

help, and anything stronger tends to worry me that I wouldn't wake up if something went wrong with Kaylee in the middle of the night.

Giving up on sleep altogether, I get out of bed and head over to the window. There's a faint light on in the guesthouse and I glance at the clock to see it's two in the morning. Is Meredith having trouble sleeping too?

I debate going down there and checking on her, but then decide to stay put. We've come to a truce of sorts, and things have been easier since our talk after breakfast yesterday, but it seems like a tentative understanding and I don't want to misstep with her again. So instead, I just stand at the window and look out at the view of the Los Angeles skyline in the distance. There's the faint haze of smog that always seems to be there, even when it rains. It's only barely visible from the ambient lights that never turn off. Looking up, there's the twinkle of stars—only the brightest ones to compete with the lights of the city.

I never thought much about death until Sydney died. Now I think about it all the time. I wonder if there's really a heaven or if people only live on in the memories their loved ones have of them. Is Sydney up in the stars right now? I'd like to believe she is, that she's always looking down on Kaylee and me, watching out for us.

"I hope I'm making you proud, Syd," I whisper, hoping with every ounce of me that she can hear me. That she's proud of how I've raised Kay, even if I question every parenting choice I make every single day. Do other parents feel this way? Or is it just me because I have to do it alone?

"I wish you were here," I murmur.

Movement below pulls my attention from the stars. Meredith steps out from the guesthouse, a knee-length sweater wrapped around her. She sits down on one of the lounge chairs and stares up at the same stars I was just staring at. Her mouth moves like she's talking, but she's too far away for me to try to figure out what she's saying.

Without really thinking about it, I make my way downstairs and out onto the patio. As soon as I slide open the back door, she turns her head to face me and then sits up.

"Sorry, did I wake you?" she asks.

"No. I was having a hard time sleeping and saw you out here."

She seems to relax at that and lies back on the lounge chair, her gaze going back to the faint stars above us. "Must be something in the water. I was having trouble sleeping too."

I take a seat in the lounge chair next to hers and mirror her pose, staring up at the sky. Neither of us speak for a long time, both of us focused on the stars and lost in our own thoughts.

Except this time it doesn't feel as lonely as it normally does. I can pick up her gentle breathing beside me, and just knowing she's next to me offers a comfort I didn't know I needed.

"Were you talking to yourself?" The question comes out quiet, and my cheeks heat once the words are out. I shouldn't have asked her that, but I can't seem to stop my curiosity when it comes to Meredith.

She doesn't seem embarrassed or even fazed by my question. "I was talking to my mom," she admits.

I turn my head toward her so I can see her better. "Your mom?"

She continues to stare up at the sky, but her pink lips tilt up in the softest smile. "Yeah. I never knew her, but I talk to her all the time." She faces me, a slight pucker between her brows. "Do you believe in heaven?"

"I don't know. I want to."

She looks back at the stars. "I do. Or at least that there's something beyond death. I don't know what it looks like exactly, but I believe there has to be something else. Just looking up at the stars, at the vastness of the universe, makes me feel like there's so much we don't know—that there has to be something else, right?"

She doesn't give me enough time to respond. "I've always imagined my mom up there in the sky, watching me. I've been talking to her as long as I can remember." She lets out a little laugh. "I guess I kind of treat her like a diary, telling her about my life, asking her questions she can't actually answer. Maybe that's foolish—"

"It's not." I don't like the thought of her feeling stupid for wishing her mom heard her. "I do the same thing with Sydney."

Now it's my turn to face the stars, but I hear her shift and can feel the weight of her gaze as she turns it on me. "Your wife."

It's not a question, but I answer like it is.

"Yeah." My thoughts tumble out of me unfiltered. "I talk to her all the time, asking her if I'm doing right by Kaylee, telling her I love her." I whisper the last part, but I know Meredith hears it anyway.

"My dad loved my mom so much, he never let her go." She shifts again, but I don't face her. "I've always wanted a love like that—knowing my person loved me so much they'd never forget me. Sydney is very lucky."

It's the first time in a long time I've heard someone use Sydney's name and the present tense in the same sentence. My heart tightens in my chest.

"And she's definitely proud of you, and how great you are with Kaylee. I have zero doubts about that," she adds.

We sit there for a while longer, neither saying a word until the lump of emotion in my throat finally subsides enough for me to speak.

"Thank you, Meredith."

When I look over at her, her gaze is already waiting for me. She offers me a small smile, but doesn't say anything else.

We sit together in silence, staring at the stars, at the vastness of the universe, and yet for the first time in a long time, the loneliness that has held me in a choke hold is nowhere to be found.

TWELVE

Meredith

On my first day off, I decide to get away from Romel's house for the day. Something has shifted between us, especially after last night under the stars. Unfortunately, that moment alone together did nothing to stymie my attraction to him. If anything, hearing how much he still loves his wife just made me realize what a loyal man he is. Three years he's been alone, but he didn't run off and try to drown himself in booze or women to forget his pain. I know how popular the Fierce Four are and have no doubts that he has women throw themselves at him on a regular basis, and yet he's remained loyal to his wife. There's something very admirable about that level of dedication and devotion.

But it also made it painfully obvious that this crush that has been growing for him will always be one-sided. I know from personal experience that a man in love with his wife that much will never let her go, even after death—my dad never did.

As soon as I pull up to my dad's house, I let out a breath I wasn't even aware I was holding. I get out of the car and head inside without knocking.

"That you, Meredith?" he calls out from the kitchen.

"Yeah, Dad," I call back, dropping my purse on the table by the front door. I head back into the kitchen of my childhood home.

I asked him once why he didn't move if it was so hard to think about Mom, but he said he wouldn't lose the memories if that was all he had left. I compare my dad to Romel, and start to really see their similarities. Is that why Romel hasn't moved out of his house? I've seen the pictures of Sydney on the wall. I know he tries to keep her memory alive for Kay, but how much of it is for himself too? After our conversation last night, I wonder if everything he does is for himself as much as he claims it's for his daughter.

"Something smells good," I say, walking into the kitchen.

Dad sticks his cheek out for a kiss, his hands busy jarring jam. "I went to the farmers' market and couldn't resist. The raspberries looked great, and I know how much you love raspberry jam."

"Need any help?" I ask, already washing my hands, assuming his answer will be yes.

He puts the pot down now that the jar is full and looks at me, his brows furrowed. "Everything okay?"

I grab a spoon and take a scoop. "Yeah, can't I just help my dad make my favorite jam?"

"Of course you can, but you look stressed."

After blowing on it to cool it down, I stick the spoonful in my mouth. "Mmm, this is good."

He shakes his head. "Fine, if you want to deflect, then sure, you can help. But remember, you're going to tell me anyway; might as well just get it out of the way."

"I don't tell you everything, you know." Even though it's true I don't tell him *everything*, I do usually tell him the big things. And he's never failed to miss when something was on my mind.

But my dad's greatest superpower is knowing when to let the silence linger—and that I'll always fill it. "Hey, Dad?"

He smiles. "Yeah?"

Dammit. Swallowing my pride, I tell him what's going on. "The family I'm nannying for is actually a single dad. Kaylee is three and her mom died just a week after she was born."

Dad stops everything he's doing and faces me, his brows slanted with pain. I can only imagine what this conversation is going to bring up for him, and maybe it's not fair for me to ask, but we've always had a good relationship, and there's no one else I would want to talk to about this.

"I love Kaylee already. She's such a sweetheart and so incredibly smart, but I really don't want to overstep. It's clear having me there has been kind of hard on him. I guess I'm just wondering what kind of help you would've wanted when it was just you and me? I don't want to step on his toes, and I feel like the situation is kind of... delicate."

Dad stops what he's doing and leans against the counter, facing me. "What have I always told you about conflict or what to do when you're feeling uncertain in a situation, especially when it involves another person?"

"Talk it out," I tell him. My dad has drilled the importance—and power—of communication into my head for as long as I've been alive. Though, that doesn't mean I've always been able to follow his advice. Sometimes communicating is easier said than done.

He nods. "I'm not the person you should be asking this question. If you want to know what would help him without you stepping on his toes, you need to have that conversation with him."

He steps forward, wrapping his strong arms around me, and I accept his hug. He steps back and squeezes my bicep once before he focuses on the jam again.

"Dad, can I ask you something?"

"Always."

"Why didn't you ever date again?"

He glances at me from the corner of his eye, and I'm worried he can read me too well and understands why I'm asking. If he does, he doesn't say anything about it, but there is concern in his furrowed brow that gives away his worry for me. "I loved your mom more than I'd ever loved anyone. She was my whole world until you were born. That kind of love can't be replaced."

He says it like it's a fact. I frown. "You wouldn't have to replace her though. Couldn't you love someone else, equal but different?"

He tilted his head back and forth, thinking about my question. "I suppose it's possible, but when you've loved someone that deeply, it's hard to open yourself up enough to hurt again." Now it's his turn to frown, and for a second I worry that I've opened a can of worms that maybe should've stayed closed. "Losing her nearly destroyed me, Meredith, and I couldn't put myself in that position again, especially not when I had to take care of you. You were my priority after I lost her."

"Do you think it's possible to love someone again when you've had that kind of big love?"

He stares at me, and I know for certain he definitely knows why I'm asking. "I think any man would be lucky to find two big loves in his lifetime, but he has to be open to it.

And when there's a child involved, that child will *always* take priority over a relationship."

My heart sinks, but his words aren't any different from the conclusion I've already come to. My crush on Romel will never go anywhere, because his priority will always be Kaylee—as it should be.

Which means it's time to bury this crush as far down as I can and focus on the reason I'm in their life at all—to take care of Kay.

THIRTEEN

Romel

There's something about stepping on a football field that makes all the chaos inside me go quiet. It's been this way my whole life, although it seems the older I get, the more of a mess my head becomes, and the more I need the reprieve I find on the field.

After Sydney died, I wasn't sure if I should keep playing. Gabe, Dom, and Ty were the ones who convinced me to get back on the field. I'd told myself I'd give it a handful of games before I decided what I'd do. The first game back after her death felt like an out-of-body experience. My body knew what to do, and I essentially went on autopilot. It wasn't my best game, but it wasn't my worst either. The second time, my head cleared and I took all the grief—the pain, the anger, the loss—and let it fuel me. I played harder, stronger, faster than I ever had before. It only took those two games to learn that I could channel my grief instead of letting it eat me alive like it had been.

It doesn't mean it's not still there when I'm off the field, but playing football allows me to expend the worst of it instead of being buried by it. It allows me to be my best self —or the post-Sydney version of myself—for my daughter.

Three years later and it still gives me the same feeling. Only tonight feels a little different because Kaylee gets to be here to watch me play, which isn't something she's gotten to do very often.

It was Meredith's idea to help with the separation anxiety, and after our talk the other night, I wanted to show her I was open to her suggestions. To show her I wasn't the closed off asshole I'd been when she started two weeks ago.

Meredith isn't quite what I expected, but I think she might be exactly what I need. I'll admit, I was surprised when she confronted me. I was also impressed as hell. It's been a long time since someone called me out. I can't think of a single time it's happened since Sydney's death. Everyone's always careful with me, whether they mean to be or not. Even my brothers—the other members of the Fierce Four—started treating me differently after Sydney died. We've joked that it's because I'm the "dad" of the group, but that's not true anymore now that Ty has his own daughter.

I don't think they do it on purpose, and it never really bothered me before. Not until Meredith. Now I'm seeing all the ways that I've shut people out—ways I wasn't conscious of until now.

But Meredith hasn't just called me out, she's also offered quiet comfort with her presence like she did that night under the stars. She's given me something I didn't realize I was missing—having someone to share my burdens with, without any of the judgment or sad looks I get from friends and family. Everyone thinks I should move on from Sydney and put myself out there again, but Meredith seems to understand without any pressure of what she thinks I "should" do.

She's a breath of fresh air when I didn't realize I'd been suffocating.

"You good?" Gabe asks me as we sit on the sidelines watching our offense get a first down.

"Do you think I've been more closed off since Syd?" I ask, glancing at him.

He arches a brow. "Is this a trick question?"

I pinch my lips together and face the field. Gabe twists his body, resting his arm on the back of the bench. "You're serious." His brows furrow. "What made you ask?"

I've never lied to him, and I'm not going to start now. "My new nanny called me out, and I haven't been able to stop thinking about what she said and how right she was."

He grabs his chest and bursts into laughter. "Man, I never thought it would be your nanny."

I twist my head and arch a brow, which makes his laughter slowly subside. He pats me on the back. "You've been grieving, Romel. There's no time limit on grief. We've let you handle it however you needed to. Honestly, we thought it would eventually be Kay that pulled you out of it."

"Out of grief?"

"Well, just out of that layer of grief. Not to sound like Shrek or anything, but in my experience, grief is like an onion." Gabe lost his dad when he was thirteen, so he knows about grief, and he's one of my best friends which is why I let him continue, even if I already think this is a ridiculous analogy.

"There's the first layer right after the loss. It's the darkest and hardest to get through—essentially that's the core of the onion that no one can get to without the outer layers being removed. But only you can move through those layers. No one can force you from one to the next, but maybe someone says something or you hear a song and it gives you a sense of closure that allows you to move out to the next layer. Or time. Sometimes you just need time to move out of that first layer, but the length of time can be different for everyone. For you, it was clear you moved out of that core layer when you really took over caring for Kay. You stayed in that second layer though for a long time. Then over the last year or so, you've moved on to the third layer—you socialized a bit more, started smiling a little bit, but you were still under more layers of grief. And now you've moved out to the next layer, and of all the people to push you, it was your new nanny." He shakes his head, then grins at me. "Is she hot?"

I push his arm and he bursts into laughter. "That's not even funny. You know there's no one else for me but Syd."

He sobers. "You're only twenty-seven, man. You really think Syd would've wanted you to be alone for the rest of your life?"

"I'm not alone. I've got Kay."

He shakes his head, getting sad. "You know it's not the same. Your child will always have a piece of your heart, but the love you have for a partner is different. And even if you're still in denial, deep down you know Sydney would've never wanted you to be single for the rest of your life. She'd want you to fall in love and find someone who will love Kaylee as much as she did."

"No woman could ever love her as much as her own mother," I say, my chest getting tight at the thought. Falling in love with someone else is never going to be on the table for me. No one will love me or Kay as much as Sydney did, and I'll never disrespect her by filling her place with a woman who doesn't belong there.

"You sure about that? There are plenty of kids out there

who've been adopted or found great foster parents who loved them better than their birth parents did."

I glare at him. "My situation's not the same and you know it. Sydney died for Kay. There's no greater sacrifice she could make to prove her love for our daughter."

Gabe rolls his lips between his teeth like he wants to say more but is biting it back. Thankfully, a whistle blows and we look out to the field to see our team needs another first down or it will be our turn. We both watch silently as the opposing team's defense holds back our forward progress. Gabe and I grab our helmets while Ty and Dom get into their own positions, along with the rest of our defensive line.

Before play starts, I do something I never do and look up at the stands where I know Meredith and Kaylee are sitting. Meredith has Kay in her arms, both of them smiling wide and cheering. My breathing gets shallow as my heart rate picks up. I shake my head, hoping I can shake off the unsettled feeling that I've never felt on the field before and then focus on the play.

FOURTEEN

Meredith

Kaylee and I laugh and cheer as I point to where her dad just tackled the opposing team's player. She claps while I hold her on my hip so she can see over the adults in the row in front of us.

My jaw practically hit the floor when I saw the seats Romel got for us. I suppose I shouldn't be surprised—I mean, he's a player so I'm sure it's no big deal for him to get second-row seats like this—but I've never been this close to the action. The last time my dad and I attended a football game together was when I was in high school. They were nosebleeds, but I still remember having the best time.

I've tried to make the experience similar for Kay. We bought snacks and hot dogs—which I cut up into much more manageable bites for her—and we've cheered every time her dad gets on the field. I make sure to point him out so she can see him, and she always gets the biggest smile on her face whenever she does.

I have to admit, watching Romel play is mesmerizing—and distracting. His football jersey does nothing to hide the way his muscles flex as he moves, the power he puts into his tackles, and his speed when he runs toward an opponent; it's all doing things to me it absolutely should not be doing.

We watch as he makes a tackle, and almost instantly, I know something's not right. The crowd around us grows quiet as we watch the guy he tackled get up, but Romel stays down. His right hand is gripping his left shoulder, and I hold my breath as three other players run toward him, one getting down on a knee to check in. The team medic runs out onto the field.

"God, I hope Watson's not hurt," someone says nearby.

Worry fills Kay's face. "Is Daddy hurt?" she whispers, her words already wobbling with the threat of tears. I hug her tighter against me, wishing I could offer her the reassurance she needs, but I also won't lie to her.

I point out to the field and the people surrounding her dad. "There's a doctor checking him out right now. We just need to wait a few minutes and then we'll know more, okay, KayBear?"

She wraps her arms around my neck and rests her head on my shoulder, her gaze still locked on the field. She doesn't lift her head, or loosen her hold, until Romel stands. Then we both let out a heavy breath as he walks over to the sidelines. His gaze searches us out in the crowd, and his brows furrow in worry once he finds us.

I point to him. "Look, Kay, he's okay."

"He's okay?" she sniffles.

He waves with his good arm—the one he was gripping on the field is still held lax at his side—and gives her a smile.

I brush away the few tears that escaped her eyes and hug her tighter. "He's going to be okay, Kay."

"Promise?" she asks, staring me down.

My chest tightens painfully at the fear I see in her eyes —how scared she is of losing him. She might not know her mother, but it's clear she recognizes what she's lost in a weird abstract way and doesn't want to lose her dad. I rest my forehead on hers. "I promise that your daddy will always do whatever he can to come home to you." It's not a lie. In just the few weeks I've worked for him, I've seen that he will always do everything in his power to be there for Kaylee.

She must believe me because she relaxes against me.

Even though Romel gets back on the field and plays, it's clear Kay is no longer having any fun. Even when I try to get her to dance with me to one of the songs they play during halftime, she barely cracks a smile.

"Do you want to go home?"

She shakes her head, and I let out a sigh. The rest of the game feels like it drags on forever. Romel plays great, but it's clear his shoulder is still bothering him when he rubs at it whenever he's on the sidelines. He's trying to be subtle about it—probably to avoid the other team taking advantage and making it worse—but it still has me worried. I try to think if I've seen ice packs in the freezer at home.

By the time the clock runs down to the end of the game, my arms are exhausted from holding Kay, who clung to me like her life depended on it whenever I tried to put her down after her dad got injured. We go to the area of the stadium Romel told me to take her after the game where the players exit.

By the time Romel comes out with three other guys, Kay is half asleep in my arms. She wakes up as soon as she hears her dad's voice.

"Daddy!" she shouts, squirming out of my arms and running straight for him.

He scoops her up in his good arm and gives her a kiss to the side of her head. The three other guys, who I now recognize as Gabe Romero, Dominic Smith, and Tyler Russell of the Fierce Four, all coo over her. Despite the stress of worrying about Kay's emotional state for most of the game, a smile breaks out on my face to see these four giant guys turn to mush for this little girl.

"You okay, Daddy?" Kay asks, her tiny brows furrowed as she touches his shoulder gently.

He glances at me before he answers her. "I'm okay, baby girl. Just fell on it wrong, but it'll be fine after a little ice."

She doesn't look convinced.

I'm about to speak up when Romel says, "You know what would really make me feel better?"

"What?" she asks.

"Ice cream," he says with a big smile, and her face splits into a huge grin.

I let out a sigh of relief. Of course, he'd pick up on how worried she really is and be able to defuse it almost immediately.

Sometimes a girl just needs her dad.

He walks closer to me, still talking to Kay. "You still had a good time, though?"

She nods her head and her smile grows. "Miss Mere got us so much food," she says, giggling.

"Oh, did she now?" Romel asks, his own smile growing as he directs it my way, and I have to remind myself to breathe because this man is handsome on a regular day, but when he smiles, he's like "Sexiest Man Alive" levels of handsome.

"My dad used to always treat us to all the sports park goodies when he'd bring me to games, so I thought I'd carry on the tradition with Kaylee," I explain.

He nods and then mouths a "thank you" before walking past me with Kaylee in his arms and letting her tell him about all the food we ate. I watch them for a second too long when I realize the other three guys are watching *me*.

Waving awkwardly, I dash off to follow Romel and Kay, but not before I hear one of the guys say, *"That's* his new nanny?" Then they all laugh and another voice says something, but by that time I'm too far away to hear the distinct words.

Romel drives us all home, and it's no surprise to either of us when Kaylee is already passed out by the time we get there.

He carries her inside and I follow them in, but when Romel heads upstairs to put her in bed, I head to the kitchen and check the freezer. It takes me a minute to find what I'm looking for, but I shouldn't be surprised to find ice packs in an athlete's freezer. I doubt this is the first time he's ever been injured, even if it's only minor.

Next, I head to the cupboard where Romel keeps ibuprofen on the top shelf and grab a couple. I'm filling a tall glass of water when he comes into the kitchen and stops in his tracks when he sees the ice pack and medication on the counter.

He glances at me. "What's this?"

"You've been favoring your right arm, which made me think your left is still bothering you from when you landed on it wrong. I figured a little ice and ibuprofen might help."

"I was just coming in here to grab exactly that." He says his words slowly like he doesn't know how to handle someone else taking care of him.

I know it's not my job, but it is my job to take care of his daughter, and I know how much she worries about him, so in a weird roundabout way, taking care of him feels like taking care of her. I place the full glass of water next to the pills and then step back.

"Well, I guess I'll head to bed," I say, gesturing with my thumb in the direction of the back doors.

He's still staring at the ice pack and meds. "Sure, good night," he says absentmindedly.

"Good night." I don't linger.

I'm halfway across the patio and beating myself up for making things awkward again when the back door opens and I spin around. Romel stands there, illuminated by the dim lawn lights he has set up along the edge of the walkway to the guesthouse.

"Thank you," he says, his voice carrying across the yard.

"You're welcome."

"You didn't have to do that and I appreciate it. It's been a long time since someone tried to take care of me."

"It was nothing, really."

The air between us feels weighted. "It was something to me."

My breath gets stuck in my lungs as we stare at each other.

"Sleep well, Meredith."

I swallow thickly. "You too, Romel."

He nods with his chin. "I'll stay out here and make sure you get in safely."

That brings a smile to my face. "In this neighborhood?" We're in a gated community and he's got security cameras all around the exterior of his house.

"I'd rather be safe than sorry."

My smile falls as something else fills my chest. I don't say anything else. I don't think I can over the lump in my throat. Instead, I turn around and walk the rest of the way to the guesthouse. I don't look back until I'm inside and have closed the door.

Then and only then do I turn around and find him still standing in his doorway, staring at me, his brow furrowed slightly. Except the longer I watch him, the more I realize he's not staring at me. He's staring at where I was, lost in thought. He shakes his head and then looks up at the dark sky, only the faintest glimmer of stars visible here in the city, before he finally closes the door and disappears from sight.

I spin around, leaning my back against the wall, and try to catch my suddenly shallow breath. I don't know what that was back there, but a part of me hopes I'm not the only one feeling this off-kilter.

FIFTEEN

Romel

Exhaustion hits me hard as soon as I pull up to the house. Leaving for this away game was rough. It's always rough on Kay, but this time she had a meltdown of epic proportions. Meredith was forced to pull her off me, and it killed me to walk away from her while she was calling for me, tears streaming down her face.

I'd been hoping I could walk in the door tonight and hold her close, reassuring her that I would always come home to her, but our flight back was delayed due to weather, and now that I'm home and the lights are all off except the front porch, it's clear I missed my opportunity to see Kaylee before she went to bed.

Grabbing my duffle bag, I head inside. The light under the kitchen cabinets is on and there's ambient light coming from the family room that I wasn't able to see from the driveway. I figure Meredith left it on for me before she went to bed in the guest room where she sleeps when I'm away— I've noticed she always does considerate things like that. Dropping my bag by the foot of the stairs, I walk in there to turn it off.

Except when I enter the room, I almost run right into Meredith. "Hey, I figured you'd already be asleep."

It's after eleven, and I know she's typically in bed by nine. Not that I track her movements or anything, but it's obvious when I walk by the patio doors and see the lights in the guesthouse off.

"I waited up for you. I was hoping I could talk to you about something."

I gesture to the couch and we both take a seat. "What's up?" My body tenses with the slight fear that she might be about to quit on me. I know we started out on the wrong foot, but the thought of losing her now leaves a foul taste in my mouth.

She pulls the sleeves of her thin sweatshirt over her fingers and tucks her legs underneath her. "I had an idea I thought might be good to try for Kaylee—to help with the separation anxiety."

"Okay."

"What if we come with you?" She holds up her hands. "Now, hear me out before you say no. We wouldn't fly with you because I'm sure that's not allowed, but we could stay in the same hotel and come to the game. She could see that you're playing, and get to be a part of it. We could try it for a game or two to see how she does, and it might help her see what it looks like when you're playing away games. It's the not knowing that gives her anxiety."

"She told you that?"

She tilts her head to the side and then straightens it again. "No, and maybe I'm projecting from my own experience, but I do think it might help."

When I just stare at her to continue, she explains.

"When I was little, I had pretty bad anxiety whenever my dad went to work. He was the only parent I had, and the more I became aware of that, the more I had this irrational fear that if I couldn't see him, then something bad would happen to him and I'd be alone. He got his boss's permission to bring me to work with him one day."

"And that helped?" She has my full attention now, and I understand why Larissa thought she'd be a good fit. I'd never have considered bringing Kay with me to an away game so she could see what I'm doing when I leave. If it'll offer her reassurance, I'll do it.

"Yeah, because I was bored out of my mind," she says as she laughs. Her smile is infectious and my lips tilt of their own accord. She continues, "Once I knew where he was going, what his day looked like, it didn't scare me as much when he'd leave. It's not really rational, but most kids aren't rational. Based on how she freaked out when you left, I think it'd be worth trying."

"I'm on board. You don't need to convince me. I'll call up the team offices tomorrow and see who makes the travel arrangements and if I can pay for an additional room to be booked for you and Kay. I'm not sure they'll be able to do it for the next away game, but I'll see what they can do."

She smiles, her body sagging against the couch in clear relief, and once again my cheeks tighten as my own lips lift in a smile.

Huh, twice in one night and Kaylee isn't even awake. She's the only person besides the guys who can usually get me to smile.

Meredith stands from the couch, her hands twisting in her sweatshirt again. "Well, that was all I wanted to chat about. I'm sure you're exhausted, so I'll let you get some sleep. Good night."

I stand and I don't know what compels me to call her

name and stop her, but I do. She twists to face me, her expression open, her brow arched slightly in question.

"Yeah?"

I don't know why I stopped her. I don't really have anything to say, so I just say the first thing that comes to mind. "Thanks. For always thinking of how to make things easier for Kaylee."

Her smile is soft. "Of course. She's a really amazing person, Romel. You've done really good with her."

I swallow thickly and nod once. She has no idea how her words affect me, especially when I constantly worry that I'm failing Kaylee in some way that I won't be able to see for years to come.

With a final little wave, she walks out the patio door, closing it quietly behind her. I watch her walk down the well-lit walkway and then into the guesthouse. I stand there, staring at the door she disappeared behind for who knows how long, trying to figure out what this sensation coursing through me is.

My gaze shifts from Meredith's door to the wall next to me where I've hung a few pictures of Sydney—one from our wedding day, one when we were in college, and one with her holding Kaylee who was only a day old at the time.

That sick sensation slithers through my gut, and I glance back at the guesthouse. Was it attraction I felt?

No.

I move my body closer to the pictures of my wife and out of sight of Meredith's door. My fingers trace over her face from our wedding photo.

"I won't be disloyal to you," I whisper. There's no one here to hear me, but saying the words out loud reminds me of my purpose in life—to keep Sydney's memory alive and raise our daughter to be as exceptional as her mother was.

I will never love anyone the way I loved Sydney. Never.

SIXTEEN

Meredith

It takes two more away games—with Kaylee having an epic meltdown for one and a complete shutdown for the other—before the plan I discussed with Romel falls into place.

The flight was mostly uneventful. Kaylee was a little nervous about flying, but like most things, she was quiet and reserved about it. She watched out the window seat with wide eyes filled with wonder. Getting to the hotel was another eventful experience since she'd never been to a hotel before. She bounced on the bed and giggled which was probably the first time I took a breath since we'd left the house.

Now she's coloring in a coloring book I bought for her and nibbling on her favorite snack while we wait for the game to continue. I forgot how much down time there is in football games when you're watching them in person, and I guess it wasn't as noticeable when we went to Romel's home game.

She's doing great until about the fourth quarter when she starts to get cranky, which is my first red flag that something is up because Kay is the happiest, go-with-the-flow kid

I've ever met. Leaning down, I make sure she's looking me in the eyes. "Are you ready to go?"

She looks out on the field and then back at me, her eyes filled with exhaustion, but it's clear she's torn. She likes when I point out her dad playing even if she doesn't really understand the game at this age and is busy coloring more often than not.

"Your dad will understand."

She's still torn, her eyes darting between me and the field.

I lean closer and whisper. "Can I tell you a secret?"

"What?" she whispers back, mirroring me.

"I'm bored," I tell her, like I just committed the worst offense known to man.

She giggles and puts her hands over her mouth, her eyes shining. "Me too," she whispers.

I sag dramatically. "Oh, thank God. Okay, here's the deal. Let's go and we'll get in our comfy pj's and watch some TV at the hotel, and then your daddy can come and say good night when he gets back. How's that sound?"

"Yes," she says, nodding her head.

I pack up our stuff and then take her hand in mine and we head out to the rental car Romel got for me, and once she's buckled in her car seat, we head back to the hotel.

She only makes it through one episode of a cartoon before she's passed out on the bed. I text Romel to let him know, but don't get any response back. Instead of changing the channel, I keep watching her show while I snack on the popcorn I bought down in the hotel snack bar.

A knock on my door startles me an hour later, and I check on Kay to make sure she's still asleep before I head to the door and check through the peephole to find Romel standing on the other side. The first thing that hits me when

I open it is how good he smells. He's freshly showered from his game and wearing his long-sleeved black button-down that hugs his pecs. Whatever cologne or soap he uses is wreaking havoc on my lady bits. He smells like the woods and man. My stomach tightens in a way it never has as I step back and let him pass me so he can come in and see Kaylee.

He walks over, his strides long and confident, and my chest squeezes at the expression of pure love on his face. He brushes his hand over her hair and then bends down to drop a kiss to her forehead.

"How was she?" he whispers as he walks back over to me.

Keeping my voice low, I tell him, "She was great. Got a little cranky at the start of the fourth, so we came back here and she passed out pretty quickly. I can't get over how well behaved she is."

He smiles, and for the first time I notice he's got a small dimple on one side of his cheek when he smiles. My stomach swoops as I wonder how the hell I missed that. "Yeah, she's always been that way. I don't know if she's just always known I was barely hanging on and needed her to not be a terror child, or if I just got really lucky."

He leans against the wall and looks over at her. I catch myself still staring at his strong jaw and force my gaze to look at the sweet toddler sleeping soundly only a few feet away.

"Do you think this helped?" he asks.

"I think so. She seemed a little overwhelmed with the travel, which I expected, but she seemed less stressed than she is at home when you leave."

He chews on his lip while he thinks. "Think we'll need to keep doing this?"

His expression is open and earnest like my opinion matters to him, and I have to remind myself to breathe.

"Maybe one more time, but we'll see how she does your next away game to know for sure."

"I'll follow your lead. I don't want her to start to expect that she always gets to travel to these games because I don't know if that's sustainable either."

"I agree. I think we stay home your next away game and then maybe travel for one more game."

He nods, still staring at me, and my breath grows shallow in my chest as my heart rate starts to gallop. I don't know what it is about him that makes me feel like this, but I can't stop responding to him, even if I know I shouldn't. It's stupid and won't ever lead anywhere, but I can't stop myself either.

It doesn't help that he's starting to treat me like we're a team when it comes to taking care of Kaylee, and that makes me feel as if I mean more to him than I probably do.

"Thank you," he says. He keeps thanking me as if I'm doing him a favor instead of doing my job—although I'd probably do this even if it wasn't my job because I care about Kaylee so much now.

"You don't have to thank me, Romel."

"I do. I wasn't sure about a nanny. It was Larissa's prodding that made me give in." His smile grows a little wider. "And like always, she was right. You are exactly what we needed. Kaylee's been more outgoing just in the short time you've been around. So, I do need to thank you. Thank you for bringing some light into our life that we didn't know we needed."

My stomach tightens as emotion clogs my throat. This man has no idea what he does to me, what he makes me feel, or the power his words have to ensnare me further—even if it's clear he'll never be mine. He's still too in love with his wife to let me in that way. To let anyone in really.

"I'm glad you don't regret hiring me," I say, trying to remind myself that I work for him, that this is a job, and that someday neither of them will need me in their life.

A pit forms in my stomach thinking about when that time will come, how devastated I'll be to leave both of them, but it's too early to think about that.

He pats me on the arm like I'm one of the guys, and my heart shrivels up inside my chest at the platonic gesture.

"Well, I should let you get some sleep too. Flight is early tomorrow," he whispers, already reaching for the door handle.

"Good night," I say, holding the door open for him to walk through. I close it behind him and flip the extra lock before leaning back against the door.

I wanted to feel again, and now I feel all the things I shouldn't for the one man who I can't have.

I'm so fucking screwed.

SEVENTEEN

Romel

There's a freshness in the air that hasn't been there in a long time as I make my way down the short walkway to the guesthouse.

Meredith answers on the first knock, her long, dark hair falling loose around her shoulders.

"Hey!" she says, her eyes wide like she wasn't expecting me.

It's technically her day off and I'm sure she has plans, but Kay insisted on inviting her, and I figure it can't hurt to ask her.

"Hey, I know it's your day off, but Kay and I were going to go on a little adventure today to the aquarium, and I came to see if you wanted to join us."

She leans against the edge of the open door, a soft smile on her face. "You'd think Kay would be sick of me already."

"Nah, she loves spending time with you. So, what do you say?"

There's a hesitation in her eyes that has my stomach tightening. I don't know why I want her to come along so badly, but it feels important that she does. After what feels like an eternity, but is only a few minutes, she nods. "Let me grab my purse."

In the car, she asks, "So is this one of the adventures you guys do every week?"

I glance at her quickly before facing the road again. "How'd you know about that?"

"Kaylee."

Looking in the rearview mirror at my daughter, I smile. "Kay, are you giving away our family secrets?"

She giggles. "Dad-dy," she says, breaking the word into two distinct syllables and sounding very much like she's scolding me even as she laughs.

I can't help laughing with her. Directing my words to Meredith who's sitting next to me in the passenger seat, I say, "Yeah, we've had a weekly adventure pretty much every week since Kaylee was two. Sometimes it's just going for a drive; other times we do something based on what she's currently into."

"Like the aquarium," Meredith says knowingly.

"Yeah."

Kaylee's been obsessed with sea life since she saw a starfish when we went to the beach this summer. I figure she'll love going to the aquarium and seeing all the different sea creatures they've got there. It shouldn't be too busy today since schools are in session. We didn't go this summer because I wanted to avoid the tourist crowds we get that time of year.

When we arrive, Kay automatically stands between Meredith and me, her tiny hands holding each of ours. I stare a little too long at her hand in Meredith's, an unsettled, but not unpleasant sensation filling my chest. When I glance up at Meredith's face, she's staring down at Kaylee, her smile wide, her eyes shining with pure joy, and that feeling in my chest gets more intense.

Kay's excitement is infectious and I soon stop worrying about anything and just enjoy watching her look at each new critter with that wide-eyed wonder that kids have. I try to look at the world from her point of view—the endless possibilities, her excitement about the little things.

Kay points to things she recognizes from her books, and Meredith and I take turns saying the names of things she doesn't know. We both look over her head at each other, soft matching smiles on our faces when she mispronounces something in the most adorable way—like crocodactyl instead of crocodile when she sees a picture of one painted on the wall.

Meredith's cheeks flush slightly before she looks away, and my chest gets tight. I find myself looking at her more often as we keep walking through the aquarium, catching her gaze several times, and feeling my own body respond in a long-forgotten way—in a way I never thought my body would react to a woman ever again.

The lightness she brings out in Kay—and me, if I'm truly honest with myself—seems even more powerful today. Like for the first time in years, I feel alive. I'm not just going through the motions or living life through the lens of grief like I've become so accustomed to.

It feels good, but unnatural at the same time.

We're wandering the fish exhibit when an older woman smiles at us. "You have an adorable family," she says to Meredith, who's squatting down pointing to the different fish in this specific tank.

Before I can respond, Meredith stands, shaking her head. "Oh, no. I'm just the nanny."

She says it with a gentle smile, but the old woman still flushes in embarrassment. "Oh, I'm sorry."

"You're totally good," Meredith reassures her, then looks down at Kaylee, her hand running over Kay's hair that's up in a bun. "You're right that she's pretty adorable." The look she gives Kay is filled with love and tenderness.

The woman nods in agreement and then wanders off while Meredith goes back to pointing out fish with Kay, who doesn't seem at all fazed by the interaction. I faintly catch that they're making up stories about the fish, but I'm still stuck on the exchange with the woman.

Nothing Meredith said was wrong, but it doesn't feel right in my gut. She *is* the nanny, but she feels like so much more than that. In the nearly two months that she's been with us, she's made our house feel warmer. She's made *me* feel more alive. Like I was walking in a dark room before she walked in, let out that throaty laugh she has, and then turned on a light switch, illuminating my world like it was no big deal when really she was bringing us all back to life.

I struggle to let the feeling go—the feeling of wrongness at her being "just the nanny"—and find myself distracted by trying to figure out what about it bothers me the most.

We're walking out of the aquarium and back to the car when Meredith and Kay walk ahead of me, their arms swinging dramatically in a way that makes Kaylee laugh hysterically. It brings a smile to my face, and then like being hit by a semitruck, I realize this is the first outing we've had where I didn't think about Sydney. I didn't think about what she would say to Kay or what their interaction would look like. I didn't imagine her here with us the way I have with every other adventure we've taken.

My steps falter and my brain seems to be frantic to redo the whole day, but properly. I'm not supposed to leave Syd out of these adventures. She's supposed to be part of everything we do. If I don't at least think of her, I'm not upholding my promise to keep her memory alive.

A hand on my arm pulls me out of my inner turmoil, and I look at Meredith as if she's a stranger. Her dark brows are furrowed. "Romel? Are you okay?"

I swallow thickly. What is she doing to me that she made me forget my wife for a whole outing? I pull my arm away from her and walk to the car, ignoring her calling my name again. I help Kaylee get strapped into her car seat, but I can't look at Meredith. I can't speak to her because I don't know if any of the words that want to claw their way out right now would make sense to her.

They barely make sense to me.

All I know for sure is that in three years, I've never gone this long without thinking about Sydney, and that feels an awful lot like cheating on her, even if she's not alive to know it.

EIGHTEEN

Meredith

The night after our aquarium outing, I'm texting my friend
Addy about a girls' night she's organizing when there's a
gentle knock on my door. A smile breaks across my face as
soon as I catch sight of Kaylee standing at the door.

"Hey, KayBear."

Her smile fills her whole face and it makes my heart
soar. I love seeing this girl so happy and carefree.

"Will you come to dinner?"

My stomach does a somersault and I glance behind her
at the patio door that's open. I can't see Romel from this
angle though. He barely spoke to me after the aquarium
yesterday, and I have no idea what happened, but maybe
this is his way of waving a white flag.

I tuck my phone into my pocket and then take Kay's
hand. "I'd love to," I tell her with a big smile on my face to
match hers.

We walk hand in hand back to the house and enter the
dining room right as Romel calls out for Kay. His voice dies
as he catches sight of us and his face goes blank—not the sad

look I'm used to seeing on him or the soft smiles he's given me lately, just perfectly blank.

That's about the same time I look at the table settings and realize there are only two plates—one for him and one of Kaylee's princess plates.

Oh crap.

Spinning to face the sweet little girl next to me, I squat down so I'm on her level and keep my voice low. "KayBear, did you ask me to dinner without your daddy's permission?"

"Yeah," she says in that carefree way that toddlers have when they don't think there would be any reason for the adult to say no to them.

Oh boy. No wonder he's now glaring at me—I'm the interloper on his daddy-daughter time with Kaylee. Or he's still pissed about whatever happened yesterday, although if it's something I did, I really wish he'd talk to me about it. I feel like all the progress we've made just disappeared, and now I'm back to walking on eggshells around him.

"Meredith can't have dinner with us tonight, Sweetie," Romel says, his voice soft toward his daughter, but his eyes are still coldly looking at me.

"Why not?" she asks her dad with a pout.

If things were different between us, I would probably tease him by saying, "Yeah, why not?" But considering I don't want to get fired and I don't get the impression he'd find it humorous, I bite my lip to keep from smiling and stay focused on Kay.

She's got the cutest pucker between her brows, and she's staring at her dad like he just started speaking a foreign language for no reason and she doesn't understand him.

Romel looks like a deer caught in the headlights, and it hits me that maybe he doesn't have a good reason. Maybe he just doesn't want me here, which burns after he'd included me in their weekly adventure like I was part of the team.

Maybe it was stupid of me to think we were all bonding, but it felt right being with him and Kay. There were a few moments early in the day where he smiled wide enough that I caught another glimpse of the slight dimple in his cheek. His brown eyes would catch mine and it would be like we were sharing a secret. All day long, I felt like I was floating, my crush taking a dangerous leap into full-on longing every time our gazes caught.

And then he'd been distracted and it wasn't until we were walking to the car when I realized something was actually wrong. But I wasn't about to ask him in front of Kaylee.

Romel's jaw twitches like he's gnashing his back teeth. "She just can't, Kaylee."

Kaylee blinks several times, her mouth wobbling as she picks up on the tension in the room. She looks up at me with the saddest eyes, her voice soft and weak. "You don't wanna eat with me?"

I can't take the heartbroken look on her face, and I immediately wrap her up in my arms and shoot daggers from my eyes at her dad. Then I focus solely on the only person in this room who matters and doesn't infuriate and confuse me. "KayBear, I would love to eat with you, but I think your dad wants this time with you."

She sniffles. "But what will you eat?"

I pull back, and the rims of her eyes are pink and watery like she's on the verge of tears. "I've got plenty of food. Tell ya what. How about tomorrow when your dad is at practice, we can have a picnic together. How's that sound?"

There's still doubt and confusion in her gaze. She doesn't understand the tension she feels in the room. I'm even more pissed at Romel right now because he could very easily have just gone with the flow for tonight. It wouldn't have killed him.

"Okay," she whispers and then glances at her dad.

I catch him reaching out his hand for her from my periphery and she walks over to him. He sweeps her up in a tight hug, and it takes a second for his gaze to move from the wall he was staring at to meet mine.

At least he's not glaring at me, but I don't love the closed off expression on his face either. There's no warmth there at all.

"I'll see you tomorrow, KayBear." Then I dash out the patio doors and toward the guesthouse before either of them can say anything.

I spend the next few hours baking a couple of treats for my picnic with Kay tomorrow and snacking on a charcuterie board I bought. And I think about all the things I want to say to Romel as soon as I know Kaylee is down for bed. Because he and I clearly need to have a talk, and if he won't be man enough to tell me what's going on, then I'll start the conversation. What happened tonight wasn't fair to me or Kaylee, and if he doesn't care about me, I *know* he'll care about how his actions impact his daughter.

I wait until I'm sure she's in bed and then march across the yard to the patio doors. I grab the handle to slide it open, but it doesn't budge and I stare at it like it burned me. Not once since I moved here have these doors ever been locked.

What the hell is going on?

I knock, irritated, but underneath that irritation is unease and, worst of all, hurt. What the hell happened yesterday that's changed Romel so dramatically? I've tried to rack my brain over the last few hours to figure it out, but I can't think of anything that stands out. We were having a great time and then suddenly he checked out.

I knock again until I finally see him come from the hallway that leads to his in-home gym. He's in gym shorts and no shirt, his dark chest glistening with sweat. Around his neck is a chain I've never noticed before with two rings on it—wedding bands. My stomach tightens with nerves and a stupid mix of lust and heartbreak. I shouldn't want a man who is so obviously emotionally unavailable.

He opens the patio doors, the muscle of his jaw tensing and the muscles on his stomach flexing in a way that absolutely should not make my mouth water at this moment.

Talk about bad timing to be turned on. Jesus Christ.

My lips part, but no words come out. My brain has turned to mush at the sight of this man's body.

"What?" he grumbles.

I look into his deep brown eyes, wishing so badly for the warmth that was there just yesterday. "What's going on?"

"What do you mean?"

"You know what I mean." I'm not letting him try to gaslight me into thinking there hasn't been a change. There's no way he could miss it, especially when he's the one who's changed.

"I don't have time for this, Meredith. I need to get a workout in before bed."

I push myself past him, brushing against his firm body. God, he's broad and fit and so fucking droolworthy, it's not even fair. "I'll make this quick then," I say as he turns around and crosses his arms. "We were fine yesterday at the aquarium and then we weren't. Did I do something?"

His jaw clenches, but he shakes his head.

I step closer to him. "I don't believe you," I say, hating how my voice shakes. "Something happened and I deserve to know what it was. What happened tonight with Kaylee wasn't okay."

Anger sparks in his eyes and he steps forward, closing the distance so we're practically toe to toe as he stares down at me. "Do not talk to me about my daughter."

"I'm her nanny. It's my job to talk to you about your daughter." I want to add *asshole*, but don't.

"You know what I mean."

I plead with him now because I want to understand what the hell is going on. "Romel, please. What happened yesterday? Why are you shutting me out and being cold all of a sudden?"

His gaze darts back and forth between my eyes, his chest heaving as he drops his hands. His head lowers slightly, and I suck in a shuddering breath as he stares at me with such heartbreak and self-recrimination.

"Romel," I whisper, my gaze dropping to his mouth.

He takes in a labored breath. "I will not cheat on my wife."

His dead wife.

My heart stalls in my chest as my gaze darts back to his, seeing the seriousness in his expression. My nose burns with the threat of tears, and emotion builds in my throat.

At least I got one thing answered tonight—I wasn't alone in feeling a spark between us. I'm only alone in wishing it would turn into a wildfire, while he's wishing his wife was still alive.

"I never asked you to," I choke out and then move around him and walk out the door back to the guesthouse.

I don't look back because if I do, he'll see the tears streaming down my face as a confusing mix of emotions slams into me. Or worst of all, I'll look back to find that he's not looking at me at all.

NINETEEN

Romel

My whole body is tense—battling itself between my loyalty to Sydney and the desire to grab Meredith and yell at her for making me feel things I was never supposed to feel again. Red rims her eyes and my heart splinters as her words slice into me.

"I never asked you to," she says before pushing past me and out the door back to the guesthouse.

I fight the urge to turn around and watch her, but give up immediately and spin around, gripping the door frame in a lame attempt to keep myself from rushing after her.

She doesn't deserve the way I've treated her since the aquarium. It's not her fault I feel unfaithful to Sydney. It's not her fault that I'm so weak, I've started feeling emotions for her that I thought were dead and buried with my wife.

I swallow down the lump in my throat as Meredith enters the guesthouse and closes the door without so much as a glance back at me. This is for the best. Let her be mad at me.

My gut tightens though as I realize it wasn't anger in her eyes but hurt. I don't like the idea of hurting her.

"Fuck," I mutter. The curse word feels good, albeit unfamiliar since I stopped cursing because of Kay repeating everything I said.

I slam the patio door closed, pissed off at myself more than anyone else. I don't lock it this time. I don't know why I did that in the first place.

As if I could lock her out of my thoughts if she was locked out of the house.

No chance of that.

My mind is a jumbled mess as I walk to the gym room and throw all my energy into working out, hoping maybe the activity will clear my mind. But not even the burn of my muscles can stop me from remembering the look on Meredith's face before she walked out.

I put my weights back on the rack and drop my head to my hands as I sit on the workout bench. I touch the wedding bands that I always wear around my neck—mine and Sydney's. She was buried with her engagement ring, but I wanted to hold a piece of her with me always, so I kept the wedding band.

"I'm sorry, Syd. I'm so sorry." My words come out choked before tears fill my eyes and I let out all the emotions that have been weighing me down. I was supposed to do better by her, to always be the man she'd be proud of.

But I know in my heart she wouldn't be proud of how I just treated Meredith. She wouldn't be proud of how I can't get my shit together.

"I don't know what I'm doing anymore," I choke out as if she can hear me. "I wish you were here. I wish you could tell me what to do."

If she were here...

Well, if she were here, I wouldn't be in this situation. We wouldn't have a nanny. I wouldn't have been alone and single for the last three years. I wouldn't be developing feelings for someone who clearly loves our daughter because I would never have met Meredith.

That last thought causes my gut to clench. The thought of never meeting her, never knowing her doesn't feel right either.

Nothing feels right.

My gaze narrows on the receiver I'm tracking as he takes off like a shot when the ball snaps to the quarterback. I match him stride for stride, my feet digging into the turf with each powerful step as I try to close the gap between us. The quarterback releases the ball, and it spins in a tight spiral, cutting through the air and heading straight for the receiver I've already got my eyes on.

As if there's a line showing the ball's trajectory, I can see exactly where it's about to go, just out of reach of the receiver's outstretched hands. But not out of my reach. I leap, timing my jump perfectly, my fingers grazing the ball's edge. For a heartbeat, it feels like the world stops as I will the ball to slip into my gloved hand.

Using my own momentum and guiding the ball with my hand, I bring it down and then cradle it to my chest as I land on my feet. Our home crowd's roar of excitement swells to a fever pitch.

The ref calls out, "Interception."

The other members of the Fierce Four, as well as some of our defensive line, run over to pat me on the back or arm or grip my shoulder in excitement. My cheeks pull up into a small smile, but my gaze focuses on the seats where Meredith and Kay sat last time they watched a game.

Strangers are sitting there now because Meredith and Kaylee are at home. Disappointment settles heavily in my gut, and it takes some of the excitement out of my catch.

I want them here.

Both of them.

And I'm not sure what it says about me that despite telling myself over and over again not to feel anything for Meredith, I still feel things for her.

Feelings that might not even matter since I've been such a giant dick to her.

TWENTY

Meredith

An Uber takes me to the club Addy chose for our girls' night. I use the drive to check my lipstick in my phone's camera before we pull up and I thank the driver. It feels good to dress up and go out, especially since I desperately needed to get away from Romel's house.

This girls' night came at the perfect time. Romel and I have barely talked to each other since our confrontation two nights ago, and the tension is nearly suffocating.

But the worst part is how Kay has pulled back in on herself because of it. She doesn't say that's why she's gotten quiet, but the way she glances at her dad and me for the few minutes that we have to be in the same room together makes it clear she knows something is going on. I hate that she's being affected, but at the same time, I don't know how to fix it.

I don't even know if it's possible for me to fix it. How do you fix the issue when the issue is that your boss thinks being attracted to you is being unfaithful to his dead wife?

I didn't learn how to handle this type of situation in college.

When I get inside the venue, I send a text to Addy because this place is packed and I have no idea where she is. She texts me that she's in a booth in the back, and after pushing through the crowd of bodies, I finally see her standing and waving. I rush over and give her a hug, a smile splitting my face.

"You look amazing! I love this dress," I say, gushing over the form-fitting red dress that makes her look like an absolute bombshell. Her smile is wide, her blonde hair falling in perfectly styled waves down her back.

"Thank you! You look great too! Here, come meet everyone."

Her last words don't fully register until I find myself in front of a booth filled with people I've never met before. I keep my smile pasted to my face as I turn to her. "I thought this was a girls' night with Chelsea and Kate?"

"Oh, they couldn't come so I decided to invite my work friends." She leans closer to my ear so only I can hear. "Plus, I've got the worst crush on Jake and am hoping he'll finally make a move tonight." She pulls back with a smile and a wink as my heart drops to my stomach.

So much for a girls' night.

I take a seat at the end of the U-shaped booth on the outskirts of a dance floor. Addy introduces everyone and then they all start talking about something that happened at work.

"I'm going to go get a drink," I shout across the table to Addy. She smiles and nods and waves me off, so I slip out of the booth and head back to the bar.

For a second, I consider just going home. The thought of being social with a bunch of strangers does not sound appealing, but unfortunately, going home means possibly running into Romel, which sounds about as fun as having a root canal.

He was gone at a barbecue at a friend's house when I left, but I have no idea when they'll be back and I'm not willing to risk it. So I woman-up and order a drink, then head back to the booth and mentally prep myself to make new friends.

When I slide into the booth, the guy next to me scans down my short dress, and I fight the urge to roll my eyes at his blatant perusal. That is not the way to seduce me, buddy.

You want to make me melt into a puddle on the floor? Look at me like I'm beautiful, funny, and bring light to your life. Having a cute little dimple that only appears when you *really* smile helps too.

I take a big swallow of my lemon drop. It's sugary sweet, but masks the alcohol so I can take a big gulp without feeling the burn right away. *I will not think about Romel tonight*, I tell myself for the millionth time.

"Hey, I'm Chad."

I bite back a laugh. Of course, the dude-bro who looks like a stockbroker is named Chad.

"Hey, Chad. I'm Meredith."

I figure it can't hurt to be nice. I also expect him to ask me something about myself after this because that's my experience with most guys, but instead he immediately starts talking about his new car and the condo he was able to buy. When he's not talking about himself, he's leering at me. I start to make a game of how many times he looks at my body—taking a drink every time he talks to my boobs instead of my face.

I finish my first drink in record time. The rest of the

night starts to blur together as I drink more—much more than I planned on.

As Chad drones on, I don't know what possesses me—alcohol, most definitely—to pull my phone out of my purse and drunk text Romel, but I do.

ME

ur a jerk

Dots immediately pop up.

ROMEL

What?

ME

You r Jen

My phone starts ringing and Romel's name flashes on the screen. Panicked, I say to Chad, "Gotta take this. It's my boss." Or at least that's what I try to say. It comes out a little more like "Gutta tuh this. S'ma boss."

I walk away from the loud tables and down a short hallway where it's somewhat quieter. "Hello?" Fuck, is my voice slurring?

There's a pause, and then his smooth, deep voice comes through the phone and makes warm tingles burst to life between my legs. "Are you drunk?"

"No," I say too quickly and with a slur so it comes out more like "nuhhh."

Jesus, I'm drunk. I didn't think I had *that* much to drink.

His voice gets hard. "Where are you?"

"Like you care." There. That came out mostly clear, so I can't be that far gone.

"Meredith. Do not play with me. Where the hell are you?"

His voice is so deep, so demanding. I want to wrap myself up in it like it's a blanket and fall asleep.

I mumble the name of the club as my eyes grow heavy. "So sleepy," I murmur. How did I go from taking sips to sleepy drunk in just a couple of hours? Damn Chad and his stupid wandering eyes.

"Don't fall asleep, and don't hang up. I'll be there in..." His voice gets distant like he pulled the phone away from his face. "Fifteen minutes, twenty tops. Where are you in the club?"

There's a rustle in the background of wherever he is and I think I tell him where I am, but my eyelids are getting so heavy. I should go back to the table. Definitely back to Addy and see if she wants to blow this popsicle stand. Maybe get some Del Taco like old times.

Oh man, tacos sound so good right now.

"I gotta go," I mumble and hang up. I stumble back to the table thinking about tacos, but when I get back to the group, Chad is waiting with that hooded look in his eyes as he once again stares at my boobs, and I'm quickly reminded that I have, in fact, had way more to drink than normal because of that stupid game I created.

Addy giggles as she stands up and hugs me, mushing her mouth to my cheek. Then very loudly she says, "You should totally go home with him. He's hot."

"Yeah, I am," Chad says with all the confidence in the world, and I wonder if he thinks his smile is supposed to look seductive when all it looks is smarmy.

Why am I here? Why did I even stay? I don't really like any of these people—not that I know them all that well to begin with—and right now my pajamas and my bed are looking way better than staying in this noisy and crowded club with a bunch of people I don't know and a guy who looked at my boobs so much, I lost count of my drinks.

I pull my arm out of Addy's grasp. "I gotta go."

"Noo!" she whines.

"Yeah." I give her a hug and then pull away.

"Fine. Text me when you get home."

I nod and then quickly walk away before Chad gets any ideas about following me. That's not happening, ever.

I stumble a few times as I make my way toward the exit, pulling out my phone to request an Uber from the app. It's late and I don't love the idea of being driven home by a stranger when I'm this wasted, but I need to get home.

I open the app when Romel's name lights up the screen. Shit. I already forgot I texted him. What the hell is wrong with me tonight?

Plugging one ear, I hold my phone to the other and answer as I keep making my way to the exit. "Hello?"

I can barely hear him over the crowd, but I'm almost at the door, so I tell him to hold on and push my way through the last big crowd of people until I get to the bouncers and the exit doors.

"Coming back in?" one of the bouncers asks.

"No."

"Alright, have a nice night."

"You too," I say as I walk out and take a breath of fresh air.

Romel's deep voice breaks through the quiet of the night outside the club. "Where are you?" he demands.

"Outside the club."

"Stay put. I'm almost there."

My steps falter as I come to a stop a few steps away from the club doors. "What do you mean you're almost here?" My words are still a little slurred, but the cool night air is clearing my head a little more.

"I told you I was on my way. Don't move, and stay on the phone with me until I get there. GPS says I'm three minutes away."

I'm speechless. Completely speechless as I stand frozen on the sidewalk.

"Talk to me, Meredith," his voice rolls over me and sends tingles to my core.

I hate how much I respond to him when he wants so little to do with me. More than that, I hate that I've just become a burden for him. God, what if he fires me over this? I feel the sudden desire to explain myself.

"He kept staring at my boobs," I say, tears of drunken frustration burning at the corners of my eyes.

"What?" he growls.

"Chad."

"Who the fuck is Chad?"

Damn, he sounds pissed. That should not turn me on, but it does. I love the protective edge to his voice.

"I made a game out of him looking at my boobs every time he looked I drank I didn't expect it to be so bad I don't drink like this please don't fire me." I heave in a breath after rambling all my words.

His car pulls up to the curb, and he stares at me through the passenger window, his dark eyes holding me hostage.

"I'm not going to fire you."

TWENTY-ONE

Romel

She drops the hand holding her phone to her side as she steps forward to the edge of the curb and opens the passenger door.

"You're not going to fire me?" Her voice sounds so sad, so unlike the Meredith I've grown used to over the last few months.

I'm here worrying about her safety and well-being and she's standing there worried I'm going to fire her. And why shouldn't she be? I haven't given her any reason to think I care about her beyond her role as my daughter's nanny.

"Get in the car, Mere. I'm taking you home."

She blinks twice and then gets in the car without argument. She's quiet for the first five minutes before she sits up and rotates abruptly to look at the backseat where Kay's car seat usually is.

"Where's Kay?" There's panic in her voice and it does something to me to hear her concern for my daughter, even knowing she's inebriated.

"She's at Gabe and Danae's house. She fell asleep while we were all hanging out, and instead of waking her up,

Danae and Gabe offered to let her sleep over. They'll bring her by in the morning. I would've been here faster if I hadn't had to take out the car seat."

"You didn't have to come and get me. I could've gotten an Uber."

I throw a glance at her, and her cheeks flush red before she looks away. I swallow thickly as my cock jerks in my pants. It's been a very long time since it's responded to a woman—to anything really.

"There's no way I would've let you do that knowing what state you're in."

"I'm sorry again, about getting so drunk. I don't usually drink like this."

"You don't have to apologize for letting loose and hanging out with your friends. I get it. Honestly, when you called and you were slurring, I was worried someone had drugged you. I know you're not the type to drink like this."

"That's why you came to get me?" Her voice is soft, and when I glance over, her eyes are heavy-lidded like she's about to fall asleep.

"I was worried about you." I don't know why I repeat myself instead of just saying yes, but a part of me needs her to know that she's not just the nanny. Despite how cold I've been to her lately, I can't deny that she brings to life something inside of me I thought was long gone.

She doesn't respond, and the next time I look over, she's fast asleep. We get to the house twenty minutes later, and she looks too peaceful to wake up, so I walk around to the passenger side, unhook her seat belt, and lift her up—one hand under her knees and the other behind her back. She protests slightly for a second—just a murmur, even though she never opens her eyes—before she wraps her arms around my neck and lets me carry her around the house to the guesthouse. I push open the unlocked door and make a mental note to remind her to keep it locked for her safety. Once inside, I carry her to her bedroom.

This is the first time I've been in here since she moved in. There are fresh flowers on the windowsill, and the closet door is open with all her clothes inside. A couple of pairs of shoes are strewn across the floor, and the bench seat at the end of the bed has a pile of clothes that were clearly discarded—I'm guessing they're outfits she was trying on for tonight since I've never seen her wear these before.

My gut churns slightly at the thought that she was getting dressed up for someone else, which I know is stupid since I've made it clear to her that nothing can happen between us.

Apparently, I haven't made it clear enough to myself because my body responds to holding her so close to me. It's the first time I've held a woman like this since Sydney—touched another woman at all. Apart from the occasional hug to my friends' wives, I've had no desire to touch another woman.

But with Meredith, my fingers practically itch with the urge to feel her whenever I see her. It doesn't make sense, and the guilt that eats at me for feeling something for a woman who isn't Sydney only confuses me further.

Now that I've got her in my arms, I'm reluctant to let her go. When she nuzzles her face against the curve of my neck, the need to hold her tighter only gets stronger.

"I wish this was real," she murmurs, her breath brushing against my neck and causing goose bumps to rise on my skin.

"It is real," I say, my voice quiet like hers.

Her arms tighten around my neck. "No, it's not." She

sounds so sad it makes my heart ache. "You would never hold me. You'd never let yourself."

My body stiffens. "What do you mean?"

"I wish..." her sentence fades, uncompleted.

"You wish what?" I ask her, a hint of urgency to my tone.

"I wish you could be mine."

I don't think she could've said anything that would shock me stupid more than those words. I swallow thickly, not sure what to say. Not that it matters. She's plastered. How much of this conversation will she even remember?

Instead of trying to fill the silence, I push her blankets back and lay her down in the bed. Her face is slack with sleep as I cover her with the comforter. I brush a few strands of dark hair away from her face. Her light skin contrasts dramatically with my dark skin, and there's something that feels so right about caressing her face. Even as I embrace that feeling, it's tainted by the sudden doubt I feel. Doubt and guilt, but this time it's not guilt for wanting her; it's guilt for suddenly *not* feeling guilty that I've developed feelings for someone when I promised Sydney it would only ever be her.

I step back from the bed, my gaze still locked on Meredith's face. I leave the guesthouse and head straight to my room, trying not to think about her words, but unable to get her voice out of my head.

I wish you could be mine.

I've only ever been Sydney's. I don't know how to let anyone else in. I don't even know if it's possible to love someone else the way they would deserve because of how much I still love Sydney. It wouldn't be fair to her.

And yet, I still can't stop thinking about it and wondering what it would be like if I could be hers.

What would it be like if *she* was *mine*?

TWENTY-TWO

Meredith

I wake up with the hangover of all hangovers.

Even with the curtains drawn, it feels like the faint light coming from the slight gap where the curtains don't quite meet is stabbing my eyeballs.

With a groan, I throw my comforter over my head, but even the groan hurts my aching brain.

Jesus, how much did I have to drink last night?

Stupid Chad.

I can't really blame him for the decision *I* made to make a stupid drinking game out of his actions, but with my hangover making my skull feel like someone's using it for a drumbeat, I decide he deserves partial blame.

My mouth feels thick and dry, and I'm hit with the urge to drink something, but I really don't want to get out of bed. With another groan which I regret instantly, I throw the covers off and push myself up to sitting. The room spins briefly and my stomach churns with queasiness.

I think I'm going to be sick. I push up and dash to the bathroom, making it just in time to empty whatever was left in my stomach into the toilet. Sagging back against the side of the bathtub, I wipe my mouth with some toilet paper. Staying seated on the floor sounds like a solid plan until I'm certain my stomach is settled. Once I'm sure nothing else is going to come up, I push myself up to standing and brush my teeth to get the thick, cottony feeling out of my mouth. A shower sounds incredible right now, but first I need aspirin for this headache.

Walking out of the bathroom, I stop in my tracks when I notice the glass of water, two little pills, and a note on my nightstand. I pick up the note first, and my cheeks heat with mortification when I see it's from Romel.

Take these and then come over to the main house when you're up. I'll make you a hangover breakfast.

I don't know what a hangover breakfast is—my friends and I usually just got Del Taco when we were drunk or hungover because it was open twenty-four hours. I close my eyes as pure embarrassment throttles me. I don't remember anything after Romel showed up outside the club. I barely remember walking out of the club in the first place.

I need him to know I'm not that irresponsible. Last night was the first time I've ever gotten so drunk outside of a couple times when we got plastered at a frat party near our dorms. But in those situations, I'd always been with friends and could walk home. Last night was next level irresponsible because I was with people I didn't really know, apart from Addy. I can only imagine what Romel thinks of me now.

I toss back the aspirin and drink most of the water before I get in the shower. Once I'm showered and dressed, I'm starting to feel marginally better, but dread still curls in my stomach at the thought of facing Romel. I have no idea what I said or did after he picked me up, and I'm not sure I want to know. I'm humiliated enough that he saw me shit-faced.

Reluctantly, I slip on my sandals and walk over to the main house. Romel's already in the kitchen when I slide open the back door, and the smell of bacon instantly hits my nose. He looks up at me at the same time my stomach grumbles.

A small smile forms on his face, and now my stomach clenches for a whole new reason. God, I swear this man's smile is my kryptonite.

"Morning," I say, giving him an awkward wave and then I briefly close my eyes and take a deep breath. I need to be an adult about this. When I open my eyes, he's already watching me. There doesn't seem to be judgment on his face, but there's something I can't quite name. At least he doesn't look angry, and I'm not getting that blank expression I hate so much. "I'm sorry about last night. I've never gotten so drunk like that, and I hope you know I'm not normally that irresponsible."

He sets down the tongs he was using to move the bacon from the sheet pan to a plate with a paper towel on it. "You're allowed to go out and have fun, Meredith. I'd be a hypocrite if I judged you for that. I've been shit-faced myself plenty of times when I was in college."

"But I'm not in college anymore," I point out. "And I don't want you to think I'd ever be irresponsible around Kay."

"I've never thought you would."

I nod. "Okay, good."

This conversation is going way better than I was expecting. I wince. "I didn't say anything embarrassing last night, did I?"

His gaze turns thoughtful. "You don't remember everything?"

I shake my head with regret. "The last thing I remember is getting in the car with you."

He looks down at the counter, and for a second it seems like he's disappointed.

"Did something happen?" I ask cautiously. I hope to God I didn't say or do anything horrendously embarrassing.

When he looks up at me, his expression is a bit more distant than it was before. "No. You fell asleep in the car and I carried you to the guesthouse. You were still passed out when I put you to bed."

I cover my face with my hand. On the one hand, I'm grateful I didn't say anything—like admitting how much I like him in a way that is completely unprofessional—but on the other hand, I'm still ashamed I got so drunk, he had to carry me to bed.

"Here," he says, picking up a plate of cheesy eggs, buttered toast, and adding three slices of bacon to it. He sets it down on the counter in front of one of the tall stools and I take a seat and dig in. He pours me a glass of orange juice and then turns around to pour a cup of coffee which he sets next to the juice.

My mouth is full of delicious food, so I can't ask him if he's got any milk or sugar, but apparently I don't need to because he pulls out a bottle of my favorite hazelnut coffee creamer. I swallow my bite and then stare at him in disbelief. How did he know this was my favorite?

That soft smile reappears and my heartbeat picks up the pace at the sight.

"Kay insisted we get your creamer when we were at the grocery store."

My own smile breaks across my face. "She's a total sweetheart, Romel."

I don't think I can tell him that enough because so often it seems like he thinks he's failing her when it's the exact opposite.

He sets down his own plate and locks his gaze on mine. "I owe you an apology."

"For what?" I hate how my voice cracks.

"For what I said to you after the aquarium." He takes a deep breath, and the movement causes his chest to expand and his shirt to stretch across his pecs. I can see the outline of the rings he wears around his neck underneath the fabric. Now that I know they're there, I can't seem to stop noticing where they slightly lift his shirt whenever I see him. "Sydney has been with me every day since she died. I think about her constantly."

What is it like to have a man like this love you that fiercely? Sydney's life might've been cut too short, but God, was she lucky to have a love like this. A man like this one.

I hate that I'm jealous of a dead woman. There's no point in feeling the emotion, but it still tangles up with my own feelings and knowing he'll never allow himself to let her go enough to let someone else in.

"I didn't think about her at the aquarium," he says, his voice heavy with guilt.

I furrow my brow. "I don't understand."

"It's the first adventure I've had with Kaylee where I haven't imagined Sydney with us—haven't thought about her at all."

I shake my head, still not quite understanding why that

made him react to me the way he did, but he speaks before I can ask.

"I enjoyed the day with you and my daughter and didn't once think about my wife, and it felt like a betrayal to her." He looks down at the counter when he says the last part like he's ashamed of himself, or maybe just can't look me in the eye.

My heart aches as I finally start to get it, and I reach my hand out and place it on his. He stiffens slightly, but doesn't remove his hand from under mine. "I didn't get the chance to meet Sydney, but I can't imagine she would want you to feel guilty for enjoying a day with your daughter and not thinking about her. I'm sure she would understand."

He looks at me then with torture in his eyes. "But it wasn't just with my daughter."

We stare at each other as a heaviness settles between us. "You didn't think about her because you were with *me*?" I ask, trying to understand if I'm way off base here.

He nods.

What does that mean? My stupid, hopeful heart starts racing.

We stare at each other, the tension between us thickening, but before either of us gets a chance to say anything more, the front door opens and Kaylee's voice shouts down the hall. "Daddy!"

We both pull our hands away as if the touch suddenly burned, and just in time since Kay comes racing into the kitchen seconds later, followed by Gabe Romero and a woman. Both adults dart glances between Romel and me. I try to calm my racing heart, but it's hard when Romel squats down just in time to catch Kaylee as she runs into his arms, wrapping her arms tight around his neck.

She sees me and smiles. "Miss Mere!"

"Hey, KayBear. You hungry?"

She nods and squirms until Romel sets her down. She runs over to the stool next to me, and I help her up where she sits on her knees and grabs a piece of bacon off the paper towel, taking a bite with a big smile.

"Sorry if we interrupted," Gabe says. He extends his hand. "We haven't formally met. Gabe Romero. This is my wife, Danae," he says, gesturing to the dark-haired woman next to him.

"Meredith. I'm the nanny."

Gabe looks at Romel. "Awfully nice of you to make breakfast for your nanny."

My cheeks flush. "Uh, yeah, I had a rough night," I say, not wanting to be more detailed with Kaylee sitting next to me. "But greasy bacon is just the cure. And coffee. Can never have enough coffee."

Danae smiles kindly at me, while Gabe keeps darting glances between Romel and me. "Coffee is definitely a necessity in our house too," she says. "Anyway, we just stopped by to drop off Kaylee. Car seat's by the front door. We'll get out of your hair." She grabs Gabe's hand and gives him a look when it's clear he wants to stay and say something.

He shakes his head and drops a kiss to her forehead that makes my chest ache. Do all these guys love their women as fiercely as Romel loves Sydney?

If so, I hope they all realize how lucky they are.

Because a love like that doesn't come around every day, and unfortunately, I think for Romel, he's convinced it can only come around once. Which means it doesn't matter if hanging out with me made him stop thinking about Sydney, because I can tell by the torment in his eyes and what he said to me the following day that he sees that as a betrayal.

And I won't push him to let her go if he doesn't want to.

TWENTY-THREE

Romel

Meredith's name flashes on my phone just as I'm getting ready to leave my hotel room. Their flight was delayed for this away game, so she's probably just calling to tell me what room they're in.

"Hey, you get settled in okay?"

"We have a problem," she says, her voice strained.

"What's wrong?" All my dad instincts go on high alert.

"The hotel apparently lost our reservation. All the rooms are booked."

I grab my keycard and exit my room. "I'm on my way down. Be there in a few minutes."

It takes me exactly three minutes to get downstairs where I find them standing in front of the reception desk. I walk up to the counter next to them, my hand automatically finding Meredith's back in a soothing touch. She spins to face me and her face is lined with weariness. Kay looks equally worn out. What the hell happened?

I'll ask them when we get this sorted. Turning to the hotel concierge, I say, "Their reservation got lost? They were supposed to be added on with the team."

"I'm so sorry, Mr. Watson. I'm not sure what happened, but there's no reservation under her name or yours, apart from the room block for the team that's already full. There's another event happening downtown, and we're all booked this weekend."

I look at my girls—I mean, Meredith and Kay, only one of which is mine.

Not the time, Romel. I rub my forehead trying to get my shit together when the obvious solution hits me. "They'll stay in my room. Can we get a cot?"

I'll let Meredith and Kay take the bed and I can take the cot.

The concierge nods quickly. "We'll get that up right away."

"Great, thanks." I reach out for Kaylee who lifts her hands to be picked up. "Hey, Sweetie. How was the plane ride?"

"Rough," Meredith says, dragging her suitcase and Kaylee's behind her as she walks next to me.

"What happened?"

She shakes her head. "I don't think my trick to help Kay's ears pop worked this time, and she was miserable the entire flight."

Sympathy fills her features as she looks at my daughter, and my chest tightens. She's always concerned for Kay, almost on the same level I am, and for the first time, I allow myself to admit that I find it attractive.

I find a lot of things about Meredith attractive.

We make it back to the room and I let them get settled before I leave to head to the stadium.

When I exit the locker room after our game, Meredith is waiting with Kaylee asleep in her arms. She gives me an exhausted smile. "I think she'll probably be fine with you leaving for away games from here on out. This trip has exhausted her."

"So your plan worked?"

She smiles wider. "I guess it did. Did you have doubts?"

"About your ideas? Never."

We share a moment, and the tension I felt between us the other day when I made her breakfast roars back to life.

I drive us back to the hotel in the rental car I got for Meredith, but when we get back to the room, the first thing I notice is the cot that got delivered is definitely not made for an adult.

"I'll call down to get a full-sized cot up here if you can get her put to bed," I tell Meredith. She nods and takes over getting Kaylee changed into her pajamas while I call down to the concierge.

I hang up five minutes later with a new problem to address.

Meredith stands up from tucking in Kaylee—who's still fast asleep—and puts her hands on her hips. "So, what's up? Are they bringing another cot?"

"They don't have anymore."

Her eyes go wide. "What?"

I rub at the back of my neck. "Turns out they only had the one kid's cot left. All the large ones are being used." What I don't tell her is the concierge assumed Meredith and I were a couple and would only need a kid's cot.

"So...we have to share a bed?" she asks, her dark brow arching.

"Looks that way. You okay with that?" I mean, at least it's a king-size bed, so it's not like we'd be forced to cuddle.

"Are *you?*" she asks.

I shrug. "Yeah, I mean I'm exhausted and you're exhausted. It's not like you'll take advantage of me," I say with a smile.

Her jaw drops. "No, I wouldn't."

"So, it'll be fine."

"Fine."

I let her use the bathroom first and spend the five minutes that she's in there moving Kaylee to the cot and then staring at the bed. Panic starts to swirl in my gut—or maybe it's nervousness, which is something I haven't felt in a very long time—the longer I stare at the king-size bed which suddenly seems much smaller.

The bathroom door opens and Meredith comes out wearing pajama shorts and an oversized T-shirt. Nothing about her attire screams sexy and yet it's hard to pull my gaze from her bare, toned legs. I brush past her, careful not to touch her, and then close the bathroom door.

Okay, this is going to be fine. We'll sleep on our separate sides and it'll all be fine.

I brush my teeth and then realize it won't be fine.

I didn't pack pajamas. I always sleep in my boxer briefs and wasn't planning on having anyone else in the room with me.

My hand is heavy on the door handle as I press it down and open it, walking back into the room. Meredith's gaze catches mine, her bottom lip trapped between her teeth, and the words just fall out of my mouth.

"I sleep in my underwear and didn't pack pajamas."

Even in the dim light, I can see her cheeks flush. "Oh," she says, her lips parting to make the shape of the word. They look glossier than I'm used to seeing, probably from when she licked them. Her gaze drops down to my pants, and my stomach tightens as I beg my body not to respond to her stare.

I do not need to embarrass myself in front of the first woman who's stirred up anything remotely close to feelings in over three years.

She puts her hand up. "I'll cover my eyes so you can get undressed." Her voice shakes a little, and I wonder if she's feeling the same nerves I am.

I quickly strip out of my pants and dress shirt, and get into the bed. We lie there on our backs, neither of us saying a word, but I can't help but notice her breathing seems to be as uneven as mine. I can't get my heart to settle down, and my ab muscles are flexed like my body is bracing itself for a tackle.

"Is this awkward?" I ask her.

"No?"

I turn my head to face her, a smile on my lips. "Were you asking me or telling me?"

She mirrors my position and then covers her face as she laughs. Her laugh is light, but a little throaty like her voice and it's infectious.

She rolls her body to face me, and this time it's my turn to mirror her pose. Despite how big the bed is, our pinkies from our hands nearly touch where they are placed beside our heads. Her dark gaze stares into mine as her smile fades into a thoughtful expression.

"You're nothing like I expected when I took this job."

"Right back at ya."

"Romel?"

"Hmm?" Both of our voices have gotten quiet, but there's something freeing about talking in the dark, something that brings down all the walls I've held up to protect me from ever getting hurt again.

She rolls onto her back, her eyes facing the ceiling. "Never mind."

I don't know what compels me, but I cup her cheek with my hand, turning her to face me again.

"What are you doing?" she whispers.

"I don't know," I whisper back, closing the space between us, and for this one minute I forget who I am, who she is, my past, all of it. I'm just a man attracted to a woman and wanting to see what she tastes like.

I close the gap and press my lips to hers. She moans and then wraps her hand around my neck, holding me in place as our kiss deepens, taking on a life of its own.

TWENTY-FOUR

Meredith

My alarm goes off at five and I turn it off immediately, glancing to make sure it didn't wake up Kaylee, but she's still fast asleep on the cot, one leg sticking out from under her blanket and both her arms over her head, her mouth slack with sleep. A soft smile lifts my lips as I stare at her, and then I look at the man next to me and bite back a laugh when I see him sleeping in almost the exact same position as his daughter.

I roll over, facing him, and tuck my hands under my cheek as I stare at him. His face is much more peaceful when he's asleep than it is when he's awake.

I touch my lips, recalling the kiss.

The kiss that was earth-shattering and yet peacefully soothing at the same time. We didn't do anything more than that one kiss, but it felt like it permanently altered something inside of me.

No man's lips on mine have ever felt as right as Romel's. And the way he looked at me like I was a gift when he pulled away, before we both fell asleep, was more than I ever dreamed I'd get from him.

A part of me can't wait for him to wake up so we can figure out where we go from here, but the other part of me just wants to live in this blissful peace for as long as possible.

I don't get to enjoy the bliss for long because a few minutes later his phone alarm goes off and he turns it off with a groan. The thick muscles in his arms flex as he scrubs his face and then turns to me.

"Morning," I say, keeping my voice low, but unable to stop my smile.

"Morning," he says, his voice still thick with sleep.

He rolls out of bed and heads to the bathroom, grabbing his clothes on the way there.

Okayyy. That was not the reaction I was expecting this morning. While he's in the bathroom, I quickly get dressed, and then stare at the bed wondering what happened between him kissing me and us waking up.

Is it always going to be one step forward, three steps back with him? I don't know if I can take that, always wondering when he's going to pull away from me.

Maybe we shouldn't have crossed that line. Maybe it would've been better to keep professional boundaries in place.

He comes out of the bathroom and stops when he sees me standing at the foot of the bed already dressed. "We should wake up Kay, so you guys can get to the airport with plenty of time to get through security and everything."

Is that really all he's going to say to me?

"Uh, yeah, I guess we should." I turn to wake her up, but stop and spin back around to face him. I take two steps toward him. "We should talk about last night first."

He looks down at the floor. "Maybe it was a mistake."

It feels like an elephant just sat on my chest. I can't

speak over the shock and hurt. It would be one thing to tell me he needed time to think about things, but to call it—*me*—a mistake is devastating. But I bury my feelings.

Without another word to him, I turn around and focus on Kaylee. "Hey, KayBear, it's time to wake up."

I get her dressed while Romel orders room service so she can eat breakfast before we need to leave. Neither of us talk much to each other as Kay eats and we pack up. I guess there's nothing to say. Words burn in my gut, all the things I wish I could say if Kaylee wasn't here and I didn't value my job.

The flight home is uneventful, and we arrive home shortly after Romel does.

"You can take the rest of the day off," he says, his voice still distant.

I stare at him longer than I should, hurt and confused. He breaks our stare, and his gaze darts to the wall behind me. I know what's there. I've lived here long enough to know where all of Sydney's pictures are hanging up. Kay and I sometimes look at them. Lately she's been curious about what features she shares with her mom, so I've spent more time than usual looking at the beautiful woman who's left such a gaping hole of grief in this house.

Pain flashes across his eyes, and I hate that I understand what's holding him back.

I would never ask him to stop loving her, but I wish he could see that it's okay to let someone else in.

Kay's in her room which is the only reason I step forward and cup his cheek. "I understand, Romel. I get it." The words come out slightly stilted with emotion, but I need him to know I understand. I may not like it, but there's not much I can do about that.

His eyes dart between mine, a slight pinch between his

brows. Pushing up on my tiptoes, I kiss his cheek—just one last time before I don't let myself touch him anymore—and then head out the front door. I'm not going back to the guesthouse today. I need space from him, from the feelings he stirs up in me that will never be returned.

So, I go to the only person I can when I'm confused and heartbroken—my dad.

He looks up from the car he's still tinkering with, and as soon as he sees my face, he sets his tools down and holds his arms out. I burrow into his hug. "I think I'm falling for him, Dad."

He doesn't say anything, but his arms tighten around me. I pull back just enough to look up at his face, his beard more full of gray than I remember. "Do you think someone can love two people at once?"

"I don't know. I think it's possible, but the person has to be open to it."

I rest my head back on his chest, my heart sinking. "Yeah, that's what I thought you'd say."

And I know Romel will never let himself be open to loving anyone but Sydney.

TWENTY-FIVE

Romel

Nothing feels right.

Watching Meredith walk out of the house has my gut clenching painfully. Telling her it was a mistake was supposed to ease the guilt, but it's only made the feeling worse.

I stare at Sydney's picture—her smiling face as she stares off into the distance, her eyes holding that spark that used to always make me feel like the luckiest guy in the world. I thought what I felt when I kissed Meredith was guilt for being unfaithful when I promised Sydney that she would be the only one.

Now I'm second-guessing myself because telling Meredith it was a mistake has left a gaping hole in my gut and not eased any of the negative feelings swirling inside me.

I pull out my phone and text Ty.

ME

Can Kay and I come over to visit?

I don't want to be at the house today, especially if Meredith isn't here.

He responds almost immediately.

TY

Hell yeah. Come on over. Lex just put Lana down for a nap.

"Kay! Wanna go see Uncle Ty and Auntie Lexi?"

"Yeah," she squeals and then I hear the slapping of her shoes against the hardwood floor as she comes racing down the hallway.

At least things with my daughter are normal, even if nothing else feels that way anymore.

Ty opens the door with his typical charismatic smile. Of all of us guys, he's the most authentically nice guy I know. We used to tease him that it was because he was Canadian, so he couldn't help himself, but I think it's just him. Since meeting Lexi, he's become even happier. They had a bit of a rocky start, and then a rough go when his brother meddled in a way that left us all shocked. His brother apologized and has done his best to make amends, but it's clear he's still fighting some inner demons and self-doubts that arose after that whole scandal. He plays pro for another football team in the league, but there have been rumors swirling that he might retire soon, especially after all the stuff that went down.

"Hey, man, long time no see," Ty teases since we flew home together this morning.

God, was it really just this morning when I woke up

next to Meredith after kissing her last night? It feels like it happened so long ago.

Lexi comes around the corner, a smile on her face as wide as Ty's. He immediately wraps his arm around her waist and pulls her against his body, kissing the top of her head. It's good to see him in love. It's even better to see that love returned because anyone who looks at these two can't deny how real and genuine their feelings are for each other.

"Hey, Romel. Hey, Kay, wanna come hang out with me and we can let the boys talk?"

I don't know if she's psychic or can just read me like a book because it only took one glance at me for her to know I needed to talk to Ty alone.

Kay smiles at Lexi and takes her hand without a glance back at me. My chest swells with love for that little girl and gratitude that I've surrounded her with people who love her as much as I do.

And then my gut tightens with that anxious, guilty feeling again because that includes Meredith.

Would she quit after what happened between us?

The sinking feeling gets worse.

Ty closes the door behind me and pats my back. "Come on, we can chat in the den."

He takes me to the room that used to be his man cave, but now there are baby toys everywhere.

"Did Lana take over this room?" I ask with a laugh.

He turns to me. "Don't babies take over every room in the house?"

We both grin. "Fair enough."

He gestures to the couch and grabs us both waters from the mini fridge he's got in here before we take seats at opposite ends. "What's going on? You look like you saw a ghost."

I pick at the label of my water bottle. "Didn't see one, but I feel like I betrayed one."

He leans forward, putting his elbows on his knees. "Romel, we've told you before that Sydney wouldn't want you to be alone. No matter what you did, I can guarantee you didn't betray her."

"I kissed Meredith."

His eyes go wide. "Your nanny?"

I nod.

He sits back against the couch. "Damn, I owe Dom ten bucks."

I glare at him. "You guys were taking bets?"

He shoots me a look. "Come on, you know Dom. He'll make a game out of anything. As soon as he saw what your nanny looked like, he figured eventually you'd slip. You've been so closed off to women—" I open my mouth to respond, but he holds up his hand. "And I get it. I do. If something happened with Lexi, I wouldn't move on easily either. That woman is my whole world." He leans forward again. "But you deserve to find happiness, Romel, and it's easy to ignore women when you never let yourself spend any significant time with any of them."

"I didn't kiss her because she was there," I grumble, a frown on my face. He makes it sound like I succumbed because she was the nearest woman around, but that couldn't be further from the truth. I've been around plenty of women when the guys and I used to go out. None of them interested me, even when they threw themselves at me.

But Meredith got under my defenses. Maybe because my only good defense is my daughter and Meredith has made Kaylee so happy these past few months. She's brought her out of her shell in a way no one else has, and she clearly loves Kay as much as I do.

"Then why did you?" Ty asks, no judgment in his tone.

Why did I kiss Meredith?

"Because I couldn't stop myself. Because she's infiltrated my mind, and she was looking at me with that soft way she has about her where it's like she really sees me. It just felt natural to lean forward and kiss her."

"And how did it feel?"

I swallow hard. "It felt perfect," I choke out, remembering the moment our lips touched and it felt like coming home. The way she grabbed my neck and seemed to melt into the kiss only made it even better. I look down at my hands. "But I promised Syd—"

He cuts me off. "We all know what you promised Syd, but you know she'd never let you make that kind of promise. Think about it, Romel. Think about Sydney. Do you seriously believe she'd want you to be alone? Answer me honestly."

"I can't," I say, my voice hoarse.

"And why not?" he asks like he already knows the answer.

I glare at him. "Because you're right, okay? No, she wouldn't want that, but—"

"No more buts, Romel. You have an opportunity here, a second chance at a real relationship with someone who loves your daughter. Who cares about you. Are you going to risk that because you're afraid of what might happen?" He reaches over and grabs my shoulder, holding me steady. "You're always the one giving us fatherly advice and calling us out when we've been immature idiots. It was long overdue for us to do the same to you, but in this, you're being an idiot.

I know it's scary to put your heart on the line like that, but it's also scary to live in 'what-if' land. What if you *don't* take the risk and you lose out on a second chance at love?"

"But what if that's not what this ends up being and then I'm setting up Kay to get hurt?"

His eyes narrow. "Kay? Or yourself?"

"Both."

"Here's what I know—you don't know unless you take the risk. No risk, no reward. You could keep doing what you've been doing and risk being lonely for the rest of your life and having nothing once Kay is grown and out of the house. Or, you could take a chance, put yourself out there, and maybe you get the partner Sydney would've wanted you to have."

I stare out the window as I ruminate over his words, and I hate that they ease some of the feeling that's been swirling in my gut since I woke up.

Because it means the only mistake I made was pushing Meredith away, and now I have a lot to make up for.

TWENTY-SIX

Meredith

Addy texts me while I'm hanging out with my dad and asks me to come with her for mani-pedis. I cave because I can't just mope around my dad's house all day, even though I'm still uncomfortable with how our last hangout went at the club.

Apparently so is she, because as soon as I get out of my car, she's holding out a coffee cup and her face is filled with remorse. "I'm *so* sorry about the club. I got way drunker than I planned and feel like a horrible friend because I just left you to fend for yourself with a bunch of people you didn't know."

I pinch my lips between my teeth and nod. "Pretty much."

"I'm the worst friend." Her shoulders drop. "I don't know why I even invited them. I've been under so much pressure at work, and I felt like I needed to behave a certain way for them to like me, which is stupid."

I grab her hand and give it a squeeze before releasing it. "It's okay. You're forgiven. Besides, it's on me for how much I drank last night. I never should've had so much to begin with. Honestly, post college has been a weird phase for me too. I feel like I figured out who I was in college, and now I've got to figure out who I am as a fully grown adult."

"Yes!" she says, her eyes wide with relief that I get it.

"Come on, let's get our nails done. I haven't done this in ages, and I deserve to be pampered today."

We go inside and get settled in our chairs as the ladies start on our pedicures.

"So, what's been going on with you?"

I debate telling her about Romel, but hold my tongue. I love Addy, but she's right that we aren't the same people we were when we met in college. We have new pressures and new social circles. I don't know if she'd let it slip, but with Romel's fame and how much he values his privacy, I don't feel like risking telling her something that doesn't even matter. He made it clear we would never be anything more than boss and employee, and I need to move on.

So instead I just tell her about the great little girl I'm nannying. She tells me all about her job and the pressures to wear the right clothes and snag the right clients. The more she talks about it, the happier I am I didn't tell her about Romel.

After our mani-pedis, we go get lunch at one of our favorite cafés we found sophomore year of college. We've just ordered our croissant sandwiches when the door opens and Cameron walks in holding hands with a woman.

Addy's eyes narrow. "Well, that was fast."

"It's been a few months since we broke up, so it's not really that surprising."

"Uh...is that a diamond ring on her left hand?"

Before I can look, Cameron catches sight of us and walks over. "Hey, Meredith, Addy. Funny running into you guys here."

"Yeah, hilarious, since Meredith was the one who showed you this place to begin with." I bite back a laugh at Addy's snarky response. This is why I'm still friends with her.

He glares at Addy and then looks at me. "Meredith, this is my fiancée, Lauren."

Addy chokes on the drink of lemon water she'd just taken. "You move on fast, Cam," she says, her voice hoarse from her coughing fit.

Cam's fiancée hugs his arm and stares up at him with stars in her eyes. "Well, when you know, you know, right?"

I stare at them both and then smile. "Congratulations. Genuinely." And it really is because looking at these two, I don't feel anything. I don't feel sad that he moved on so quickly. I don't even feel much of anything seeing him for the first time since we broke up.

He doesn't stir butterflies in my stomach like someone else does. He doesn't make my heart race or stir up any of the confusion and desire that Romel does. Even when things were good with us, Cameron didn't stir up butterflies. Maybe that should've been my first hint that things would never work out with us in the long haul.

"Enjoy your meal," I tell him with my smile still on my face. There's no reason for us to continue a conversation, and clearly he feels the same way because he gives us a head nod and then they walk away.

Addy, however, isn't so quick to let it go. She leans forward and whispers, "How are you not enraged that he moved on so fast and got *engaged?*"

I shrug. "Because I haven't felt anything for him for a long time, and the longer we're apart the more I can see that we were never the right fit to begin with. Good for him for finding someone he wants to spend the rest of his life with.

Honestly, I'm glad he didn't think it was me because I might've actually said yes, and that would've been terrible."

"You really think you would've said yes to him?"

The waitress drops off our sandwiches, and Addy takes a bite as I try to think of how to answer her question. "I probably would've. I don't think I would've gone through with it, but this last year has been so weird for me. I felt apathetic toward everything, including my relationship with Cam."

She looks at me more closely. "You do seem more... animated than you've been the last few months. I'm sorry. I should've checked on you sooner. I figured you were just dealing with the same senior stress as the rest of us."

"I was, but I think it just hit me differently. I spent so long just going through the motions—doing the next level of school because that's what I was supposed to do. I don't know. Maybe I was having a quarter-life crisis or something."

"You seem more yourself, or maybe that's not quite the right word because honestly you seem more sure of yourself than I ever remember you being."

I smile softly. "Yeah, maybe I am. Nannying has been good for me. Nannying Kay at least. I don't know if I'd feel this way if I'd nannied for anyone else, but she's such a happy and smart kid."

"Do you think you'll ever go back to school for PT?"

"I think so. I'm still glad I took a break, but I've been thinking about it more and more. Right now, I'm just kind of going with the flow and that's working for me. We'll see what happens."

It feels good to admit that I like where my life is right now, I don't love the turmoil I've felt about Romel, but I am overall happy with the choice I made to take a break before deciding whether I'd pursue my PT degree or not.

Maybe my life hasn't gone how I thought it would, but I'm starting to think that everything has happened the way it has for a reason.

Later that night, I pull up in front of Romel's house. The lights are on inside, but I still decide to go around the outside path to the guesthouse instead of through the main house. I pass one of the windows and catch sight of Kaylee dancing and singing off-pitch to one of her favorite cartoons. But what really brings a smile to my face is seeing Romel dance and laugh with her. There's a strong pang in my heart as I watch them, feeling like an outsider. They've both lost so much, but still find these moments of happiness together. A fierce longing stabs me in the gut, and I know with certainty that any chance I had of escaping these two without a broken heart is long gone.

Someday, they won't need me anymore.

And I'm going to be devastated when that day comes.

TWENTY-SEVEN

Romel

I pause at the foot of the stairs and watch Meredith lean over and paint Kaylee's toes the same bright pink as hers. My chest tightens at the sight of them smiling and giggling. Sydney always talked about doing things like this with her daughter—even before we knew we were having a girl, although she'd had a feeling early on that it was a girl. It hurts to know Syd will never get this experience, but at the same time, it's nice to see Kay get to have moments like this with a woman I know she looks up to.

Right as I have the thought, Kaylee looks at Meredith, her eyes bright and happy like she thinks Meredith is the best thing in the world.

I imagine it's not far off from the look I often have when I look at Meredith. I've been thinking about what Ty said ever since we left their house, and something is shifting inside me. I spent a lot of time talking to Syd's picture last night—the one I keep on my bedside table— and trying to remember her and what she'd say in this situation. It gave me some clarity, but I'm still wrapping my head around the confusing swirl of feelings stirring inside me after so long of feeling nothing but various layers of grief.

Meredith looks up when I clear my throat, and her smile becomes a little forced when it's aimed at me. I haven't had a chance to talk to her without Kaylee around, and I'm not sure if she's done that on purpose or not.

I wouldn't blame her if she did.

"I'm heading out for guys' night, but I won't be out late."

"Okay," she says.

Kaylee wiggles her toes and hits me with a megawatt smile. "Daddy, look!"

"Pretty," I say as I walk over and drop a kiss to the top of her head. "Be a good girl for Miss Mere, okay?"

She nods, but she's already focused on her toes again. Meredith is smiling at her with such a serene expression on her face, and I'm hit once again with how much she loves my daughter.

"I'll see you when I get home."

She nods, but is already focused on Kay. I leave with an uneasy feeling in my stomach and a certainty in my veins that I need to find the words before I mess this up further.

Ty sets down the card with a smile. "Uno."

But his smile is short-lived when Dom lays down a reverse and then +2. "Not quite."

Gabe chuckles as Ty grabs the cards and grumbles before he looks at me. "So, have you talked to Meredith yet?"

Both Gabe and Dom look at me expectantly. Too expectantly. I narrow my eyes at Ty. "Did you tell them?"

"I told Dom he owed me money, and you just confirmed

he does by insinuating there's something to tell. So tell them the details and then catch us all up on what happened when you went home."

I take a drink of my bottled water—none of us are drinking tonight—and then face my three best friends. "I kissed her, then told her it was a mistake, and she didn't stop by the main house when she got home last night, so we haven't talked except about Kay."

"You kissed her and then immediately told her it was a mistake?" Gabe asked.

"No, we fell asleep and then when I woke up I told her I thought it might've been a mistake."

"Hold up," Dom says, setting his cards face down. "You slept with her?!"

"We actually slept. Nothing sexy happened apart from me kissing her."

"Was it a bad kiss?" Gabe asks, looking completely confused about how I fucked this up so badly.

"No, it wasn't," I admit, my voice low. Quiet descends, none of them sure what to say.

I tip my head back, staring at the ceiling before facing them and admitting the truth, because if I can't admit it to these three, then I can't admit it to anyone. "I was freaked *because* it wasn't a bad kiss. It was a great kiss. One of the best, even though it's not like we were making out or anything. It was a pretty simple kiss, all things considered, but there was something in it that made it feel like it packed a punch, ya know?"

They all nod their heads with knowing grins. Of course they know. They're all happily married to the women they've shared those kisses with.

So, now I guess it's time to admit something else to

them. "Sydney was the only person I've shared a kiss like that with."

"That should be a good thing, right? It means Meredith is special."

I rub my forehead and let out a heavy exhale. "Sydney's the only woman I've *ever* kissed. And now Meredith."

They all stare at me, jaws dropped.

Dom puts up his hands in a stop gesture. "Hold the hell up. Are you trying to tell us that Sydney...that she was the first girl you ever kissed? The first girl you had sex with?"

I nod.

"No fucking way," he says in clear disbelief.

"I was focused on football and getting scholarships in high school. I didn't want to disappoint my parents. It's not like there weren't girls around who were clearly interested, but I wasn't willing to risk my chances of getting a full-ride scholarship, and girls were a distraction. I met Sydney freshman year of college and there was just something about her. I couldn't have stopped myself from falling for her if I tried. I think I knew I wanted to marry her after our first month together, but we still waited until after college to get married. And as you know, there's been no one since her." I scratch my jaw. "So to say I'm a little out of my depth here would be an understatement."

"You married the first girl you had sex with?" Dom asks, clearly still trying to wrap his head around this. Considering he's a reformed playboy, I'm not at all surprised he's the one so shocked by this. The others seem to be taking it in stride.

I smile. "Yeah. Got a problem with that?"

He shakes his head. "Man, you could've had so many girls. Especially in college. You missed your player days. Are you sure you don't want to maybe date around before you start thinking seriously about a woman again?"

"I'm not really the date around type. I watched my parents' marriage and knew I always wanted something similar to theirs. I don't think I'd be all that good at no strings attached. Especially considering there are so few women who catch my eye to begin with."

"But Meredith did?" Gabe asks.

I slide my thumb back and forth on my cards lying face down on the table in front of me. "Yeah, she did." I scrub my hands over my face. "I ignored it for a long time because it felt like being unfaithful to Sydney."

They all speak at the same time. "You're not being unfaithful."

"Yeah, I finally got that. It just took a while to sink in. But I've already shoved my foot into my mouth with Meredith and I need to fix it, but as you've now learned, I don't exactly have massive game with women. I don't know what to do here. I can't guarantee I won't freak out again. This is all new territory."

"But you do want to date her?"

"Yeah, I do. It's a delicate situation because of Kay. She loves Mere and would be devastated if things between Meredith and I led to her losing Meredith. I don't want to put her through that, but is it really fair to ask Meredith to keep it a secret when I've already told her it was a mistake? I don't want to make her feel like she's a side piece or something."

"I think you should probably tell her everything you just said to us. Women like when we talk to them and tell them how we're feeling, even if it's confusing and shows that we're a hot mess," Ty said.

Dom and Gabe nod and hum in affirmation.

"Then I think it's time I go home and see if I fumbled

this past the point of no return or if she's willing to give me another chance."

TWENTY-EIGHT

Meredith

The second Romel leaves for guys' night, I feel my body relax. He hasn't mentioned our kiss again and neither have I. What is there really to talk about anyway? Knowing the man you've been falling for thinks kissing you was a mistake is next level humiliating, and I'd rather not drag the awkwardness out if possible.

I put the finishing touches on Kay's toes, and she wiggles them and squeals with pure joy. Thank God for quick-dry nail polish.

"Alright, next on the girls' night checklist is face masks."

"Yay!" she squeals although I don't know if she even understands what a face mask really is. I did some research when I got home last night and found a recipe for a home-made cucumber aloe face mask that's supposed to be great for sensitive skin and had simple ingredients so it was safe for Kaylee to put on her face. The last thing I wanted to do was accidentally buy one that gave her a rash or something and ruined the experience for her.

I grab the mask mix that I whipped up earlier today and

start by putting a blob on her nose. She giggles, and the sound brings a smile to my face.

God, I love this girl so much. She's such a ray of sunshine when everything feels like a mess. Even though I had a moment of jealousy of Sydney, right now all I feel is sadness that she'll never get to see the incredible kid she created. She brought this beautiful gift into the world and doesn't even get to enjoy her and watch her grow. It's the greatest travesty of losing a parent at such a young age.

I remember wanting to always do things like this with my mom, especially when I was around ten and my friends would tell me about the fun mother-daughter things they'd do. I don't want Kay to miss out on any of those things, so I'll give her as many memories as I can while I'm in her life.

Once I've got the mask spread in an even layer on her forehead, nose, cheeks, and chin, I do the same to myself. We run to the bathroom and laugh at how silly we look.

I even snap a few pics of us and debate sending one of them to Romel, but decide against it. He's probably busy with his friends anyway. I tuck my phone into my back pocket, and then after a few minutes, we rinse off our faces.

"Gorgeous!" I say to our clean faces in the reflection in the mirror.

"Gorgeous!" she mimics.

"Okay, now it's time for popcorn and a movie. What do you think we should watch?"

She shouts the name of her current favorite movie and grabs my hand to pull me out to the living room. I get it started on the TV before I go to the kitchen to make the popcorn.

Despite her energy when we were doing face masks, she only makes it halfway through the movie before her eyes start getting droopy with sleep.

"You gettin' sleepy, KayBear?"

"No," she murmurs, half asleep.

I chuckle and hit pause on the remote. "Let's go read a couple of stories before bed."

The fact she doesn't fight me on it only confirms how exhausted she is. We go through her bedtime routine— putting on her pj's, brushing her teeth, and then getting into bed for story time.

The first story she picks out isn't one I've read before, and immediately my heart feels like it tugs in my chest. It's about a mama bear and her cub. The rhymes are simple and sweet, but still, my voice gets throaty as the sentiment under the words hits me right in the chest.

"Miss Mere?" Kay whispers, snuggling closer to me.

"Yeah, KayBear?"

"I wish you were my mommy."

My nose burns as tears fill my eyes. I put the book down and wrap my arm around her shoulders, holding her tight. I don't tell her that she feels like mine, and that being her mommy would be the greatest title I'd ever have because I won't get her hopes up for something that will never happen, even if we both wish it could. I could never replace Sydney, but I could honor her memory by loving her family.

I pick the book back up and finish the story, fighting back tears the entire time. I read her one more after that before she falls sleep and I extricate myself from her bed. I brush a loose curl away from her face. She has no idea all the hard days in her future without her mom—the days when she'll miss her so fiercely because she'll ache to know simply what it would be like to have one. I wish I could save her from all those days, that I could hold her hand when she misses her mom and tell her how proud Sydney would be. I press a kiss to her forehead, make sure her night-light is on, and then leave the room, closing the door behind me.

I'm picking up the living room and putting things away when the garage door opens.

Shit. Why is he back so soon? I thought I had at least another hour so I could get the house clean and be ready to walk out the door as soon as he got home. Things are going to be so awkward without Kaylee awake to ease some of the tension.

I'm about to throw the last few remaining toys in the toy bin in the living room when he walks in. Taking a breath, I stand up and face him.

"Hey," I say.

"Hey," he says back, dropping his keys on the counter and taking off his coat.

"I was just picking up. I'm almost done."

"Okay." He stands there, staring at me, and that familiar tension that always seems to arc between us flares up once again.

Dammit. It's too soon for me to be alone with him after what he said to me. I've never been called a mistake before, and I'd like to avoid reliving the memory for as long as possible.

I toss the handful of toys left into the bin and then look around the room. It's all clean and nothing's been left out. I already put our popcorn bowl in the dishwasher.

"I think I'm all done here. Have a good night," I say with as much fake cheer as I can muster and then rush out the patio door.

He calls my name, but I don't look back. I can't. Not tonight. I'm too weak after Kaylee told me she wished I was her mom. I can't deal with Romel's emotional issues on top of my own.

But I forget that he's an athlete who works out and can run faster than I can. He catches up to me before I can escape into the safety of the guesthouse.

"Meredith." He says my name like a plea at my back, and I close my eyes, already knowing I'm going to give in and turn around, even if I know what he's about to say will probably only add to the hurt I feel.

I turn around, internally bracing myself for pain. He closes the space between us, his gaze fierce on mine. "I'm an idiot and that kiss wasn't a mistake. Nothing about you could ever be a mistake."

And then before I have a chance to respond, he kisses me like a man who's been starved of affection his entire life and this kiss is the only thing that will save him from eternal misery.

TWENTY-NINE

Romel

Her lips are even softer than I remember as I kiss her deeper, wishing *this* was our first kiss and I hadn't messed up the last one. Her hands grip the material of my shirt where it rests against my hips as her body melts against mine. I slide my fingers in her hair and lick across her lips, needing to taste her. She moans as I lick inside her luscious mouth.

My pants get tight as my cock hardens against my zipper. Damn, it's been so long since I've responded like this, and I can finally admit it feels like coming back to life. It's scary—terrifying—in the way a free fall might be. There's exhilaration humming through my veins as I kiss Meredith with everything I have and she gives it all back.

"Wow," she whispers when we finally break the kiss, her eyes glazed and heavy-lidded, and then her cheeks flush that bright pink color I'm growing so addicted to. She has nothing to be embarrassed about. "Wow" was exactly what I was thinking too.

Leaning my forehead against hers, I let out a heavy exhale and already regret that I have adult responsibilities which means I can't keep kissing her like I want to. "I should go back inside. I've got an early practice tomorrow."

She nods but doesn't pull away, and I love that she doesn't. I'd deserve it if she did after I kissed her last time. "I won't regret this in the morning," I say, wanting to reassure her in case she's worried.

She peers up at me and gives me a soft smile. "I'm gonna hold you to that."

I kiss her once more, wishing I could kiss her all night, but I do have an early practice, and the last thing I need is to be dragging tomorrow because I stayed up late kissing my nanny.

I can just imagine the way the guys would tease me.

The next morning, I'm down in the kitchen when Meredith walks in through the patio doors. Her hair is up in a messy bun and she's wearing skintight leggings and a loose top, similar to what she wore last night. She looks beautiful.

"Kay still asleep?" she asks, looking around.

"Yeah, she must be going through a growth spurt or something. That's the only time she really sleeps in."

It's already after six a.m. I can't remember the last time Kaylee slept past five thirty.

"I need to head out." I glance up at the stairs to make sure Kaylee hasn't woken up and might be coming down the hall, but the coast is still clear. "Can we talk more tonight after Kay goes to bed? About us?"

She keeps her face carefully neutral, but there's still some caution in her tone. "Is there an *us*?"

"I'd like there to be."

Her dark brown eyes flick back and forth between mine.

"Okay," she says, her voice low. I hope I can convince her to let down her guard, even if I know it's my fault it's up so high in the first place.

"I'll see you after practice."

I seal my mouth over hers, kissing her one more time because I can't have her this close and not kiss her, and then I leave for practice.

Two hours later, I'm on the field running drills when a whistle blows and our defensive coach, Alison Fairbright, calls my name.

"There's a call for you, Romel. From your nanny. Sounds like it's an emergency with Kay."

She doesn't need to tell me any more before I'm rushing off the field into the locker rooms. A trainer is standing by one of the office phones and hands it to me as soon as I run in the room.

"Mere?"

Her panicked voice makes my blood pressure skyrocket before she even gets all her words out. "Romel, I'm at the hospital with Kay. I went to check on her—"

"Which hospital?"

She names a local hospital, and I tell her I'll be there as soon as I can. I grab my bag and race out of the training center to get to the hospital.

When I arrive, I'm quickly directed to where she is. They haven't been moved yet from the ER, but the nurse gives me a rundown of what's going on. Kaylee was admitted with a fever of 104.3 and unresponsive when attempts were made to wake her up. They've given her fluids and medication to break the fever and are now monitoring her.

The nurse moves the curtains aside and I find Meredith sitting in a chair next to Kaylee's hospital bed, her eyes red and wet from tears, her hand covering Kay's. She stands up when she sees me, and I immediately wrap my arms around her. She's blubbering as she rushes to explain what I wouldn't let her explain over the phone. "I went to check on her after you left and she seemed fine, but then she still wasn't up by seven-thirty, so I went into the room to try and wake her up. She was burning up, so I took her temp and it was 104. I called her pediatrician's after-hours line and when they heard she wasn't responding to me trying to wake her up, they told me to bring her to the hospital to get checked out."

I hold her tighter. "It's okay. You did the right thing."

"I feel so helpless," she cries as fresh tears fall down her cheeks.

"I know, but the nurse said she's going to be okay. They're just worried about breaking the fever now and getting her to wake up." Truth is she's not the only one feeling helpless, but I'm going to choose to trust the professionals in this situation.

I pull back and brush away her tears with my thumb. "You did the right thing, Mere," I tell her again because it's clear she feels awful when she has nothing to feel bad about. She did everything right in this situation—it's exactly what I would've done too. "Thank you for loving her so much," I whisper, emotion starting to clog my throat.

She stares up at me, her watery eyes filled with so much worry and love for my daughter. "She's easy to love."

There's something in her eyes that makes me wish she thought *I* was as easy to love. That I could be worthy of the love she so freely and easily gives to my daughter. I don't know if I'm ready to be quite that serious with someone yet, but I've also never been a casual kind of guy. I don't know if I know how to do anything besides go all-in with a woman.

"Yeah, she is," I say instead of saying any of the other thoughts swirling around inside my head.

We both take a seat next to Kaylee, and I hold Mere's hand, each of us offering comfort to the other, while my other hand rests on my daughter's.

I've had help and support from friends and family Kay's entire life, but it's never felt like this. Like I don't just have help, but a partner.

Over the next hour, I watch Meredith stare at Kaylee, hold her hand, and fuss over her. Another piece of the boundary I've held on to so tightly disintegrates. Something about seeing Meredith love my daughter like her mother would removes the doubt I've clung to.

I hate to think it, but maybe the guys were right, and it's time to honor Sydney the way she would've wanted—by letting someone in who could love her family as much as she did.

THIRTY

Meredith

A week later, I'm putting away the peanut butter and jelly while Kay eats half the sandwich I just made when the front door opens and her grandma walks in.

Larissa greets me with a huge smile and then wraps her arms around me in a hug, even as I stand there wondering if this is awkward. I'm the nanny she hired to watch her granddaughter, not secretly kiss her son-in-law.

"Hey," I say, trying not to be surprised that she's here.

She pulls back with a knowing twinkle in her eye that has me immediately on alert. "I hope you don't mind, but I'm stealing my granddaughter for the day." And then lower so Kaylee won't hear. "I think you're about to have other plans anyway." She gives me a wink, and I start to wonder if I've entered an alternate reality.

Romel didn't seriously tell his mother-in-law that he and I were...well, whatever we're doing, did he?

But I get my answer when he comes down the stairs with a smile on his face. He kisses Larissa's cheek and thanks her for coming.

"Meredith, can I chat with you in the other room for a sec?"

"Sure," I tell him, knowing if he set this up on purpose, he doesn't want Kay to know what's going on. We've agreed to keep this quiet and between just us for now. Although apparently "just us" now includes Larissa.

We walk to another room far enough away that we won't be overheard. He rubs his hands together in front of him like he's a bit nervous and then says, "Do you want to go out with me today? I thought we could grab a bite to eat and then maybe go to a movie or something."

"A meal and a movie? That's a very old-school date."

He looks a little embarrassed. "It's been a long time since I've dated, so I'm not really sure what's standard procedure here."

"You got Larissa to take Kay out so we could go on a date." It's not really a question because that's obviously what's going on here, but he acts like it's one.

"Yeah, I knew if they stayed around here, then Kay would wonder why we were both gone, and I'd rather not lie to my daughter."

"Unless it's a lie of omission."

"Not telling her about us isn't a lie of omission; it's just keeping this private since it's new and I don't want to get her hopes up in case..."

I get it. "Okay, let me go get changed and I'll be ready to go."

His shoulders sag with relief and he nods once. I dart back out to the kitchen to say bye to Kaylee and then head back to the guesthouse to change and get ready. Since he's wearing jeans and is dressed fairly casually, I decide to go casual too. Once I'm changed into my favorite pair of skinny jeans and a cute top I bought the last time I went out with Addy, I head back to the main house to find it silent.

It's crazy how different the house feels when Kaylee isn't here.

Romel is pacing back and forth in the den, and I bite back a smile at how nervous he looks. I know it's been at least three years since he last went on a date—assuming he took Sydney out on dates until she was too sick to enjoy them. But dating your wife is very different from dating someone new.

I wonder how weird this is for him—dating someone new after thinking he was going to be with Sydney for the rest of his life.

He stops his pacing as he catches sight of me, and all thoughts of his past with Sydney evaporate as he smiles at me—the same smile that causes a slight dimple to form in his cheek. Butterflies cause a flurry in my stomach as I try to catch my breath and slow my heart's reaction to him.

"Ready?" he asks.

"Yep." I'm definitely ready to take this next step and see if he can drop his walls enough to let me in.

I'm cautiously optimistic, but I'm also the daughter of a man who could never let go enough to let anyone else stand by his side.

My dad always saw someone else as a replacement—which he said was impossible, and to an extent I agree. I don't think the person that comes after you lose a loved one is a replacement. That makes them sound like a stand-in for the person you lost, which they're not. I think they're someone new for the new you that was created from the loss you experienced. They take the place by your side as an equal and act as the glue to your heart.

In other words, I have no desire to replace Sydney. I

could never live up to that pressure. But I can heal the hurts her family has experienced and hold their hands as we move into this next phase of life. I can love them like they deserve and still honor her memory.

Or I can, if Romel will open up his heart enough to realize it's big enough to love both Sydney and me.

He takes me to a taco stand off the beach. "Ty found this place when Lexi was craving Mexican food and told us all about it. Gabe came with his sisters to try it out and gave his seal of approval, although no tamale compares to Mama Romero's." His eyes roll to the back of his head as he lets out a groan. "They're seriously the best tamales I've had in my life."

"Well, now you're just making me jealous."

He bumps me with his shoulder. "Well, if you're lucky maybe I'll convince Gabe to ask his mom for some to share with you."

I push up on my tiptoes, putting us almost nose to nose, and my heartbeat speeds up at the heat in his eyes. "I'm a pretty lucky girl, so I think my odds are good."

And then I drop down before I'm too tempted to kiss him. He lets out a huff of breath and then a deep chuckle as he shakes his head and watches me with a sexy grin on his face.

We get our order and move to one of the picnic benches. It's probably a little too cold to eat outside, but we both brought jackets, so we decide to rough it. The benefit of it being so chilly is that not very many people are eating around us.

"Do you ever get recognized when you're out in public?"

He swallows his bite. "Sometimes. More often if I'm at a bar or restaurant where there might be fans, but just running my day-to-day errands, not very often. If the other guys from the Fierce Four are ever with me, then we always inevitably run into fans who want pictures with us. We love our fans—they're the best in the league—but it's one of the reasons we started having game nights at each other's houses. We try to rotate to keep it balanced, although it's always Ty who brings the game, but it's the one time we can all let loose and just have fun without really worrying about other people snapping our picture or coming over to ask for autographs."

I set down my taco, my brows furrowed as I think about a new concern. "Do you ever worry about someone snapping Kay's picture?"

His gaze softens at my worry for his daughter, but it shouldn't surprise him, especially after he saw me have a complete meltdown over her well-being last week. "Not usually. They're more worried about the other guys. They like drama. A single dad who's just hanging out with his daughter doesn't really sell papers."

I don't know about that. I'd buy the hell out of a magazine watching this man dote on his daughter. He's hot, and watching him be such an amazing dad with Kay is panty-melting levels of sexy. Clearly the media doesn't know what women want because every woman I know would be drooling over those types of pictures.

"Being out with my nanny might raise a few eyebrows," he adds before he takes another bite of his taco.

I glance around us, expecting to find cameras or cell-phones pointed our direction, but there's only one other couple eating at a table across from us and they're deep in conversation.

"Maybe we shouldn't be out in public."

He frowns. "How am I supposed to take you on dates if we can't do it in public?" He leans forward. "Mere, I'm not putting my life on hold because of the potential that we become media fodder for a week. I have a strong enough reputation and I know we aren't doing anything wrong. The only person I'm worried about is Kaylee, which is the only reason we're keeping this mostly under wraps."

We both take another bite and then he asks, "What did you go to school for?"

"Kinesiology. I wanted to be a physical therapist."

"*Wanted?* As in, you don't anymore?"

I shrug and pick at the meat that fell out of my taco. "I do. I think I just got too in my head about things and lost sight of why I loved it in the first place. My last year of college, I was hit with this horrible apathy. Nothing seemed to have any point, and I questioned my entire future. It's why I didn't apply to grad schools and instead looked into becoming a nanny. I needed to do *something*. I'm not very good at sitting and doing nothing."

He smiles. "I've noticed that about you."

"I miss it," I confess. It's probably stupid to tell him that when he's still technically my boss, but it also feels nice to tell someone. It wasn't as noticeable when I first started being a nanny for Kay, but that desire to learn, that interest in how the human body works and how to help it heal has come back slowly. It's gotten even stronger since Kaylee got sick. I may not want to be an ER doctor, but I do still have the desire to help people heal from injuries or find renewed strength in their body.

"I loved learning about the human body and was

excited about going into physical therapy and helping people. I'd forgotten how much I loved that feeling because it was completely gone during most of my senior year."

"You could go to grad school next year, couldn't you?"

"Yeah, but that would mean leaving Kay now and I'm not sure I can do that. Your daughter is entirely too easy to love."

He smiles wide. "Agreed." Then his face gets more serious. "She'd understand, though. And it's not like we wouldn't still see you."

It's the first time he's implied there's a long-term future here, and it's giving me a stupid amount of hope. "Really?"

He must hear the underlying question because he's very serious when he responds. "I'm not a casual dating kind of guy, Meredith."

"Good to know."

"And you?" he asks, and he actually looks nervous for my answer. Does he really not see how hard I've already fallen for him? I suppose that might be a good thing because it might be embarrassing if he realized.

"I'm not a casual kind of girl either. I've only had three serious relationships, one in high school and two in college. The longest one was almost two years, although I knew after a year that we probably weren't right for each other. But it was during senior year and I think I stayed with him because I knew what to expect from him. It didn't shake anything up."

"When did you guys break up?"

"A few months ago. Shortly before I started nannying for you."

He nods and then frowns. "Does that make me a rebound?"

I nearly choke on my soda. "No. But shouldn't I be asking *you* that question?"

Based on the look he gets on his face, I suspect his cheeks would be a deep pink if his skin wasn't dark enough to hide his blush.

But then he speaks, and once again he makes my heart race with possibilities. "You're not a rebound."

"Good to know."

Our conversation gets lighter as we talk about our childhoods, mine here in LA and his up in Washington. He grew up in Tacoma, a city south of Seattle, and his parents still live there. I learn more about him on this date than I have in the several months I've been working for him.

And everything I learn only makes my feelings for him grow deeper.

But one doubt still remains, and I don't think about it until we get back to the house later that night after Kaylee goes to bed. We walk in the front door, and like he does every day, he puts down his keys and then looks at the picture of Sydney he has hanging on the wall.

And despite our incredible date where I felt like we got closer to each other, I know we have a long road to travel for him to let Sydney go enough to be able to love me too.

THIRTY-ONE

Romel

This game feels different from any other game I've played in this stadium, and it has nothing to do with what's happening on the field, and everything to do with the woman holding my daughter while she wears a jersey with my name and number on it.

It doesn't matter how many other people in this stadium are wearing Watson jerseys. It only matters that Meredith is. A fierce caveman-like pride swirls in my gut and makes me play harder than ever.

"Trying to impress someone?" Ty asks with an arched brow and a smile when we run off the field.

"No," I say, but I'm smiling and he knows that's exactly what I've been doing.

I grab a water bottle from the trainer and take a drink as I scan the crowd for my girls.

My girls. Damn, that feels good to think about Meredith as one of my girls.

As mine.

My eyes land on them and they both wave, which immediately makes my smile grow even wider. I'm on cloud nine the rest of the game, feeling lighter than I can ever remember feeling and having fun on the field. It's not work, and it's not about channeling my grief; it's just about having fun and playing a game I'm not only great at, but one I've loved for almost my whole life.

When the game's over, I'm eager to get showered and changed in record time so I can get out to Meredith and Kaylee. The guys all look at me with knowing grins, but they're all speeding out of there too to get to their women.

It feels good to walk out of the locker room and see Mere standing beside the other Fierce Four wives—not that she's my wife. My brain stutters on the idea.

Why couldn't she be my wife someday? I already told her this isn't casual for me. I never planned to get married after I lost Sydney, but I never thought I'd meet someone like Meredith either. My throat gets tight and my stomach clenches, still holding on to the residual guilt of moving on.

I'm putting the cart before the horse and need to focus on the here and now. I know better than most that the future is unpredictable.

Kaylee lets go of Meredith's hand and comes racing toward me. "Daddy!"

God, I live for that sound. Her laughter, calling me her Daddy. Pride surges inside me at how smart and incredible my daughter is. No matter what I do in life, raising her will always be my greatest joy and the thing I'm proud of the most. I don't care how many championship football rings I have. None of them come even close to Kaylee's simplest accomplishment.

I lift her up, throwing her into the air and causing her to squeal. The guys all give her smiles and then go to kiss their wives. My stomach tightens again, wishing I could wrap my arms around Mere and kiss her, but I can't with Kaylee here. Not with this thing between us still new and us finding our footing.

Instead, I give her a smile and a wink, hoping she knows I'll make it up to her later when we can be alone.

As soon as Kaylee falls asleep, I head out to the guesthouse with the baby monitor tucked in my back pocket so I can hear Kay if she wakes up. I knock on the door, and the second Meredith opens it, I reach out and grab the back of her neck at the same time that she grabs the sides of my shirt at my waist. We collide in a hungry kiss. Without breaking our lips apart, I move us farther inside the guesthouse and kick the door shut.

She moans against my mouth.

"God, I've wanted to kiss you all day," I say before her mouth parts and I slide my tongue along hers. All the blood in my body rushes south at how badly I want her. I forgot about this feeling, the hunger to feel her lips against mine, to lick up her neck as she shudders in my arms, the way the vibrations of her moans light all my nerve endings on fire.

I walk her backward until the back of her legs hit the arm of the couch and she tumbles over it with a squeal. We both start laughing, which only slightly tempers the need brewing between us. But maybe this is good because there's something I need to confess to her before we take this any further.

"I need to tell you something."

"Okay?" She sits up on her elbows, her face suddenly filled with trepidation.

"I've only ever been with Sydney." Her brows furrow in

confusion, so I push on. "She was my first everything, and there's been no one since her."

Understanding dawns on her face. "Ohhh."

"I just thought you should know before we go any further."

Her gaze softens. "Were you worried I'd think less of you?"

Before I can respond, she says, "Because I don't. I think it's really sweet that you've only been with your wife. Does that make this harder for you?"

She gestures between us, and the concern for me is just one of the many reasons I never stood a chance keeping my guard up with her.

Feeling more confident, I walk forward and push her knees apart, placing my body between her legs and leaning over her, not stopping until my lips meet hers.

When I pull back, I tell her, "You are making this a lot easier than I ever expected, just by being you."

"Are you sure? Because we don't have to do anything."

It's sweet of her to suggest, but my mouth is watering at the thought of tasting her orgasm as she comes all over my face. For over three years, I've had barely any sex drive, and now I'm hard as stone and desperate to taste her like it's my last fucking meal.

"I'm absolutely sure that I don't want to talk anymore. I've got better ideas of what my mouth could be doing."

I grip the edge of her leggings and tug them down her long, toned legs. I throw them behind me, and my gut clenches at the smile that lights up her face at my actions.

"You like that, huh?" I find myself smiling back.

She laughs—the sound music to my ears. "Oh yeah, very caveman, which is hot."

Chuckling, I push her knees apart and get harder when

I see that she's already glistening wet, her pussy bare except for a small triangle of dark hair. Her smile falls as her eyes heat and her breathing becomes uneven.

I get on my knees, putting my face right where it belongs between her legs. Anticipation thrums through my veins—heady and eager. I lick up the seam of her pussy and groan as her flavor bursts across my tongue. Her hips move as she moans, and I wrap an arm around her thigh, holding her still while I feast on her.

I take another long lick, then swirl my tongue around her swollen clit. Her hand grips my head as she lets out another moan. "God, Romel. That feels so good."

"Tastes good too," I murmur before focusing back on her pussy.

Fuck, she tastes divine.

Pushing her legs nice and wide, I hold them apart as I fuck her with my tongue and suck on her clit. Her thighs tremble under my grasp as her moans reach a crescendo, and then she's holding my head tight against her as she rocks her pussy against my lips, the taste of her orgasm flooding my mouth.

Pleasure hits me hard and fast, so intense it completely blindsides me, and as her moans fill my ears and her taste floods my tongue, I come in my pants.

Fuck, that's embarrassing.

I slow my licking as her orgasm begins to fade, her shaking legs falling from where they'd squeezed my head, and then I kiss her thighs as she comes down.

"Oh my God, that was amazing," she says, her voice breathy and her chest heaving as she lies on the couch, sated and happy.

I kiss my way up her body, wishing I'd taken her tank top off too. Wishing even more we could take this even further, but I don't want to leave Kay in the house alone for too long, despite having the monitor and knowing she's fine. So instead, I seal my mouth over hers and let her taste herself on my tongue, loving how she rubs her pussy against my jean-clad cock. I'm hopeful she won't be able to tell I came in my pants like some overeager teen boy.

If she keeps kissing me like this, I'm not going to be able to stop. Hell, she's already making me hard again.

"Damn, I wish we could keep going, but I need to get back in the house," I whisper against her lips.

She sags back against the couch. "I know."

I kiss her again. "But don't think for one minute that I'm done with you because I'm not done by a long shot. Someday very soon, I'm going to stretch your pretty little pussy with my big cock until you're addicted to it."

I bite back the words that want to follow that declaration—that I feel like I'm getting addicted to her and the way she makes me feel.

She moans against my mouth and then wraps her hands around my neck, holding my mouth to hers as she kisses me with so much passion, it reassures me that I'm not in this alone. She's feeling this just as strongly as I am.

THIRTY-TWO

Meredith

The next night, I decide to take a late dip in the pool. It's heated, so I don't feel the slight chill in the air, and the sky is clearer than usual due to the rain we had yesterday. Instead of my usual black one-piece, I opt for my red bikini because with the way Romel was looking at me today, I'm pretty sure he's going to come out here as soon as he puts Kaylee to sleep.

I haven't been able to stop thinking about how hard he made me come last night. Like, seriously, way to go, Sydney for training him so well because I had a hard time believing I was only the second woman he's done that to when he did it so incredibly well. Like, best oral I've ever had by a landslide.

The only downside was watching him walk away, especially before I was able to return the favor.

I only make it through five laps in his pool before the patio door slides open and he steps out. His shirt sleeves are pushed up to his elbows, revealing his strong forearms with pronounced veins that I've never paid much attention to on guys before. But with Romel, I can't help noticing everything about him—from his strong body, chiseled jaw, and sexy brown eyes to the way he takes care of everyone around him, not just his daughter. Romel is one of the most naturally caring men I've ever had the pleasure of knowing, and even if this ends up being too much for him, I'll never regret getting to experience him like this—to pretend that he's really mine, even if it only ends up being temporary.

He walks over to one of the lounge chairs near the pool and takes a seat, his heated eyes watching my every move-ment as I swim closer to him. I push myself out of the pool and don't miss the way his hungry gaze narrows and his throat bobs. Giddy excitement pulses through me that I'm able to make this man react to me in a way I know he hasn't reacted to any woman in so long.

"Come here," he says, his voice deep and husky. I don't hesitate to follow his command because there's nothing I want more than him and whatever pleasure we can have together during these stolen moments.

As I get closer, he spreads his legs, indicating I should stand between them. He grabs my hips and leans forward, kissing my stomach with a tenderness that makes my chest ache. God, I wish this man was mine in every way possible. I've never felt like this before—nervous, excited, scared, yet exhilarated.

His hands slide around my hips and down to cup my ass. "God, I've wanted to touch you like this all day. You have no idea how hard it is to keep my hands off you now that I've tasted you."

"I have a pretty good idea," I whisper, my voice embar-rassingly breathy. He's not the only one who's struggled to keep his hands to himself.

I can practically see the wheels turning in his head, the way his brown eyes go nearly black with desire as he plays with my bikini bottoms, but tonight it's my turn to give him pleasure. I slide my hand around the back of his neck and squeeze just enough to get his attention. He lifts that deep gaze to meet mine, and the seductive words I've been thinking all day get stuck in my throat.

But he must see my desire, and maybe we're on the same wavelength after all because with his husky voice he says, "Get on your knees for me."

Desire curls in my belly at his demand, and I lower myself to my knees. My hands go to the waist of his sweats and he doesn't stop me. Instead, he lifts his hips so I can pull them down over his ass and his thick thighs. I quickly realize he's not wearing any underwear, and something about knowing he was going commando is so hot. How long has he been walking around the house in sweats with no boxer briefs?

And then I can't think about anything else but his thick cock that's already hard and glistening with precum at the tip.

His eyes burn with desire and need, his chest rises and falls with his unsteady breaths, and his arms are straining as he grips the edge of the lounge chair. He looks so wound up that a wicked grin pulls up the corners of my lips knowing I'm about to make him completely unravel.

Without looking away from his face, I dip down and lick up his shaft, not missing how he shudders and lets out a heavy exhale. His eyelids close as bliss streaks across his face and he tips his head back. "Fuck," he mutters so low, I almost miss it.

I swirl my tongue over the tip, licking off his precum, and he opens his eyes, his lids hooded, to watch me do another swirl around the head of his cock. "You look so pretty with my cock in your mouth."

I open my mouth and let him slide against my tongue. "Oh fuck, that's so good, yes," he says, his voice tight.

Wrapping my lips around his cock, I take him as far into my throat as I can, although it's a challenge. He's thicker than any guy I've been with before. I use my hand to compensate for what my mouth can't reach and find a rhythm of gripping and tugging his shaft while my mouth works the head of his cock.

"Oh, that feels good." His hands find their way into my hair as his thighs tense.

I pull my mouth off his cock with a pop. "You like that?"

His eyes are so dark, they look nearly black. "I fucking love it."

My heartbeat speeds up as I take him back in my mouth, loving the sharp inhales and low grunts he makes. I lick up and down his shaft and then around his balls, taking them into my mouth when his breathing stutters.

"God yes, that feels so fucking good. I love the way you do that."

His praise makes my pussy contract, wanting him with a desperation I've never felt before.

I maintain eye contact with him as I take him back in my mouth and attempt to take him farther into my throat, gagging a little. "God, you look so hot," he says, with such awe, like he can't fully believe this is happening.

I moan around his length and then suck the head of his cock again while my fist finds the rhythm he seems to like best on his shaft.

His grip on my hair tightens and his thighs start to shake. "Oh God, you're gonna make me come. Yes, just like that. So *fucking* good."

And then with a loud groan he comes. His body shudders as I continue to fist his cock, getting every last drop of his cum on my tongue.

With a final unsteady exhale, he collapses back on the lounge chair. "Holy shit. Holy fucking shit, Mere. That was..."

He trails off and I can't help but smile. It's a nice compliment when the guy you just sucked off can't even form coherent sentences afterward.

He only takes a minute or two to catch his breath before he lifts his head, his gaze still hungry. "Now get over here and sit on my face so I can taste how wet you are from sucking my cock."

Yes, sir.

THIRTY-THREE

Romel

The next morning, Meredith walks into the kitchen while I'm making breakfast. Kaylee is in the other room watching cartoons, and I can't help myself. I grab Meredith's hand and pull her into the pantry, closing the door behind us and kissing her before it's even closed all the way. My fingers twine in her hair, and I seal my mouth over hers, desperate to kiss her, to connect with her this way.

She moans and her body melts against mine. My cock grows hard as she slides her tongue against mine, deepening the kiss.

I can't get enough of her. I want to kiss and lick her tits and feel her pussy tighten around my fingers. I can't even let myself think about how amazing she's going to feel on my cock or else I'll take her right here.

A sound outside the pantry door alerts me, and I break our kiss just as the door opens. Kaylee stands on the other side, her gaze darting between Meredith and me.

"What're you doing?"

I grab the nearest thing on the shelf as an excuse. "Just grabbing this and talking to Miss Mere about something."

Kay's face lights up. "Cake!"

I look at the box in my hand and then at Meredith who's nibbling her lips, fighting back a smile. Sure enough, out of all the things for me to grab from this shelf, I grabbed the box of Funfetti cake mix I bought on a whim.

I shake my head at Meredith, who loses her battle with holding on to her laughter and lets out a little laugh. "Well, looks like we're making cake for breakfast," I say, giving in to my own smile.

Her eyes shine as she smiles wider. "Sounds delicious."

I'd rather have her for breakfast. I'm becoming a little obsessed with the taste of her, the feel of her body against mine, the way her thighs shake when she comes.

This woman is turning me into a sex addict—and we haven't even had full-on sex yet.

Meredith is clearly not nearly as obsessed with me as I am with her because she turns to my daughter and asks her to go into the kitchen and get a bowl to mix everything.

"Okay!" Kay shouts and then races away.

I grab Meredith's hand, stopping her before she can follow Kay. "Sorry."

She tilts her head like she doesn't understand why I'm apologizing. "For having to keep this a secret," I clarify.

She shakes her head. "I get it, Romel. I don't want to get Kaylee's hopes up just in case you decide this isn't something you're ready for."

My gut tightens. "What if you're the one who decides this isn't something you want?"

Her brown eyes seem to stare into my soul. "If you really think I would ever feel that way then you haven't been paying attention."

She keeps her words low, but they have the impact as if she's screamed them. I'm left reeling in the pantry while she grabs the box of cake mix out of my hand and works with Kay in the kitchen. I push the door wider so I can see them and watch their interaction.

It's not the first time I've watched them together, but it hits different now that Meredith and I are...well, whatever we are.

I don't like the idea of minimizing what she is by thinking this is just physical when it's not.

Meredith makes me feel alive. She makes the days brighter and easier. She makes my daughter happy. She makes me happy. She's everything we didn't know we needed, and I'm scared out of my mind of losing her now that she's become such an integral part of my daily happiness.

I step out of the pantry, and we spend the morning making cake and a healthy breakfast of scrambled eggs. Despite Meredith being here for the past few months, it's the first morning where I feel so in sync with her, like we're a real partnership. We could have this every morning.

My gaze catches on one of the pictures of Sydney across the room, and I wonder what she would think about me moving on. Would she be as okay with it as everyone says she would be?

A sensation tickles the back of my neck, and I turn my gaze right as Meredith looks down at the cake she's frosting. She smiles at Kay, but it doesn't reach her eyes the way her smiles did earlier.

She's made it clear we'll take this at my pace, but what if my pace ends up being too slow? What if I can't let go of the way my wife's memory haunts me to let Meredith into my heart the way I know she deserves?

THIRTY-FOUR

Meredith

A few days later, Romel comes down the stairs with his suitcase in hand. He sets it by the front door and then comes over to the kitchen island where Kay and I have play-dough out and are making food shapes.

"I gotta head out, Sweetie. You be good for Miss Mere, okay?"

"Okay, Daddy." She stands on her chair, which I know Romel only allows because he's right there to catch her if she falls. She hugs him tight and pooches out her lips for a kiss. He gives her a quick kiss and I just barely catch him murmuring, "I love you."

He waves at me, and I can see the tension in his eyes. We kissed and said our goodbyes this morning before Kay woke up, but it's a struggle to keep my body still instead of running over to him and hugging him one last time before he takes off.

Kaylee grabs some of her red playdough. "You kiss Miss Mere too?"

We both freeze and stare at each other in mild panic before Romel grabs the back of her chair with one hand and the counter with the other and leans forward, so he's face-to-face with her. "Why would you ask that?"

"Cuz you kissed in the pantry." She doesn't say the word "duh" after her sentence, but her tone is so straight to the point that she might as well have.

So much for thinking we hadn't been caught. I should've known better. Kaylee is one of the most observant kids I've ever met. I swear she never misses a thing.

My breath gets uneven as panic starts to fill my veins, and I brace myself to hear him deny it. We haven't discussed how we would tell Kaylee, because we didn't plan to tell her any time soon. I honestly wasn't sure we'd ever tell her because I'm still not certain he'll be able to move on from Sydney enough to make this a real relationship.

Sure, we've been kissing for nearly a week now, and the orgasms he's given me with his mouth and fingers are better than any I've ever had, but physical stuff doesn't mean this is a relationship. And we haven't had the conversation defining what exactly "this" is.

Romel glances at me, his expression thoughtful, and then he faces his daughter. "Would you be okay with that? With me kissing Miss Mere?"

She turns her face to him, her expression open and curious in the way only little kids can be. "Like Uncle Ty and Auntie Lexi?"

"Yeah, kind of like that."

She shrugs and goes back to her playdough. "Sure."

My mouth drops open at how easily she's accepted this —hell, how easily he was willing to be honest with her about it. He looks at her for a moment, a subtle smile on his face before he stands back up to his full height and walks around the counter.

Despite just watching their interaction, my eyes go wide in alarm. "What are you doing?" I whisper.

He smiles, and damn him, it's that adorable smile that shows off his dimple and instantly makes me weak in the knees. "I'm kissing my girlfriend before I leave for my game."

My heart races as I stare into his eyes, trying to gauge how he's really feeling. "Are you sure about this?" I ask, keeping my voice low. "Because we don't have t—" I'm cut off by his lips on mine. It's not a deep kiss or even a passionate one. It's a familiar kiss like he knows he can come back for more later.

"I'm sure," he says against my lips, kissing me one more time before walking toward the front door, grabbing his suitcase, and walking out the door with one last goodbye.

I lean my hip against the counter as I stare at the door he just walked out of. Did that really happen?

"Are you my mommy now?" Kaylee's voice pulls me from my conflicted thoughts. She's pressing the green playdough into a pickle mold, not even looking at me.

"Uh, no, KayBear."

She pauses and frowns at me. "Why not?"

Oh boy. Forget conflicted feelings because now I'm just annoyed that Romel would drop that bomb and leave me to answer the million and one questions I'm no doubt going to get over the next day and a half that he'll be gone.

How do I explain to a nearly four-year-old the complexities of this situation?

Leaning my elbows on the counter, I decide to dumb it down but also be real with her. She's a smart kid and I won't lie to her. "Your daddy really misses your mommy."

"I know," she says, her voice getting sad.

"And sometimes when we miss people that much, we

have a hard time letting new people come into our lives. I really like your daddy. He's one of the best men I've ever met, but we need to take things slow so he doesn't feel like he can't still miss your mom. Does that make sense?"

Her little brows furrow and then she shakes her head. "Nope."

Alrighty then. Take two. "How about this. Your daddy and I like each other, and we might kiss, but I'm still mainly your nanny first. You come first, okay?"

"But what if I want you to be my mommy?"

This kid is killing me. I grab her hand. "I'd be so lucky to be your mommy, but let's be happy with what we have right now, okay?"

"Okay," she says sullenly.

"So, what are we making here?" She immediately lights up and starts talking so fast, I can only understand a handful of words as she makes up some story about her playdough food.

What a simple life it must be to move through feelings so quickly without letting them weigh you down.

If only adults had that ability, the world might be a much better place.

THIRTY-FIVE

Romel

It's been a week since Kaylee made it clear she knew about Mere and me, but instead of getting to soak in the new relationship endorphins, I've been slammed with work—either games, practices, or meetings with my agent and current sponsors.

I don't need more money, but I want to make sure I fulfill all my contracts and agreements with my sponsors to get the full payout. That money will go into a high-yield savings fund for Kaylee which she'll be able to use for whatever she wants, whether that be college, buying a house, or anything else.

While I know these meetings are necessary, all I've wanted to do all week was have some real alone time with Meredith—and not just alone time we steal after Kaylee goes to bed before I inevitably need to go to bed, so I can be a functional dad when Kay wakes up at the butt crack of dawn.

Which is why I talked Ty and Lexi into watching Kaylee tonight so I can take Meredith out on a proper date.

They show up right on time, and I help Ty get Kay's car seat strapped in.

"Text me if you need me to come get her," I tell Ty. Over the years, these guys and my in-laws have rallied around me and helped take Kaylee so I could occasionally get a break. It's a luxury I'm grateful for because it helped a ton, and I know not a lot of single parents have this level of support. But it's still always hard to see her go with someone else, to know I'm not going to be the one reading her a bedtime story. It never gets easier.

Ty slaps me on the back. "She'll be fine." In a lower voice, so no one else can overhear even though Lexi and Kaylee are still inside, he adds, "Do you have everything for tonight?"

I frown. "What do you mean?"

He wiggles his eyebrows. "You know...condoms and shit."

Jesus fucking Christ.

"We're not having sex." Although I wouldn't mind. As much as I love eating her sweet pussy, I'm aching to feel her come all over my cock. Four years of celibacy followed by a raging libido is not a good combination.

Ty purses his lips. "Dude, come on. It's me you're talking to." He opens the trunk of his SUV. "Don't worry. The guys and I figured you'd probably try to cock block yourself, so I made a stop by the store on my way here."

He throws a box of condoms at me. I look around to make sure none of the neighbors are walking by and then shove the box under my shirt. "What the hell, man?"

He grips my shoulder, staring me in the eye, his face the picture of seriousness. "You've been there for all of us when we were in new relationships and trying to find our footing. It's our turn to be there for you. You're more emotionally mature than the rest of us, so we figured where you'd struggle would be the bedroom department and going slower than molasses."

I shake my head. "You guys are insane."

He smiles wide. "It's what you do for your brother." He points to the box. "Those are good for a year, but I recommend breaking that box open tonight. You've gone long enough, my friend. Time to ditch the celibacy."

Before I can respond, Lexi and Kay walk out the front door, hand in hand. Kaylee's smile is as big as her face as she laughs at something Lexi says. In her hand, she's got her small overnight bag that she typically uses for when she stays at Larissa and Jimmy's house.

"Daddy! Auntie Lexi got a fish!"

Now I get why she's so excited. Lexi looks at Ty. "Uncle Ty wanted a dog, but with the baby, we thought it was better to start with a fish before we had our hands too full."

Strapped to Lexi in a baby carrier is little baby Lana, sound asleep against her mama.

"God, I can't wait to get that woman pregnant again," Ty says low enough so only I hear him.

I shake my head and fight back a laugh. We've started teasing him that he has a pregnancy kink—which Lexi overheard once and corrected us, telling us it's called a breeding kink. Who knew that was a real thing? We'd thought Ty was joking the first time he mentioned it at the beginning of the season.

I give Kaylee one last kiss and then wave as they drive off. I turn back toward my house, and instead of the usual "what now?" feeling I used to get whenever Kay was gone on the rare night she'd sleep over with our extended family, I'm filled with anticipation.

I pull the box of condoms out from under my shirt and

wonder if maybe my friends are right. Maybe this dry spell has lasted long enough.

I take Meredith to my favorite seafood restaurant on the beach for our date. Growing up near Seattle, I was used to fresh seafood, and it's always been my favorite. Thankfully, Meredith loves it too. I was nervous she wouldn't, and I didn't even think to ask her if she liked fish before we arrived. It's been so long since I've dated, I've forgotten the basics and feel a bit out of my depth here.

As if she knows, Meredith has made this night exceptionally easy for me. She's got a carefree attitude like she's up for anything, and it's been nice to enjoy each other's company.

When we get back to my house, I walk her to the guesthouse. I don't know why I feel so nervous. It's not like I haven't seen her naked—at least partially naked—or already had my mouth on her body, but somehow the thought of having sex again is weirdly terrifying.

She's been giving me all the signals that she's down for that—lingering eye contact, a lot of touching, and she even kissed me when I opened the car door for her. Now she's looking at me with those hooded eyes that have my dick hard as stone, and yet my stomach is clenched with mild panic.

What if I come too fast?

What if it's not good for her?

What if I forgot what the hell I'm doing and she doesn't like it?

She wraps her hand around my neck, and my attention

focuses on her eyes. "What's going on in that head of yours?" she asks.

"You don't want to know."

"I wouldn't have asked if I didn't want to know." Her brows furrow. "Are we moving too fast for you?"

My relationship with Sydney was the only real relationship I had, but we were always honest and clear with each other from the get-go. It's something I want to have with Meredith too, so there's no time like the present to start.

"I haven't had sex in four years, and I'm worried it's going to be bad for you."

A slow smile fills her face. "Is that what's got you all stuck in your head?"

"Yes," I admit, wondering if I should just toss out my man card right now. I'm only twenty-seven. Coming quickly should not be my concern right now.

She steps forward, pressing our bodies together, and pulls on my neck so I'll tilt my head down where she murmurs against my lips. "I'm willing to give it a shot. And if you come before me, then you can make it up to me during round two. How about that?"

I swallow thickly, my cock stiff as hell, and there's no way she can miss it pressing against her. "Sounds good to me," I say, my voice hoarse.

And then we're done talking as I seal my lips over hers and get lost in the feel of her body against mine. Like always, she practically melts against me, and I love the way her whole body submits to me like I'm the only thing she's wanted all day.

I open the door to the guesthouse and then lift her up with my hands under her butt. She wraps her legs around my hips, her ankles crossed right above my ass. I carry her inside and straight to her bedroom. Once there, I put her down on the bed and lift up one of her legs, kissing the exposed skin up to her high heel before I pull it off. I do the same to her other foot and then push her thighs wide. Her dress rides up even farther, exposing her red satin panties that already have a dark wet spot on the crotch.

"Fuck, I need to taste you again."

I drop to my knees and pull her underwear down her smooth legs before tossing them behind me. Her pussy glistens with arousal, and knowing it's for me has me feeling a new type of high. Her heavy-lidded gaze watches my every movement as I lean forward and lick from her ass to her clit. Her head drops back as she lets out a moan and I go for gold. I'm too impatient to get inside her, to feel what I've wanted to feel since the first time I tasted her like this.

Her thighs tighten on my cheeks and her fingers grip the top of my head as she rocks her hips, grinding her pussy against my face. I shove two fingers inside her and suck on her clit until she explodes with a scream, her movements becoming stilted as her orgasm crashes through her.

Her body shudders as she sags back against the bed, her legs relaxing, and I take her recovery time to get undressed. When I'm standing at the end of her bed in only my boxers, I reach for her and help her get out of her dress and bra. It nearly takes my breath away to see her completely naked for the first time.

Even though we've messed around here and there over the last few weeks, we've never been completely naked together. Those brief moments were always tinted with an urgency knowing I needed to get back in the house in case Kaylee needed me. Even with the baby monitor, I was too paranoid that she might wake up or something while I was in the middle of things with Meredith, and it kept me from going as far as I wanted.

But now, we have the whole night to ourselves. There's no rush, nothing stopping me from savoring every single second of tonight.

"You're so beautiful," I murmur, cupping her face and leaning down to kiss her.

Her tongue licks the crease of my lips and I part my mouth, letting her taste herself on my tongue. She moans.

"Romel, please don't make me wait anymore."

I shake my head. "No more waiting." Then I kiss her one more time before I push my boxer briefs off and reach over to my pants to grab the condoms I put in my pocket before our date tonight.

I'm increasingly thankful my boys were looking out for me. Because now that I'm here, I can't imagine not burying myself inside her tonight, and I would've been completely ill-prepared.

My hands shake as I rip off the packaging and situate the condom over the head of my cock. It's been forever since I wore a condom.

Meredith's hands cover mine, and when I look up, she's watching me with nothing but tenderness in her gaze. "Can I do it?"

My heart practically gallops in my chest and I have no words, so I just nod. She takes the condom from my shaking hands, pinches the tip of it, and then rolls it over my cock. I let out a shuddering breath as I watch her movements, the way she's making this so much easier than I thought it would be.

Powerful emotions crash through me, but gratitude and need are the strongest. I need this woman—more than I've ever needed anyone.

Sliding my fingers through her hair, I lean down and kiss her. Without breaking the kiss, I move forward so she's lying flat on her back and I'm positioned over her, her legs instantly wrapping around me. I grip my cock and rub it up and down her pussy, coating it in her slickness. Even just this sensation makes it hard not to close my eyes in bliss.

With a stuttered breath, I notch my cock at her opening and then slowly—ever so slowly—push inside. I can't be sure if I'm going slow for her or for me, but either way we both moan as I push into her body, the sensation overload making my mind go blank.

"Goddamn." She feels so fucking good.

Meredith wraps her arms around my back, her fingernails clawing at me as she tilts her head back, exposing her neck to me. I kiss where her pulse thrums rapidly, loving the way her pussy tightens on my cock when I suck on a certain spot where her neck and shoulder meet.

"Romel," she cries out as I bottom out inside her.

"God, Meredith, you feel so damn good."

Her arms tighten around me. "You're so deep."

I want to be as deep inside her as it's possible for a person to be. I want to be so deep in her she'll never let me go.

I push up so I'm sitting with my knees still bent and grab her butt to help tilt her hips. I hit a new, deeper angle in this position, and she grips the pillow with one hand and the sheets in the other as if she needs something to physically anchor her to the bed.

"Oh my God."

"You like the way my thick cock stretches that pretty pussy?"

"Yes," she cries, her thighs starting to shake.

Fuck, she feels too good. I've lasted longer than my paranoia thought I would, but I won't last much longer if she keeps tightening her pussy around my cock like she is.

But I need her to come before I do, or I'll feel like a complete and utter failure.

Holding her legs to my chest, I keep thrusting inside her, loving the visual of my thick cock disappearing into her body. I take my free hand and use my thumb to rub gentle circles over her clit, and it takes only two more thrusts before she screams my name as her pussy grips my cock so tight, stars burst across my vision. My orgasm takes me by surprise—ripping through me with an intensity that makes me feel like I just got the wind knocked out of me.

I hold myself stiff inside her until my tremors start to subside and then collapse onto the bed next to her. Her chest heaves as she tries to catch her breath, and her hand is covering her eyes.

"Holy shit," she whispers. "I can't believe you were worried it wouldn't be good. That was next level."

A smile fills my face. She has no idea what she brings to life in me, how grounded she makes me feel. For the first time in years, I have hope that my future won't be nearly as bleak as I'd feared.

THIRTY-SIX

Meredith

A week later, I'm woken up in the most pleasurable way I've ever awakened. My heavy lids part as desire ripples through my core. Romel's eyes are closed as he groans and sucks my clit into his mouth.

"Oh God," I murmur, my voice groggy. Fuck, his tongue is magical.

Then he slips two fingers into me and rubs them against my G-spot as he relentlessly sucks and flicks that talented tongue over my clit until my back arches and my orgasm rolls through me like a slow, but powerful tidal wave.

He kisses his way up my naked body—I never bothered to get dressed after he left last night because I was too exhausted—until he reaches my mouth. I wrap my arms around his neck, holding him against me, soaking in the warmth and weight of his body on mine. A week of the best sex of my life and I'm officially addicted.

He notches his condom-covered cock against my core and gently pushes inside. I have no idea when he put on a condom, but I can't care less once he's buried inside me.

And then he finds a fast rhythm that shoots us both over the cliff quickly.

He sags against me, but his arms are flexed, holding most of his weight off me so he doesn't crush me.

"What a way to wake up," I murmur happily. My body is practically humming from how good I feel after the orgasms he gave me last night after he put Kay to bed and then again this morning.

"I couldn't leave without saying goodbye properly." He kisses me and while it starts light, it gets deep quickly. I can never seem to kiss him and not feel a million emotions. It's been even more intense since we started having sex. I want so much with him—a future that I'm not sure he's quite ready for, but I'm remaining hopeful.

"You'll just be gone tonight and tomorrow, right?" I ask him.

"Yep, and then I'll be home." He kisses me again and then pulls back, something tender in his gaze. "I'm going to miss you."

I can't help smiling, a giddy warmth filling my chest. "I'll miss you too."

He kisses me again, but pulls away before either of us can take it as far as we want it to go. He slides out of me, and I get dressed while he puts his clothes back on. We walk hand in hand back to the main house. He's got an early flight, so he's up even earlier than normal. He checks his watch and a frown mars his handsome face. "I wish Kay was up so I could say goodbye."

"You can video call us when you guys get settled in the hotel. I'm sure she'd love that."

He smiles and pulls me into his arms. "Sounds like a plan." He drops a peck to my lips with a smile. "Miss you already."

I laugh and push him out of the house. His answering laugh is music to my ears. I'm not sure what's changed in him, but he seems less weary, less worn down than he was when I started working for him. I'd like to think it's our relationship, but it's possible it's just the power of consistently great sex.

That would put anyone in a good mood.

Later that day, Kaylee falls asleep on the couch, and I decide to just let her nap there instead of moving her to her room. I pick up the toys we played with this morning and then go upstairs to pick up her room. It's amazing the mess a three-year-old can make when given the chance. As sweet as this girl is, she can be a tornado when it comes to wreaking havoc on this house.

Next, I sort and fold the laundry and find some of Romel's clothes in the load that I thought was just Kaylee's stuff. I fold it, and after I put Kay's clothes away, I walk down the hall to Romel's room. I don't even think twice about walking into his room—a room I've never been in before—and setting the clothes on his bed.

And then as I'm turning around to leave, my gaze catches on a framed picture sitting on his nightstand. I know it's his because the bed is still rumpled and unmade on that side. I move closer to the nightstand and then take a heavy seat as I pick up the photo.

I don't know how I feel about him still having the picture of his wife next to his bed when he's been fucking me every night.

Scratch that—it's not a good feeling. Is this why we haven't had sex in here?

My brows furrow as reality threatens to pop the blissful bubble I've been living in. In the last week, we've only had sex or fooled around in the guesthouse. I thought it was because Kay was in the main house and he didn't want to risk waking her up if we couldn't be quiet, but as I stare at the picture of his wife that he still keeps right next to his bed, another thought hits me.

What if he doesn't want to be intimate with me in the house he shared with Sydney?

Will I always be stuck in her shadow?

I'm falling hard for him—harder than I've ever fallen for anyone—and now I'm scared I'm setting myself up for heartache.

I mean, I always knew it was a possibility, but I'd convinced myself it was worth the risk of heartache—*he* was worth the risk.

But as I sit here staring at the photo of his wife that he sees every night before he falls asleep—while I've been in the guesthouse thinking of him—I can't help feeling like I should've listened to that tiny voice in the back of my mind.

Even my dad has voiced his concerns. I brushed it off as him just being worried about his baby girl, but what if he's right? I mean, after all, he was once in Romel's shoes and he could never move on. I know he loved my mom as fiercely as Romel loves Sydney.

My chest tightens as I think about the picture of my mom that has sat on my dad's nightstand for as long as I can remember.

I look down at the picture of the woman who still holds Romel's heart—how much is anyone's guess, but I would bet the majority. "You were so lucky to have his love."

But then my chest tightens even more as I think about my words. Was she really all that lucky when she died before she could enjoy the family she created with him? Sydney will never get to see Kaylee grow up, fall in love, figure out who she is.

"I want to love them both, but I'm afraid he won't love me back."

Sydney smiles through the photo, her face frozen forever, but her memory as present in this house as I am. She's everywhere, and I need to figure out if there will ever be room for me here as well.

Because if there isn't, better to know sooner rather than later—and preferably before I get my heart completely ripped out of my chest.

THIRTY-SEVEN

Romel

"Can I ask you something?" Meredith asks as we lie in her bed, my fingers playing with her hair. We don't get to snuggle after sex very often because I don't like to leave Kaylee alone in the house for very long.

"Of course," I say, although my body tenses because I didn't miss the nervousness in her tone. Why would she be nervous to ask me something if it's not bad?

"Why do we only hook up in the guesthouse?"

It rubs me wrong that she calls it hooking up which has always seemed casual to me, and nothing about Meredith and me feels casual. I feel more for her than I ever thought I'd feel again, and it scares the shit out of me. I didn't think I *could* feel this much for someone after how much I loved Sydney.

I'm also hesitant to admit the truth—that my room still feels like Sydney's space. All of her stuff is still in there and it's our bed. The idea of another woman in that space—even one who's made me feel like Meredith has—feels disrespectful to Sydney's memory.

But I've always been honest with Meredith, and I won't

change that now. Bracing myself for her reaction, I confess. "I haven't changed anything about my room from when Sydney was alive. It wasn't a priority before, and even after we started things, I didn't ever consider bringing you into that room. I should have thought about that, and I'm sorry I didn't."

"You don't have to apologize," she whispers, but her voice is thick like she's fighting back emotion, and my gut churns with worry. I don't ever want her to think she's not important.

"I do," I tell her. "You mean so much to me, Mere." The words don't feel like enough—not even close—but they're all I have right now.

Fear holds me back. The last woman I fell in love with died and left me feeling more broken and hollow than I ever thought I'd experience. To open myself up to feel that way again is as terrifying as the reality that it might be too late for me to even have that fear.

I wince as my phone beeps. It's the alarm I set to go back to the house just in case we fell asleep after we had sex. Of course, it goes off at the worst possible time for me to leave.

She pats my chest and kisses me, but the kiss feels more distant than it's ever felt before. "You should get dressed and get back inside in case Kaylee needs you."

"Mere—"

"We can talk more about it tomorrow."

I bite the inside of my cheek, but still get up and get dressed. Instead of staying naked in bed, she gets up and puts pajamas on and walks me out. Panic starts to claw at my chest because this isn't usually how we say good night. She should be in her bed, sated and sleepy, with the cute little smile she gets on her face after I kiss her good night.

Now, she's got her arms crossed and she won't look at me. I grab her chin between my thumb and fingers and gently tilt her face up. "We *will* talk tomorrow because I'm definitely not done with this conversation."

I hate the hurt in her eyes, but more than that, I hate the understanding in them. Like she expected this of me.

I kiss her once more, and like our last kiss, she holds herself back instead of melting into it like she normally does. With a knot in my stomach, I go back into the main house.

When I walk in my room, I stop just inside the door and stare around the space. If she walked in here, what would she notice?

Sydney's jewelry case on her dresser? The navy blue comforter with flowers on it that Sydney picked out? Sydney's picture on my nightstand? I think about how I would feel if I saw a picture of another man on Meredith's nightstand, and a fierce stab of jealousy slices my stomach.

I never want her to feel the way I feel right now, and I refuse to lose her, which means it's time for me to finally put some of the past to rest.

I text the guys to see who's available tomorrow. Only Dom is free, but he agrees to go shopping with me.

First and foremost, I need to get a new bed.

"This one's bouncy. Not ideal for your back, but could be fun when you're fucking," Dom says as he sits on a mattress and tests it.

"Could you keep your voice down? There are other people around."

He smiles. "Everybody has sex."

"That's not even close to true."

He cocks his head side to side. "Okay, fair enough. How about this? Everyone is a result of sex and therefore shouldn't be prudes about it."

Well, at least it's more accurate. I give him a look, and he chuckles but lets it go.

We walk past a few other mattresses. "So, what brought on this sudden need for a new bed? Haven't you been sleeping with Meredith already for like a week?"

"I don't know how I feel about you guys knowing such personal details about my sex life."

He shrugs. "Stop avoiding the question."

"We've been in the guesthouse."

His face gets stern. "You've been leaving Kay alone overnight?"

"No."

He stops walking and I turn around to face him, already dreading where this conversation is going.

"Explain."

Sighing, I tell him about how I've been "hooking up" with Meredith, as she so eloquently put it, and then afterward going back to the main house to sleep. Kay isn't usually alone in the house for more than thirty minutes before I'm back, and I always have the baby monitor with me when I'm with Meredith, so I'd know instantly if anything was ever wrong. Plus, I have a ton of security alerts set up so my phone would alert me if any of the exterior doors or windows opened. I'm not irresponsible, especially when it comes to my daughter's safety.

Dom pinches the bridge of his nose. "Dude...come on, tell me you're not this dumb."

"I know, okay? I get it. I'm screwing this up, but I'm trying to make it better. Starting with getting a new bed."

Dom steps closer and puts his hand on my shoulder, looking at me very similarly to how Ty did a week ago. "Only you would make the first woman you've had feelings for since Sydney feel like a side piece to your dead wife."

My stomach curdles as I frown. Only Dom would ever state the truth in such a brutally honest way.

I sit heavily on the nearest mattress. "Hell, that's exactly what I've done, isn't it?"

He takes a seat next to me. "Probably. I don't know Meredith well enough to know for sure, but I know Laney would skin me alive if I ever pulled what you have."

"What would you do to fix it?"

"Fuck her until she couldn't move or forgave me, whichever came last." What's incredible is that he says it with a straight face.

"Okay, that might be how you do things, but I'm buying a new bed and putting Sydney's stuff into boxes for Kaylee to go through when she's older so she can have whatever she wants."

He stares at me like he's not sure I'm serious. "Are you really putting Sydney's stuff away?"

He understands how hard I've held on to her things. I haven't touched our room at all; it's exactly as she left it. I nod.

"Wow, you must really like Meredith."

"I think I'm falling in love with her," I confess quietly.

"Seriously?"

I nod.

"Woah, that's huge, man."

"I know. But now I feel like I'm letting her down already. I don't know how to have them both. I'm not entirely ready to put everything Sydney owned in storage, but I also don't want Meredith to think I'm not taking this relationship between us seriously. I want to move forward with her, which is huge. I never thought I'd want that again. I never thought I'd find anyone who I could feel even a smidgeon of what I felt for Sydney."

"But you do with Meredith."

"Yeah, I do. She's so amazing with Kaylee and she takes care of me, not in a caretaker way, but in small ways that ease my stress and make me feel like I have a partner again. But it's also different. Before, it was just Sydney and me. We didn't have anyone relying on us, and we could do our own thing but also look out for each other. It's different when you have a kid. I never got to experience that with Sydney, so maybe that's why it feels like such a blank slate with Meredith. But I feel like I've gotten a second chance when I didn't want one. Or I didn't think I did, but now that I have her, I don't want to lose her."

I stare at my hands for a minute, my head a jumbled mess, then turn to Dom. "Do you think it's possible to love two women at once?"

There's sadness in his eyes. "I don't know, Romel. I'd like to say yes, but I've only ever loved Laney, so I'm the wrong person to ask. That said, widowers move on all the time, so it's not unheard of. Sydney doesn't have to be your only love. I guess the real question you would need to ask is if you *can* love them both, is Meredith okay having to share your heart with Sydney?"

I need to figure out the answer to the first question before I even attempt to ask myself if Meredith is okay with me loving them both. If I can't let go of Sydney enough to love Meredith, it won't matter—I'll lose her anyway.

THIRTY-EIGHT

Meredith

The next day, I'm hanging out with Kaylee playing with her stuffed animals when Romel walks into her room with Larissa behind him.

"Hey, Mrs. Brooks."

"How many times do I need to remind you to call me Larissa?" she scolds with a smile.

I return it with one of my own. "Sorry. Larissa," I correct. Then I glance between her and Romel, who's also smiling but looking a little shy at the same time. "What's up?"

"I'm taking my grandbaby for a sleepover at Grammy and Papa's house."

"Yay!" Kaylee cheers. "I gotta get my shoes," she says and then she's off running into her closet for her shoes. I furrow my brow at Romel because normally he tells me if I'm going to be off duty.

"I was hoping you'd accompany me to a sports gala tonight."

I dart a glance at Larissa whose smile has grown even

wider—and she actually looks proud of Romel. "Um, like a date?"

A sports gala would likely have press around, which would mean everyone would know about us.

He reaches out a hand to help me up and I take it. "Exactly like a date," he says, his voice low and his eyes promising all kinds of naughty things later.

I swallow. "Okay."

"Great. Then you'll want to head back to your room... there's something waiting for you there."

Now I'm intrigued.

I walk out of the room with a quick hug and goodbye to Larissa and Kaylee and then dash to the guesthouse. When I walk into my bedroom, there's a large white box on my bed with a smaller shoe box next to it. On top of the large box is a black envelope, and inside that is a cream card with gold painted edges and Romel's neat scrawl.

I hope you like the dress. I can't wait to walk into that room with you as my date. When you're ready, come back over to the main house. We need to leave by seven. See you soon, gorgeous.

I set the card down on the bed and lift open the box, sucking in a sharp breath at the beautiful red satin gown. I quickly strip out of my clothes to try it on. The material is soft between my fingers as I slide it over my body. It hugs my breasts and has a sweetheart neckline that accentuates my cleavage. Fortunately, I have the perfect bra for this dress or else I'd be terrified about my nips poking through the thin and delicate fabric.

It hugs my torso with an almost corset-like style and

then flows loosely from my waist, with a long slit on the left side that comes up almost to my hip. I'll definitely need to be careful how I sit, stand, or move so I don't accidentally flash someone. It adds a sexy element to an otherwise fairly conservative dress.

Looking in the mirror, I get an idea for how I want to do my hair and makeup. With a giddiness I haven't felt since our conversation got cut short the other night, I carefully take off the dress and get in the shower. I have a lot of work to do to make my vision come to life.

A few hours later, I walk into the main house to find Romel in a tailored black tux that makes my mouth water. I've never met a man who was just as drop-dead sexy in sweats as he is in jeans or a freaking tux. Dressed up like this, he looks like he could be a stand-in for the actor Michael B. Jordan, but taller and with more muscles.

His eyes get darker as his gaze turns heated the longer he takes me in.

I do a small twirl, not bothering to hold the slit closed at my thigh because he's already seen all the goods. "Is this what you had in mind when you picked out this dress?"

He rubs his hand over his mouth, his gaze hungry, then says, "You are better than any dream I've ever had."

Emotion clogs my throat as my heart soars and butterflies take off in my stomach. "Thank you...for the compliment, and the dress. It's gorgeous," I add, looking down at my dress.

"Yes, you are."

I meet his gaze, my heart racing. He blinks and shakes his head like he's shaking himself out of a daze.

He grabs a box off the counter and then clears his throat as he approaches me. "I got you something else too. Something to complement your natural beauty."

I arch a brow at him in question and then he opens the box and my smile falls as I stare in awe at the most beautiful diamond necklace I've ever seen. There's a large diamond in the center, with smaller diamonds on each side that get smaller until they reach the clasp at the back.

"Is this real?"

He laughs. "Yeah, it's real." Then, "Do you like it?" He sounds nervous.

I look at him like he's insane. "No. I don't like it; I *love* it, Romel. This is stunning."

He takes it out of the box and sets the box back on the counter. "May I?" he asks, gesturing to my neck.

I nod and then spin around, grateful I wore my hair up, so the necklace will stand out even more. This is the kind of jewelry you wear for it to be seen, not hidden.

He clasps it at the back of my neck, and a shiver races across my shoulders as he places a tender kiss right behind my ear when he's done. I spin back around to face him and don't miss the catch in his breath.

"That necklace has nothing on you, Meredith. I don't know how I got so lucky."

Now I'm the one who has to catch my breath. I feel like I'm living in a fairy tale, except I desperately hope my carriage doesn't turn into a pumpkin at midnight.

He holds out his elbow to me, his smile back on his face and that small dimple making my stomach swish again. "Ready to go?"

I wrap my hand around the crook of his elbow and nod. "Ready."

Romel failed to mention that this was not just a football gala, but a huge network TV sports gala. There are Dodgers players here.

"Are you fangirling?" he asks with a grin.

"No," I say, but it sounds breathy even to my ears, and then one of the best players in Dodgers history walks by and I nearly trip and fall against Romel.

He actually has the audacity to laugh at me, the jerk.

"You weren't even this tongue-tied when you met the guys," he says.

"Yeah, but you guys are football players. Football is my dad's favorite sport, not mine."

"So let me get this straight. You would've lost your mind when you first met me if I was a *baseball* player?"

"Oh, totally."

"Alright, then I'm definitely keeping you away from all the baseball guys tonight—and in the future."

I give him a sly smile. "Worried one might steal me away?"

He grabs my hand, spinning me into his arms. "Oh, absolutely, and I don't plan on ever letting you go."

My smile falls as my heart rate speeds up. Staring into his deep brown eyes, it's easy to lose myself inside them, and I hope he's right that he'll never let me go because there's nowhere else I want to be than in his arms for the rest of my life.

We walk to the table and I see the other members of the Fierce Four. Next to each one is a beautiful woman—their wives I'm guessing based on the looks of pure devotion in the guys' eyes. Romel does the introductions.

"Everyone, this is Meredith Gable. Meredith, you've met Dom. This is his wife, Alayna, then Ty and his wife, Lexi, and then you've already met Gabe and Danae."

I smile and offer a wave. "It's nice to officially meet you all."

I take a seat next to Danae and spend the rest of the night getting to know the Fierce Four wives and seeing Romel in his element. He's charismatic, but modest, and as the dinner winds down, a presenter gets up to announce the winner of the award they're giving out tonight for best sportsmanship.

"Without further ado, let's welcome up here Romel Watson from the LA Wolves!"

My jaw drops as I stare at Romel in shock. Did he know he was getting an award tonight?

Based on the bashful smile he gives me, I'd say he had a good idea.

"I can't believe you didn't tell me," I whisper as he stands.

And then he shocks me further by leaning over and placing a kiss on my lips. Camera flashes go off all around the room, and some hoots and hollers from other tables, and then Romel stands tall and walks up to the stage while I remain stunned speechless in my chair. I can't believe he just did that.

He accepts his award with the grace and humility I've come to expect from him, and then the rest of the night is spent with people coming over to our table to talk to him. It's fascinating to watch him interact with all these other super famous athletes like all of this is normal.

What on earth have I gotten myself into?

On the drive home, I ask him, "Do you get awards like this regularly?" This award seemed like a big deal based on how everyone else reacted, but Romel doesn't seem all that fazed by it.

"No. I've gotten a few in my career, mostly MVP

awards, or some accolades as part of the Fierce Four, but nothing like this."

"You just made it seem like it's no big deal."

"It's cool that my peers think I'm a good sportsman on the field. That's what I'd like to be known for—as a good guy and a strong player. But at the end of the day, it's a trophy that won't mean much when I'm eighty. My legacy is Kaylee and how I raise her." He pauses and then says, "And any future kids I have."

My head spins so fast to face him, I almost get a crick in my neck. He must catch the movement from his periphery because he glances over at me, his expression serious.

I don't say anything because I don't know what to say to that kind of declaration. Hope floods me that maybe he will be able to make room for me the way I want him to if he's thinking about a future where there are more kids.

"Can I tell you something? Something I haven't told anyone yet?" he asks quietly.

"Of course."

"I'm planning to retire at the end of the season."

I rotate in my seat so I can better face him. Well, at least as much as my seat belt will allow. "Seriously?"

I can't imagine the LA Wolves without Romel, without the Fierce Four as we know them.

He nods. "I want to be home with Kaylee. I want to figure out what my life looks like after football. And…I'm hoping we could figure that out together."

"You and Kaylee?" I ask as he waves at the gate guard and drives through the gate to his house.

"No. You and me."

THIRTY-NINE

Romel

She doesn't say anything right away, but she sucks in a sharp breath at my words.

I barrel on.

"I know I haven't done enough to prove to you what you mean to me, but I promise that I'm working on it. And I see a future with you, Meredith."

Maybe it makes me a coward to be having this conversation with her in the car, where she can't escape and I don't have to look at her the whole time.

The darkness helps ease some of my fears about opening up.

"I'm sorry I was distant," she says. "After I talked to you about us being only in the guesthouse, I realized I shouldn't have brought it up."

"No, I want you to be able to bring these things up. You should be comfortable telling me what you want. I don't want you to feel like you can't express an emotion or ask me a question."

She twists her body in the seat to face me better. "I get it, Romel. I get it probably better than you think I do."

I let out a frustrated sigh. "You shouldn't have to *get it*," I tell her. "I don't want you to feel like you have to understand my baggage. I want to be able to let you in—all the way in. Yeah, maybe it's only been a few weeks, but I see a whole future with you, Meredith. And I want that future. I want to wake up with you in the mornings, not sneaking out to see you. I want you right there next to me. I want you in my arms. I want us to make breakfast together and go on adventures with Kaylee. I *want* those things."

I glance over at her to see her nibbling her lip, her eyes uncertain.

"But?" she asks.

I hate that she asks, but I hate even more in this moment that it's there anyway.

That there is still the "*but*" lingering between us.

The *but can I let go?*

I want her, *but will I let myself have her?*

Will I open myself up to that kind of hurt? I didn't think I would survive losing Sydney. What would it do to me if I lost Meredith?

I don't ever want to find out, and yet I know I am sitting on the precipice of potentially losing her anyway if I can't pull my head out of my ass and figure this out.

I can feel the weight of her stare as she waits for me to answer.

"I don't know, Meredith," I say. "I'm sorry. I wish I could say with 100 percent certainty that we'll be able to have everything I want. But there is one thing I'm certain of. And it's that I'm trying, and I'm going to keep trying because you have brought me back to life. You have made me feel things I never even dreamed I could feel again. You've made me breathe for the first time in nearly four years. I feel like I can finally take a full breath without the weight of grief sitting on my chest. Every day that I see you, my world feels a little bit brighter. And I know that doesn't answer your question or ease your worries and your fears. But I hope it's enough for now to know I am going to try my damnedest to be the man you need and the man you deserve."

I pull up to the house and put the car in park. I don't wait for her to say anything as I get out and walk around to her side of the car and open her door. Extending my hand, I wait for her to take it, hoping she will.

She slides her smooth hand into mine, her dark gaze staring up at me. And in those beautiful brown eyes, I see all the hopes, fears, and desires I feel reflected back at me.

Without a word, I guide her into the house. But instead of heading toward the patio doors and out to the guesthouse like we normally do, I head for the stairs.

She pulls on my hand as we reach the bottom step. "Where are you going?"

"We're not going to the guesthouse. We're going upstairs to my room." I tighten my grip on her hand. "Are you coming?"

FORTY

Meredith

I nod because my words are completely gone, and he leads me up the stairs toward his bedroom. I never told him I came in here that one day. Maybe I should have, but after what I saw, I couldn't.

My stomach dips at the thought of walking in and seeing her picture.

He wouldn't do that to me after everything he just said tonight, right? No, he wouldn't. Romel's not that kind of guy.

I nibble my lip as we reach his door and he pushes it open, then pulls me inside. My eyes sweep around the room quickly, and immediately I notice two things.

One, the picture is no longer on his nightstand.

And two, his bed is different. Or at least the bedding. Where there was a navy comforter with floral print is now a dark gray comforter with black lines around the edges and matching pillows.

Taking a breath, I take a moment to see what else might be different.

I notice a couple of other changes from the last time I

was in here. There was a dresser on the far side of the room with a jewelry box on top and a couple of glass bottles of perfume. The whole dresser is now gone.

I'm not sure when he found the time to do it because usually I'm around the house if he is. But it's clear he's taken the time to make the space more his own and not his and Sydney's.

He squeezes my hand, his skin warm against mine, and cups my cheek with the other. He doesn't speak, and neither do I, because at this point I don't think either of us need words.

We need actions, we need touch, we need reassurance—both of us—that the other person is here standing in front of us. That this isn't a dream.

My breathing grows shallow as he dips his head down and seals his lips over mine.

There's nothing in the world like kissing Romel Watson.

His lips are thick but firm, and somehow with every kiss, he takes another piece of my heart, and this one is no different.

My hands move to the buttons on his shirt, slowly undoing each one. He doesn't stop me, and he doesn't rush me. He just kisses me in between every button I get undone, and watches my movements with a heated gaze.

When I get his shirt all the way unbuttoned, I run my hands along his firm pecs.

I love touching him like this, so freely, like he's really mine.

His hands wrap around my waist, pulling me tighter against him before they move up to the zipper of my dress at my back. He pulls it down slowly, the sound of the zipper sliding down the only noise in the room apart from our heavy breaths. My heartbeat races the lower it goes, until he gets to the bottom. My dress slips down my torso to the floor at my feet.

His tongue darts out to sweep across his lips, as if the sight of me makes him absolutely ravenous.

My heart pounds as I stand there, exposed, in just my bra and panties. Romel's gaze is intense, like a physical touch, as he takes me in. His eyes linger on every curve, every line, as if he's committing me to memory.

"You're so damn beautiful, Meredith," he murmurs, his voice like velvet wrapping around me. His hands cup my face, thumbs brushing my cheeks, and he kisses me again. This time it's deeper, hungrier. His tongue slides against mine, exploring, tasting. I can feel his need and it ignites my own.

I push his shirt off his shoulders, letting it fall to the floor. My fingers trace the lines of his muscles, the ridges of his abs. He shudders under my touch, his breath hitching. I love that I can do this to him, that I can make this strong, reserved man tremble.

He reaches behind me, unclasping my bra with a flick of his fingers. It falls away, and his hands immediately cover my breasts, his large palms warm and slightly rough. He thumbs my nipples, sending jolts of pleasure straight to my core. I gasp into his mouth, arching into his touch.

"Romel," I whisper, his name a plea on my lips.

He smiles against my mouth. "I've got you," he says, walking me backward toward the bed. The back of my knees hit the mattress, and I sit down, scooting back as he crawls over me. His body covers mine, his weight supported on his elbows. He looks into my eyes, his own dark with desire and something more, something deeper.

Romel's hand slides down my side, over my hip, and

hooks into the waistband of my panties. He pulls them down slowly, his knuckles brushing against my skin, sending goose bumps across my flesh. I lift my hips, helping him, and then I'm bare before him.

He sits back on his heels, his eyes roaming over me. "God, you're perfection," he says, his voice hoarse.

His words send a flush of heat through me, and the wetness between my legs grows. I spread my thighs slightly, inviting him, needing him to touch me there. He takes the hint, trailing his fingers up my inner thigh, making my core clench with anticipation.

When he finally touches my pussy, I let out a soft moan. His fingers slide through my folds, spreading my wetness, circling my clit with a gentle touch that sends sparks of pleasure shooting through me. He watches my face, his eyes locked on mine as he makes me gasp and squirm.

"You're so wet," he murmurs, his voice thick with desire. "Is this all for me?"

"Yes," I whimper. What I don't say is that it's only for him. No man has ever made me so wet before. No man has turned me on the way Romel does.

He smiles, a slow, sexy smile that makes my heart flutter. He slides one finger inside me, then another, stretching me, filling me. I rock my hips against his hand, chasing the sensation, the building pressure. His thumb stays on my clit, rubbing in slow, deliberate circles that make me see stars.

"That's it," he encourages, his voice a low rumble. "Ride my hand. I wanna watch you fall apart for me."

I do as he says, grinding against his hand, taking what I need. The pleasure builds and builds, my body tensing, my breath coming in short gasps. And then it hits me, a wave of ecstasy crashing over me, making me cry out his name.

Romel watches me come, his eyes filled with awe and

desire. "Goddamn, Mere, you're so sexy." I love how hoarse his voice is, as if he's barely hanging on. He brings his fingers to his mouth, tasting me, and the sight of it sends another shiver of pleasure through me.

He stands up, quickly shedding the rest of his clothes and grabbing a condom. His cock is hard and thick, standing proudly, and I can't help but lick my lips at the sight of it. He sees the gesture and chuckles, a low, sexy sound.

"Another time," he promises. "But right now, I need to be inside you."

He climbs back onto the bed, his cock now covered with a condom, and settles himself between my legs. He leans down, capturing my mouth in a searing kiss. I can taste myself on his lips, and it makes me even more aroused. His cock presses against my entrance, hot and hard, and I whimper into his mouth, needing him inside me.

He pulls back slightly, his eyes meeting mine. "I want to see you, Meredith," he says, his voice raw with emotion. "I want to watch as my cock fills you while you're in my bed."

My heart races at his words. This time feels different *because* we're in his bed. He's not hiding me away in the guesthouse. He's finally bringing down some of his walls and letting me in. I hold his gaze as he slowly pushes into me. I feel every inch of him, filling me, stretching me, completing me.

He groans, his eyes never leaving mine. "You feel so good, Mere. So perfect."

I wrap my legs around his waist, pulling him deeper into me. He starts to move—slow, deep thrusts that hit every sensitive spot inside me. I match his rhythm, our bodies moving in sync, our breaths mingling, our eyes locked on each other.

There's emotion in his gaze that has my chest feeling

tight. It's affection, desire, and need, and it's all for me. I reach up, cupping his face, my thumb brushing over his cheek. He turns his head, kissing my palm, his dark eyes never leaving mine.

His pace quickens, his thrusts becoming harder, more urgent. The pleasure builds again, my body tensing, my breath coming in short gasps. He slides his hand between us, his thumb finding my clit, circling it in time with his thrusts.

"Come with me," he says, his voice strained with the effort of holding back. "Let go, Meredith. Let me feel you come all over my cock."

His words send me over the edge. My orgasm hits me like a tidal wave, sweeping me under, consuming me. I cry out his name, my body convulsing around him. Romel groans, his body tensing as he finds his own release, spilling himself into me.

He collapses on top of me, his body trembling from the force of his orgasm. I wrap my arms around him, holding him close and feeling his heart pound against mine. Our bodies are slick with sweat as our breaths come out in ragged gasps. But we don't let go of each other. We can't. Not yet.

Romel lifts his head, looking down at me with such tenderness it makes my heart ache. He brushes a strand of hair away from my face, his fingers lingering on my cheek. "That was..." he starts, but words seem to fail him.

"I know," I say before he can finish his sentence. It was everything.

God, I'm so in love with this man.

Did I ever even stand a chance?

He rolls off me, pulling me with him so that we're lying on our sides, facing each other. His hand traces lazy patterns on my hip, sending gentle tingles of pleasure through me. I can't believe how responsive my body always is to his touch. It's never been like this before.

"I want you to know," he says, his voice serious, "that this isn't just sex for me. It's not just some fling. You matter to me, Mere."

I look into his eyes, seeing the sincerity there. He leans in, kissing me softly. It's a sweet, gentle kiss, full of tenderness.

And maybe it's dangerous, but his words give me hope that one day he can love me the way I love him.

FORTY-ONE

Romel

After my conversation with Meredith, I decide it's time to finally tell the guys my plans for next season, especially since we're nearing the end of the season already.

So after practice the next day, when most of the locker room is cleared out, I ask them to hang back for a second.

"What's up?" Ty asks as he straddles the bench I'm sitting on. Gabe leans against the lockers next to me and Dom stands on the other side of the bench.

"I need to tell you guys something. Something big."

"Okay, what is it?" Dom asks.

"I'm going to retire at the end of the season. I'll announce it soon since the Wolves already sent a contract extension to my agent."

Dom sits on the other bench across from me, his face the picture of shock. "For real?"

I nod.

The guys are somber as they absorb the bomb I just dropped on them. Ty looks between all of us. "So this is it? Our last season as the Fierce Four?"

We all know the name might stick around with whoever takes over my position, but it won't be the same.

Dom breaks the tension. "I don't know why we're getting all mopey about it. It's not like we won't still see him all the damn time. Unless you're trying to break up with us, you're stuck with us for life, man. Plus, we always need a fourth for our game nights."

Gabe, Ty, and I smile. Leave it to Dom to lighten the mood and remind us that we're family. We might not play on the field together after this season, but we'll always be brothers. We're family by choice, and nothing will break that bond we created on the field.

"Not to be sappy or anything, but I love you guys," I say, relief filling me that they're handling this news so well. Part of me was worried they'd be upset with me, but I should've known better.

When I get home, Meredith looks up from where she's sitting on the floor with Kaylee—an ABC puzzle laid out with all the pieces. She looks at me expectantly.

"How'd it go?"

I smile, a weight off my shoulders. "They took it well."

Her shoulders sag like her relief matches mine, and my stomach and chest fill with warmth. This woman has become my partner in every way, and I can't imagine life without her anymore. I should know better than most how quickly life can flip on a dime, but I'd been living in such a dark place for so long that I forgot.

I forgot it was possible to feel this light, this happy.

I forgot what it was like to share the weight of life with someone else.

And it's made an announcement I was dreading into something easy and freeing. I'm no longer carrying the weight of this secret. The people closest to me all know, and soon my coaches will know too.

It's time to move into the next phase of my life, and I hope, more than anything, that Meredith will be in that phase with me.

FORTY-TWO

Meredith

My dad has met every boyfriend I've ever had, but I've never been more nervous than I am right now. I already have a good idea of how my dad feels about Romel, given what I've told him and his caution about our relationship. But this will be his first time meeting Romel and Kaylee.

These two have become my whole world, but I'll always care about what my dad thinks. He's been my best friend my whole life. I'm on pins and needles hoping that tonight goes well and the three most important people in my life all like each other.

We pull up to the house, and I wipe my palms on my jeans to try to ease the clammy feeling. Romel covers my hand with one of his, and when I face him, he's smiling at me.

"It's going to be fine. Parents love me, and if your dad likes football, I'm a shoo-in."

I nibble my lip, having my doubts. I glance back at Kaylee in her car seat. "Would you like a boyfriend of Kay's just because he was a football player?"

His smile drops and his eyes turn stormy. "Kay's never dating."

Laughter bubbles out of me. That's just what I needed him to say to ease some of my nerves. "So now you understand where my dad is coming from."

His gaze moves from me to the front porch of my dad's house that we can see through the car window.

"Dang," he mutters, his brown gaze coming back to me. "Now I'm the one who's nervous."

I turn my hand over so I can clasp his and give it a squeeze. "At least we'll be nervous together."

We get out of the car, help Kay out of her car seat, and then walk down the cement walkway to my dad's front porch.

"So, this is where you grew up?" Romel asks.

"Yep. My parents bought this house when my mom was pregnant with me and then my dad said he couldn't stomach moving."

Romel nods his head in understanding. Of course he gets it better than any other guy I've dated. That level of understanding could work in his favor, or it could be the reason my dad doesn't bother giving him a chance. Those knots in my stomach tighten.

I pull my house key out of my purse and then open the door. "Dad? We're here," I shout and hear some pots clattering in the kitchen.

"In here," he hollers back.

I close the door behind Kay and Romel and then take a deep breath before walking into the kitchen with them following me. My dad looks up from the stove where he's stirring his home-made spaghetti sauce. I walk over and place a kiss on his cheek.

"Smells great, Dad."

He looks down at Kaylee, who's now hiding behind Romel's legs, and smiles at her. "I heard someone likes spaghetti, so I thought I'd make my famous sauce."

Kaylee gives him a small smile, but still stays glued to her dad's leg. She'll warm up soon enough. My dad's always been disarming with anyone he meets.

"Dad, this is Romel Watson and his daughter, Kaylee."

My dad holds his hand out to Kaylee first, that smile still on his face, and she takes it. "Nice to meet you, Kaylee. You can call me Mr. Rob."

"Hi, Mr. Rob," she says in her soft voice.

Then he faces Romel, and even though he still has a smile on his face, it's certainly a lot stiffer than the one he gave Kaylee. He holds his hand out and Romel takes it. "Nice to meet you, sir," Romel says.

"Mr. Watson," my dad says formally.

"You can call me Romel."

He nods, but doesn't say anything else. Those knots in my stomach turn into nausea as my fears start to come to life before my eyes.

"Do you need any help getting things ready?" I ask my dad, my voice a little higher pitched than normal.

"You can help set the table," he says, going back to stirring the sauce.

"Have a seat at the table," I murmur to Romel, but he places his hand on my stomach, stopping me from passing him.

"I'll help if you'll show me where things are."

Is this man for real?

"Okay," I say, giving him a soft smile and then showing him where the plates are while I grab silverware and glasses. I glance at my dad, who's still stirring the sauce but watching my interaction with Romel closely. He looks away when he realizes he's been caught.

Dinner is relatively successful. My dad is polite to Romel and friendly with Kaylee. I'm finally feeling relaxed when my dad turns to Romel.

"You like cars?"

Romel sets down his glass of water. "I'll admit I don't know much about them."

Dad pushes his chair back. "Well, come on out to the garage and I'll give you a mini lesson. I've been restoring a classic."

Romel doesn't even glance my way before he nods and pushes his chair back.

"Uh—" I start, but Romel bends down and drops a kiss to my cheek.

"I'll be fine," he whispers. Then to my dad, he says, "Lead the way."

Dad shoots me a look that fills my stomach with dread before the two most important men in my life exit the kitchen and head to the garage.

FORTY-THREE

Romel

I'm not easily intimidated. I face off with some of the NFL's finest—and toughest—players on a weekly basis. I've been loved instantly by almost all of my friends' parents growing up and Sydney's parents. There was only one parent who didn't like me, but he turned out to be a racist asshole, so it had nothing to do with *me* and everything to do with my skin color.

I don't get racist vibes from Mere's dad, but I'm definitely feeling how protective he is of her. As a dad, I get it. I would be the same way with any guy Kaylee brought home —which will never happen because she's never dating, but in theory, I'd be just like Meredith's dad.

I follow him into the garage where he turns on the overhead light that illuminates a beautiful red Corvette. He rubs the side of it affectionately and chuckles. "I feel like I've been working on this thing for as long as Meredith's been alive. But restorations like these require care, and sometimes it takes more time than you expect."

"I can imagine. It's a beautiful car," I tell him. Right

about now, I wish I knew more about cars so I could ask him questions about it.

He leans against the passenger side and crosses his arms. "As much as I love this car and have put endless hours and time into it, it's nothing compared to how much I love my daughter."

"I wouldn't expect any less."

He narrows his eyes thoughtfully. "No, I suppose you wouldn't, having a daughter of your own. So, you understand why I have my concerns about her getting involved with you?"

"Because I'm a football player?"

"Because you still love your wife."

His words land like I just got tackled. Even though I knew he would likely bring it up, for some reason I didn't expect him to just come out and say it so directly. In my experience, most people talk around death; rarely do they face it head-on.

I swallow thickly. "I do still love Sydney. That doesn't mean I don't care about Meredith."

His gaze is stern, focused, like he's analyzing every word out of my mouth, and it makes sweat break out on the back of my neck. "*Caring* about someone isn't the same as loving them. I know my daughter, and I can see clearly that her heart is already involved. If you can't love her the way she deserves, then I'm going to ask—father to father—that you let her go. Let her find a man who will love her so hard, she'll never question his feelings for her, or if he still has feelings for someone else," he adds on, his words heavy with meaning.

My heart sinks to my stomach. I can't tell him I love her —because even if I see a future with her, love is not a word I've allowed myself to associate with anyone besides Sydney or Kaylee—but I can't let her go either. Because even if I don't love her now, I want to. I want a future with her, and I'd like to believe I can get there.

If I can learn how to let go of Sydney's hold first.

"Don't break my daughter's heart, Romel. Because there's nothing harder on a father than watching his daughter suffer."

"I don't want her to suffer," I admit, my voice hoarse.

"No, I don't think you do. Hopefully you can figure it out before it's too late."

His words are ominous, but I don't get another chance to respond because he pushes off the car and walks toward me. He pats me on the back and gives me a meaningful look like he hopes we understand each other.

All I understand is that he thinks I'm going to break Meredith's heart, and I can't reassure him that I won't.

FORTY-FOUR

Meredith

My dad walks in the back door followed by Romel. Both their faces are somber, and my heart sinks to my stomach.

"Everything okay?" I ask Romel softly.

He nods his head and kisses my forehead, but his gaze is distracted—lost in thoughts that he doesn't share with me.

"You ready to go?" he asks instead.

I nod and then watch my dad give Kaylee a high five goodbye and Romel a handshake. Romel takes Kaylee out to the car while I say goodbye to my dad.

He hugs me tight and then whispers in my ear, "Be careful with that big heart of yours, sweetheart. Remember what I said before—if he can't give you what you need, then you need to be willing to walk away."

I pull back and look into his worried eyes. "What did he say to you?"

"It's what he didn't say that has me worried. Just be careful. I don't want to see you get hurt, and I'm worried that's exactly what you're setting yourself up for."

He kisses the top of my head and then walks me to the

door. My nerves had mostly evaporated, but now they're swirling viciously in my stomach, joined with something else—a sense of loss even though I haven't actually lost anything.

My dad didn't outright say he doesn't approve of Romel. In fact, I suspect if Romel wasn't dating his daughter, he'd be his biggest fan. As it is, I'm wondering if this dinner was even a good idea or if I should've kept Romel and Kaylee to myself for longer.

But I suppose this night would've happened no matter what, and now I'm left feeling adrift at sea.

The drive home is quiet, both Romel and me clearly lost in our thoughts. We go through Kay's bedtime routine together, both of us focused on Kaylee more than each other. We alternate reading stories to her, and by the third book, she can barely keep her eyes open. We both kiss her forehead and then walk out of the room.

Romel has barely spoken to me since we left my dad's, so I start to head downstairs, planning to stay in the guest-house tonight, even though it's the last place I want to be right now. But before I get too far, he grabs my hand and stops me.

"Stay with me," he says, his voice soft but filled with need.

I nod, grateful he doesn't want to be apart either. Still holding my hand, he leads me to his bedroom, closing and locking the door behind us.

It's still weird sleeping in this room with him. I want to believe it means our relationship is heading in the right direction—I mean, he got rid of the bed he shared with Sydney and put her picture away. That's a huge step. I'm not even sure my dad has done more than replace his mattress in the twenty-two years I've been alive, but that was only because the other one got too old and I finally convinced him to get a better one.

Neither of us speak as he slowly undresses me, his lips kissing my skin as he exposes more of my body. He sheds his clothes quickly and then lifts me up and carries me over to the bed. His kisses are hungry, almost urgent in a way they've never been before.

His hands roam over my body, claiming every inch as if it were uncharted territory. Each touch is electric, sending jolts of desire straight to my core. I can feel the urgency in his fingers, the need that mirrors my own. His mouth finds mine again, kissing me deeply, his tongue exploring, dancing with mine in a primal rhythm.

Romel pushes me gently onto the bed, his body covering mine. The weight of him is comforting and grounds me in the moment. His lips trail down my neck, nipping and suck-ing, marking me as his. I can feel his cock, hard and insis-tent, pressing against my thigh, and I reach down, wrapping my hand around his length, stroking him slowly. He groans into my neck, his hips thrusting into my touch.

"Meredith," he whispers, my name a prayer on his lips, but there's something else in his tone that makes my breath catch and fear slither through my veins.

He grabs a condom and sheaths his cock quickly before I pull him toward me and guide him between my legs to where I need him most. Romel looks into my eyes, a storm of emotions swirling in his gaze. Guilt, desire, need, fear—it's all there, raw and exposed. But he doesn't hesitate as he thrusts into me, filling me completely. I gasp, my back arching off the bed as pleasure rips through me.

His movements are urgent, almost desperate. Each thrust is a claim, a plea, an apology. I meet him stroke for stroke, my hips rising to meet his on every thrust. Our bodies are slick with sweat as they slide against each other in a way that feels almost animalistic.

He leans down, capturing my nipple in his mouth, sucking hard. I cry out, my hands grabbing his head and holding him to me. He moves to the other breast, lavishing it with the same attention while he continues to pump into me with abandon. My body is on fire, every nerve ending alight with sensation.

His hand snakes down between us, finding my clit, and he immediately rubs circles around the sensitive bud, his touch firm and sure. Pleasure coils in my belly, tightening with each stroke of his fingers and every thrust of his cock.

"Come for me, Meredith," he growls, his voice low and rough. "I need to feel you come."

His words push me over the edge. My orgasm crashes over me, my body convulsing around his cock as my nails dig into his shoulders, holding on to him for dear life. He buries his face in my neck, his body tensing as he finds his own release, my name a whispered chant on his lips.

We lie there, panting, our bodies still entwined. I can feel his heart racing against my chest, his breath hot on my neck. But as our breathing slows and our bodies cool, I can feel the shift in the air. He pulls back, looking down at me, and the guilt that always lingers just beneath the surface begins to creep back into his eyes.

He pulls me into his arms so my back is to his front and kisses the side of my neck. "Good night, Mere."

"Good night," I whisper.

But I don't fall asleep, even long after I feel his body go slack with sleep. Thoughts plague me for hours as I keep hearing my dad's words from earlier and then seeing the guilt creep back into Romel's eyes after we had sex tonight.

Is my dad right? Should I accept that Romel may not ever be able to give me what I need and let him go?

No matter what, it's too late for me to get out of this with my heart intact. And maybe that's what I'm afraid of most of all—that no matter what, I'm going to end up with a broken heart.

FORTY-FIVE

Romel

Kaylee's birthday always brings up a slew of mixed feelings. This year is no different, and I feel myself falling into the same funk I always do. Because of an away game, we don't get to celebrate Kaylee's birthday until a few days later which puts the party closer to the anniversary of Sydney's death. The combo of that anniversary and the constant thoughts about what Meredith's dad said to me has caused me to be in a weird headspace this last week, and I think Meredith can feel it.

But no matter how hard I try to stop feeling like I'm being dragged underwater as the anniversary of losing Sydney creeps closer, I can't stop it.

The day of Kaylee's party arrives, and everyone comes over to celebrate. Meredith and Larissa work together to put together a huge ocean-themed party since Kaylee is still obsessed with fish. Dom, Gabe, Ty, and their wives all come to celebrate my daughter. They're used to the melancholy that hits me this time of year, but for Meredith, this is something new.

I put on my happiest face for Kay's party, but I'm going

through the motions. Everything feels like it's happening through a tunnel, or to someone else—like an out-of-body experience.

Ty slaps me on the back. "Let's head outside for some air."

It's only fifty degrees outside, but I don't argue. I follow him to the backyard and find Gabe and Dom waiting. Tall heaters have been set up on the perimeter to keep the patio warm, although the women and grandparents are still inside with Kaylee.

I take a large pull of air into my lungs, but it does nothing to settle the turmoil in my soul.

"You wanna talk about it?" Gabe asks.

I shrug. I don't miss the glances they share with each other.

"How're things going with Meredith?" Ty asks.

I rub my palm down my face. "I don't know."

Dom frowns. "What do you mean you don't know? She's great."

My jaw clenches and my chest aches. It's weird to feel so hollow and yet still hurt.

I drop down onto one of the patio chairs and hang my head in my hands. "I don't know if I'm good for her."

They all follow my lead and take seats around me. "Why would you think that? You're one of the best guys we know," Ty says.

I drop my hands and let them see all the anguish inside me. "Am I? I've been in a relationship with her for a while now and I can't...I don't know if I can...fuck," I swear, my head a jumbled mess. Her dad's words whisper through my conscience. "She deserves a man who will love her with his whole heart."

"And you don't think you can give her that?" Gabe asks, his voice soft.

I almost wish they'd yell at me or tell me what to do. The thought of letting Mere go feels like someone is repeatedly stabbing me in the heart, but is it really fair to hold on to her when I don't know if I can give her what she deserves?

Before I can answer his question—not that I even know how I'll answer it—Ty says, "Maybe this week isn't the best time to be making big decisions. What with the anniversary tomorrow."

Another stab to the heart.

"Do you want us to come with you?"

I shake my head. They offer every year, and every year I turn them down. Going to Sydney's grave has become a tradition, but it's one I do alone.

"Is Larissa watching Kay?" Dom asks.

"Yeah, they're taking her home with them tonight after the party."

They always do. They visit Sydney more often than I do, so they take Kaylee off my hands so I can have that day with Sydney's memory. I don't know what it says about me that I can't visit her grave more than once a year. Even that one time emotionally wrecks me for days. I learned early on if I was going to be able to function and be the dad Kay needed, I could only see Sydney on the anniversary of her death. Any more and I'd end up in the grave right beside her.

The guys stay outside with me for a little longer, giving me the time I need to pull myself together enough for the rest of Kay's party. We should've thrown her party earlier, before her birthday instead of after. I know better by now that I'm always a wreck the closer we get to the anniversary of Syd's death.

When we go back inside, I paste a smile on my face and once again go through the motions. Worry fills Meredith's gaze whenever she looks at me, but the more I stare at her, the guiltier I feel.

She deserves a man who isn't a fucking mess over another woman. That's not fair to her at all.

She kisses Kaylee goodbye and then it's my turn. I hug her tight. "Have fun with Grammy and Papa, okay, sweet girl?"

"Okay. I love you, Daddy."

My eyes burn with the threat of tears, but I hold myself together. Hearing my daughter tell me she loves me will always be one of my favorite things in the world.

"I love you too, baby girl."

Jimmy pats me on the back and squeezes my arm, a knowing pain in his eyes. This week is always hard for him too. He walks around to get in the driver's side while Larissa gives me a tight hug.

"Call us if you need anything tomorrow, okay? We'll keep Kay as long as you need us to," she says low enough so only I can hear. She glances at Meredith, then gives me a concerned look. "Maybe you shouldn't go alone tomorrow. Maybe it's time to take someone with you."

She means Meredith.

I shake my head. No, tomorrow is my time alone with Sydney. I don't need anyone else there to witness me breaking down. Larissa frowns at me, but she knows better than to question me.

As they drive off, Meredith sidles up next to me, slipping her hand in mine. It feels foreign to have someone hold my hand right now.

"I'm tired," I say, dropping a kiss to her head, but it lacks the emotional connection I'm used to giving her. Everything feels forced tonight. I know I should explain it to her, but I can't find the words or the energy.

FORTY-SIX

Meredith

Romel was off all day yesterday, and when I woke up this morning, he seemed completely unlike himself. I know what today is—Larissa warned me, and I'm grateful she did.

I wish he'd talk to me. Truthfully, he's been more distant ever since the dinner with my dad last week, but this is on another level.

I'm worried about him.

He grabs his keys and murmurs that he'll be back later. I nibble my lip, hesitating for only a second before I decide on a course of action. Without second-guessing myself, I grab my keys, get in my car, and follow him to the cemetery. I don't really need to follow him since Larissa told me all about his typical routine—every year on the day Sydney died, he goes to the cemetery alone and then comes home. Larissa suspects that he usually gets shit-faced once he's home, but they leave him alone until he calls or comes to get Kaylee, and by then he's pulled himself together.

I can't imagine going through your grief alone like that. Maybe that's why I follow him, because I want him to lean on me and know he's not alone.

Or maybe it's because I want to see for myself if there's a place for me in his heart, or if it's buried with Sydney.

I watch through my windshield as he walks sullenly across the lawn to a spot near a large oak tree. He stands there for a moment, his shoulders hunched, and then he drops to his knees, his head in his hands and his back shaking.

Tears fill my eyes and I can't stand the distance from him anymore. I rush out of the car and to his side, dropping to my knees next to him and wrapping my arms around his back. He leans against me for only a minute before he rears back, and the devastating loss in his eyes clears and turns into confusion and anger.

"Meredith? What are you doing here?" He looks around before his accusatory gaze lands back on me. "You don't belong here."

I'd opened my mouth to tell him I was here for him, but any words I had die in my throat when I register what he said.

You don't belong here.

Another tear slides down my cheeks, and it finally hits me that this is it. He either lets me in or he lets me go, but it's not fair to either of us to stay in the in-between anymore.

"You can love us both, Romel. You know that, right? I don't need you to act like Sydney never existed. That wouldn't be real. She did exist and she made you the man you are and literally created Kaylee. I'm so thankful for who she was, and I know there's room in your heart for both of us."

More tears slide down my cheeks as my defenses crumble. This is it. My Hail Mary pass for his heart. If he can't give me what I need, then I have to take my dad's advice and walk away.

"I don't care about being the woman who came after the love of your life," I say, laying it all out there. "Maybe I should, but I don't. All I know is I love you more than I've ever loved anyone."

His mouth parts in surprise as I finally say the words that have been dying to come out for weeks. His gaze darts between my eyes and his brow furrows slightly, but he doesn't speak, so I barrel on. "I want you and Kaylee to be mine. I want to stand by your side and be your strength when you miss her. I want you to let me in, all the way in. I want you to love me."

Pain fills his eyes, and the truth I was too in denial to see shines in his gaze.

My voice is barely a whisper when I speak. "But you won't let yourself love me, will you? Because it would be a slight to Sydney's memory?"

His voice is barely a croak when he speaks. "I can picture a future with you—"

"But can you *love* me? Because what's the point of a future together if you'll never let yourself love me? And that's the real root of the problem, Romel. You *could* love me, but you won't because you don't know how to love two women at once. I'm not asking you to love me the way you loved Sydney. She was your first love, the woman who gave you an incredible daughter. She will always be those things to you, Romel, and I'd expect no less. But I need to know if there's room in your heart for *me*? Can you love me?"

He stares at me, but no words come out of his mouth. The longer we stare at each other in silence, the more I know what I need to do, even though it's the last thing I ever wanted. It's not fair to do this to him today, but I can't keep pretending.

My heart shatters in my chest as I lose any semblance of holding myself together and tears stream down my face. "I quit," I whisper.

I quit accepting less than I deserve. I quit being a stand-in mom for Kaylee when I want to *be* her mom. I quit trying because he's made it clear I'm the only one fighting for us.

Still, he doesn't say anything. He stares at me like he's frozen. And then his gaze slides to the grave marker, and my heart shrivels in my chest. I was always fighting a losing battle, wasn't I? I never stood a chance.

I was never going to be the love of his life.

Because he already had it.

A sob bubbles up my throat, and I know I'm seconds away from completely falling apart. "Goodbye, Romel," I choke out as I push myself to standing and walk back to my car.

He doesn't follow me.

I drive straight to my dad's, brushing away the tears I can't keep inside the entire drive. When I walk into the house, my dad is sitting in his favorite chair, sports high-lights playing on the TV. As soon as he sees my face, he stands and lets me run into his arms, holding me tight as I finally let myself feel it all—the pain, the heartbreak, the loss.

"I'm so sorry, Sweetie."

"I really thought he could do it. I wanted him to so badly."

"I know you did."

I sob in his arms until I have no energy left, and he walks me to my bedroom. It's just as I left it, and that only makes everything worse. I feel like I'm going backward instead of forward.

Maybe I should've gone straight to PT school instead of taking a year off. Maybe I never would've gotten my heart broken.

I can't decide if this feeling is worse than the numbness I felt before. But I guess I'll have plenty of time to figure it out.

I wake up the next morning, my eyes swollen and dry from all the crying I did last night. I roll over in the bed and stare at the pictures I've hung up on my wall over the years—of my dad and me, friends, pets, art prints I bought because they made me happy. All things that used to be important to me at one point in my life.

There are two people not pictured on that wall who have come to mean more to me than nearly anyone else. But as I stare at the pictures—my chest aching so much it hurts to breathe—I start to accept that like many of those friends I don't talk to anymore, maybe Romel and Kaylee were meant to only be part of my life for a short amount of time.

Yet they've left a lasting impact that I know I'll carry with me for the rest of my life.

There's a knock on my door, and I hate that I immediately wonder if Romel came after me.

"Sweetie? I made your favorite blueberry pancakes with lemon whipped cream."

I bury my face in my pillow and let myself feel the disappointment for a count to ten and then I take a large breath and push myself up. "I'll be right out," I tell my dad, wincing at how rough my voice sounds.

I wait until I hear him walk back toward the kitchen and then I open the door and walk across the hall to the bathroom. I splash my face with water, hoping the cold will help the swelling on my eyelids. I take a breath and then face my reflection in the mirror.

My eyes are dull and red-rimmed, my eyelids so puffy it looks like I got stung by a bee. My skin is paler than normal, my cheeks completely missing their usual rosy glow. My hair is in a messy knot on the top of my head, and I don't have the energy to make myself look more presentable.

When I go out to the kitchen, there's fresh coffee with my favorite creamer on the table next to a pile of my favorite blueberry pancakes. He used to make them for every birthday and holiday. When I was twelve and heartbroken that a boy I liked teased me and called me stupid for thinking he could ever like me, he started making them to cheer me up. He sets down a bowl of whipped cream and the maple syrup, then turns to go back to the counter for the extra berry compote he always makes. I grab his hand and stop him.

"Thank you, Dad." I hope he can see the sincerity in my eyes. I don't know what I'd do without him.

He drops a kiss to my forehead. "It kills me to see you hurting, Sweetie."

"But pain reminds us that we're alive, right?" He used to say that to me when I'd fall and scrape my knee. I don't think he ever imagined I'd turn it around on him for this type of situation.

But I've also never had my heart broken as badly as it's been by Romel, and I need the reminder that this pain will allow me to appreciate the joy I'll feel in the future.

He grabs the berries and then joins me at the table. For a while we eat in silence. When my plate is half cleared, I set down my fork and pick up my coffee mug. "I'm going to look into grad schools."

His eyebrows shoot up. "For physical therapy?"

I nod. "Yeah, and I think I might look to see if there are any programs I could start right away instead of waiting until next fall. Spring semester for most people starts end of January."

He watches me closely. "If you're sure, but you also don't have to rush into anything. If you need more time off, you can still stay here."

I cover his hand. "Thanks. I really do appreciate that, but I don't want to get stuck wallowing. Maybe this is what I needed to push myself to take the next step. I've been thinking about it for a while anyway. I've already been looking at schools for a fall start, but now I'll just move that timeline up."

"Whatever you want to do, you know I'll support you."

I feel a little lighter as I finish my breakfast and head back to my room to research what I'm going to do for the rest of my life. At some point, I need to go back to Romel's house to get my stuff out of the guesthouse, but I'd rather wait until his next away game, so I know he won't be home.

Three days later, I get an unexpected phone call from one of my favorite professors I emailed about a recommendation. "Hi, Dr. Hawes."

"Hello, Meredith. I was so happy to get your email and hear you're going to pursue physical therapy. I reached out to a friend of mine who runs the PT program at her university in Boston. I know you said you wanted to stay in California, but she said she's willing to make some room for you to start in January as a favor to me. She said you'd likely need to take some classes in the summer, maybe two summers, but you could definitely get caught up enough to graduate with everyone else in your class."

I sit down heavily on my bed. Boston. Could I move that far? I've never wanted to leave California or be that far away from my dad, but maybe it would be good for me to spread my wings. I could always move back here after grad school.

While I don't love the idea of Boston—especially in the winter—I do need a change.

"One more thing," Dr. Hawes says, pulling me from my thoughts. "She was wondering if you could come out for an interview on Friday."

"*This* Friday? As in, three days from now?"

"Yeah." I can practically hear her wince through the phone. "I know it's short notice—"

"No, I can do it. I'll be there."

I write down all the details and then go out and tell my dad. "Is this crazy?"

He smiles. "It's an adventure. You're going to be amazing."

I hope he's right.

FORTY-SEVEN

Romel

Pulling up to her dad's house, only one thought keeps repeating itself. *I hope I'm not too late.*

I've had a lot of tough conversations over the last week, and faced a lot of self-reflection. I'm not proud that it took Meredith leaving for me to finally face how I'd let my grief skew my perspective about loving again in the future.

It was ultimately Sydney herself who set me free.

The day after Meredith left, I spent the day locked in my room, finally emptying out Sydney's closet. Each item of clothing I put into a box felt like a stab in my gut. Some brought back memories of parties we went to, dresses she wore on nights out, her favorite pair of jeans that had a doodle of a flower she did during a lecture once when she was bored.

I was a mess, but I kept going instead of continuing to put it off like I had been since she died. It was when I got to her accessory drawer that I found a letter with my name on it.

I sat on the floor, my back to the rest of the drawers, and

stared at my name in her handwriting. It had been so long since I'd seen her delicate scrawl, but it brought back so many memories. She used to write me little notes before all my games in college.

Why hadn't she told me this was here waiting for me? How long would it have stayed there if I hadn't met Meredith and felt the need to finally put Sydney to rest?

With shaking hands, I slid my thumb under the sealed envelope and then pulled out the cream paper. The words blurred together several times as I read her note—and then read it again. It took a third readthrough before they penetrated the thick fog of my grief.

And all at once, the full weight of what I'd lost with Meredith hit me full force.

I spent the rest of the week making a plan, talking to my friends, and scheduling my first appointment with a therapist—because if I'm going to be my best self for Meredith, I need to do the work.

Now I'm here at Meredith's dad's house to put my plan into action.

I walk down the path to his front door and knock, my nerves a mess because I have no idea how this is going to go, and I'm not a guy who likes conflict.

The door swings open and Rob stands there, his full body blocking the door and his face in a scowl. I deserve that.

"Is Meredith here?"

"No."

Well, shit.

"Do you know when she'll be back?"

"Not for a while."

"Listen, I know you have no reason to like me after I

broke her heart, but I'm here to fight for her. I messed up. I know I did, but I'm here to make it right."

His eyes narrow, but at least he hasn't shut the door in my face. We stare at each other for longer than feels comfortable, but I'm not leaving until I have no other choice. I know her dad means the world to her. If I can get him to give me another shot, then it means I have a chance with Meredith.

His jaw wiggles back and forth like he's chewing on words he wants to say, but instead of saying anything, he steps back and gestures with a sweep of his hand for me to come inside. I don't hesitate.

The living room is just like it was the night I was here with Meredith, and I take a seat on the couch while he sits in his lounge chair across from me. The TV is on ESPN, but it's muted.

On the mantel above the fireplace on the opposite side of the room are several framed pictures, most of Rob and Meredith at various stages of her life, but there are also a few with a woman who has similar features as Meredith, except with brown hair.

"She was the most beautiful woman I'd ever laid eyes on," Rob says, pulling my attention back to him. When I glance over, he's staring at the mantel too. When he looks at me again, his gaze is curious. "I was never able to feel that way about anyone else. Not even close. I tried dating when Meredith was in junior high and she started going to sleepovers with her friends. I gave up pretty quickly. It's rough out there."

"I wouldn't know. I never even looked at another woman until Meredith came into my life." It's true. No one ever caught even the slightest bit of my attention until Meredith.

His expression gets thoughtful. "What is it about Meredith that made you pay attention?"

I've thought a lot about this over the past week. "It was the way she loved my daughter. She didn't just watch Kaylee and then check out when I was home. She was actively engaged with her and worried about her at all times. She cared about her well-being in a way that went above what I expected from someone who was doing it as a job." A smile—the first one I've had all week—lifts the corner of my lips. "She also wasn't afraid to call me out. I wasn't used to that. Most people in my life have been pretty delicate with me since Sydney died. Meredith wasn't."

Rob smiles to himself. "She's always been like that. I'll never forget when she was four years old, she came up to me and said, 'Daddy, you need to smile more.' I hadn't even realized I didn't smile that often, but she'd noticed and didn't hesitate to call me out. I figured that was just the brutal truth of kids, but she didn't really grow out of it." His smile drops. "Except for in the last year of college. She was different then. Withdrawn in a way I've never seen her." His brown gaze pierces me. "Until she started working for you. Your daughter brought the light back into her eyes, and then you brought the fire back to her spirit."

We both grow somber as the unsaid truth settles between us. I may have done that, but then I also hurt her because I couldn't give her what she needed when she needed it. It's a mistake I hope she'll let me fix and one I don't plan to make ever again.

"Do you love her?" he asks me.

"You aren't exactly the person who should be hearing this first, but I suspect you won't let me stay long unless you know the truth. So, yes, I love her, but I've done a poor job of showing it—of even figuring it out. But I do love her, more than I thought I was capable of ever loving anyone."

"Again?" he asks, tacking on a word I might have added if someone had asked me this a month ago.

But something I've thought a lot about this week is how Meredith kept trying to make me understand I could love them both—equally but different. I didn't understand what she meant until this week.

"No. I loved Sydney, but not the same way I love Meredith. I always thought love was like a well full of water, but only enough for one person. I didn't realize that well can be refilled. Maybe it's not the same spring of water, but it's still water, and it can still sustain you and keep you alive. It's different, but not less than. I love Meredith. Full stop. Not more or less than Sydney, but differently. I'm not the same man I was when Sydney was alive. I'm the new version of me that was born because of her loss. And this version of me loves Meredith with everything I've got in me."

I hope he understands what I'm explaining because I need his support if I'm going to get a chance to tell Meredith all of this.

He takes a deep breath and then gets up and walks over to a small hutch in the corner. He pulls out a pen and paper and writes something down, then comes over and hands me the piece of paper with an address on it.

"Meredith is in Boston for a grad school interview. She'll be there for two more days. If you want another chance, don't wait. You and I both know life is too short to sit on the sidelines and not act."

I take the paper, stand, and shake his hand. "Thank you, Rob."

"Don't break her heart again, Romel."

"Never again," I promise. It's one I intend to keep until my very last breath.

And then I rush out the door, my phone to my ear as I call Larissa. I need her to watch Kaylee because I have a flight to catch to Boston.

FORTY-EIGHT

Meredith

It's fucking cold in Boston. It's early December, so I shouldn't have expected any less, but holy smokes it's freezing.

I grab my to-go container from the Chinese restaurant the hotel recommended and then head back to the hotel. If I'm going to move here, I'm going to need to get a much better coat—and gloves, and insulated boots, or whatever people wear in this weather.

My phone rings and I pull it out of my pocket, stopping in my tracks when I see Romel's name flashing on the screen. My chest instantly aches, and my finger hovers over the green accept button before I shake my head and hit decline. I can't talk to him right now, not if I'm going to go through with this interview tomorrow.

I go to shove my phone back in my pocket when it rings again. With exasperation, I look at the screen only to see my dad's calling me this time. What are the odds that he would call me right after Romel does?

Instantly I start to panic and wonder if something happened with Kaylee.

"Hello?" I answer, a tinge of worry in my voice.

"Are you at your hotel?"

"I'm just heading back there now. I was out grabbing dinner. Is everything okay?"

He hesitates before he says, "Yeah, everything's fine."

"Dad," I say, dragging out the word. "Are you sure? Why'd you call?"

"Can't I call my daughter?"

"Yes, but not when you sound like you're up to something."

He huffs a breath. "How far away from the hotel are you? I'll stay on the phone until you get there, just so I know you get there safe."

I smile and shake my head. "Dad, the restaurant was just around the corner. I'm safe, I promise."

"You can never be too careful. You know that."

Growing up in a big city, my dad drilled the importance of being aware of your surroundings at all times. "I know, Dad."

I turn the corner and dash up the hotel steps. "Okay, I'm back at the hotel. I'm gonna go."

He hesitates. "Meredith?"

I slow my steps as I reach the elevator. "Yeah?"

"I love you. Don't be mad at me."

"Mad at you for what?"

"Call me tomorrow after your interview," he says, not answering my question.

"Dad, mad at you for what?"

"Have a good night, Sweetie."

"Dad!"

The line goes silent and I realize he hung up. What the hell was that about?

It doesn't take long to figure out, especially when I get

off the elevator and turn the corner to find Romel leaning against the wall outside my room.

He watches me as I get closer, my steps slowing and my heart racing. "What are you doing here?"

"It's where you are, and I had to tell you something."

I frown. "It couldn't wait until I got back to LA?"

He shakes his head.

Deciding it's better to be mad at him than find it endearing that he traveled all this way for me, I open my door without looking at him again and walk into my hotel room. He's right on my heels as I head to the small desk on the other side of the room and set down my Chinese take-out. Then I remember what day it is.

I spin around to face him. "Wait, don't you have a game tonight?"

"I told my coach I had a family emergency."

"Romel, that's insane. The guys need you."

He steps closer, and I hate that my breath catches the closer he gets to me. "I'm right where I'm supposed to be."

I cross my arms in one last lame attempt to keep myself from caving to this man who's already broken my heart once.

"What do you want to say? Just say it and then you can leave."

He winces and grips the back of his neck—a sign that he's nervous. But then his gaze gets determined, and he closes the distance between us until we're toe to toe and I'm looking up into those deep brown eyes that I so easily—and stupidly—fell in love with.

"I was a shell of a man before I met you. I thought I'd put myself together enough that I was convinced I was whole, but I wasn't. I was lying to myself. Turns out I've done quite a bit of that over the last several years. And then you came in and brought all your light and liveliness with you. I thought romantic love could only feel one way, and I couldn't wrap my head around what you were trying to tell me that it could be different. That I could love you completely and it wouldn't mean loving Sydney any less."

He cups my face, his thumb brushing away a tear I hadn't even realized was there. "I'm so sorry it took you leaving for me to see how empty my life—my heart—is without you. I love you, Meredith. I love you so much, this last week hurt to breathe without you. I don't want a life without you in it, and I'll do whatever it takes to prove I can love you the way you deserve—wholly and completely."

My gaze meets his, wanting to believe him with my whole heart, but still hesitant after getting my heart broken by him so recently. "I want to believe you," I say, my voice hoarse from the tears threatening to fall in abundance.

"Then believe me," he whispers back desperately, resting his forehead on mine.

"Romel..."

"I love you, Mere. I love you, and I'm sorry it took me so long to say the words, to understand the true depth of my feelings for you, but I promise it's real. *I love you.*"

I don't think I'll get used to him saying it so freely. "And Sydney?"

I don't want him to think I'm asking him to stop loving her. I know that's not how love works.

He pulls back just enough to stare down at me. "I love her too, but it's different."

My heart feels like it expands in my chest, filled with a dangerous hope.

He goes on. "I love you with everything I am *now*. All the lessons and pain and loss I've experienced created a different version of me when I was still holding on to the idea of the old one—the man I was when Sydney was alive. But I'm not that man. That version of me will always love Sydney. But this version of me can finally let her go enough to know I can love someone else—*you*. It's only you, Meredith. I don't want anyone else. I'm not doing this because I'm lonely. I'm doing this because you're the other half of my soul, and I don't want to live any more days without you."

Tears stream down my face relentlessly as I give in because there's nothing I want more than his love.

"I love you too," I cry and then he seals his lips over mine, and everything in my world seems to right itself with his kiss.

FORTY-NINE

Romel

This kiss is a claiming, a promise that I will never let her down like I did before. I will love her as hard and as long as I can.

Wrapping one hand around her back, I use the other to lift up her leg and carry her to the bed. I don't dare break the kiss as I lay her down, desperate to feel her mouth as she submits to me.

Her hands wrap around my neck, holding me close as I plunge my tongue into her mouth and grind my aching, jean-covered cock against her.

"Need to feel you," she pants.

I sit up and take off my jacket and pull off my shirt in record time. Her hungry eyes trace down my six pack, followed by her fingers. She leans forward and traces a reverse path with her tongue that has my eyes closing and my head tipping back.

Her hands go to the button on my jeans as she keeps peppering kisses along my abs. Every so often, her tongue darts out, and the sensation is making my mind a mess of desire.

I laugh at the visual of her frantically trying to get my pants undone while she's still wearing her big, bulky coat. She stops kissing and looks up at me and then at herself. A bright smile washes over her face and makes my chest tighten with love. How could I have been so blind to not understand what was right in front of me?

"Oops, should probably take off the winter jacket," she giggles.

"Let me," I say, my smile fading as I strip her out of her jacket and then her sweater until she's left in only her bra and pants. I lean down to kiss her as I unhook her bra and slide the straps down her toned arms. I remove her boots and socks and then slowly—teasingly—I pull off her jeans and her underwear.

Her eyes are molten by the time she's bared before me, her naked body absolute perfection. I kiss her hip, then that triangle of hair I've grown so fond of before finally kissing her pussy. I get down on my knees and use my fingers to spread her open, loving how wet she is already for me.

"This pussy is mine," I demand.

She rubs her hand over my head. "Only yours." I love how thick her voice is with desire.

I love everything about this woman, but most of all I love that she's mine. That I didn't mess it up.

I rub my fingers up and down her opening, spreading her juices around and getting my fingers nice and slick before I gently push two of them inside her. She sucks in a sharp breath, her hand tightening on my head, but I don't stop. I know what she likes, what she needs to get off.

I wrap my lips around her plump clit and suck, flicking it with my tongue as I pump my fingers inside her. Her back arches off the bed as she lets out a cry and tries to tighten her legs around my head. But I'm not having any of that, not until she comes and her taste floods my mouth.

"God, Romel, I'm s-so close."

I curl my fingers, rubbing her G-spot as I continue sucking and licking her clit. Like a bomb, she detonates, her pussy tightening on my fingers, squeezing them so tight. My other hand comes up and gently pinches one of her nipples, knowing it'll extend her pleasure.

As the last of her orgasm fades, she sags back on the bed, and I take the opportunity to pull the condoms I brought from my jeans pocket and then remove my jeans and boxer briefs, kicking them off to the side.

I stand over her, my cock hard and ready, as Meredith's eyes drink me in. Her lips are parted, chest heaving with anticipation. I tear open the condom wrapper and roll it onto my length, my gaze locked on to hers. Her eyes are a storm of desire and love, a mix that has my heart pounding.

"You're mine." I lean down, bracing myself over her, our breaths mingling. "You're mine, Meredith," I growl, saying it again as I kneel on the bed and spread her legs wider. She nods, her breath hitching as I position myself at her entrance. I need her to know, because I'm never letting her go again. A week apart already felt like an eternity, and I never want to experience anything like that again.

I rub my tip against her wetness, teasing her, making her squirm.

"Say it," I demand, my voice barely recognizable. I want her to do more than nod. I need to know she's as desperate for me as I am for her.

"I'm yours, Romel," she breathes, her hands reaching for my hips, trying to pull me into her body.

I lean down, capturing her mouth in a fierce kiss as I thrust into her, burying myself to the hilt. She gasps into my mouth, her nails digging into my skin. I start to move, slow and deep, each stroke igniting a fire within us. Her hips rise to meet mine, our bodies syncing together just like they have every time we've had sex.

"You feel so fucking good," I murmur against her neck, my pace quickening. Her response is a moan, her head tilting back to give me better access. I kiss, suck, and bite her neck, my hands roaming her body, touching every inch of her like it's sacred ground.

"Harder, Romel," she pants, her legs wrapping around my waist, urging me deeper. I oblige, my hips moving faster, my cock filling her completely. The room fills with the sound of our bodies coming together, our ragged breaths, and her soft moans.

I can feel her tightening around me, her orgasm close. I reach between us, my fingers finding her clit. I rub it in time with my thrusts, her moans growing louder, her body tensing.

"Come for me, Meredith," I command, my voice hoarse. "Let me feel you come all over my cock."

And she does. Her body convulses, her pussy clenching me so tight I see stars. I keep thrusting, riding out her orgasm, until I can't hold back any longer. My own release crashes through me, a wave of pleasure so intense it steals my breath. I groan, my body shuddering as I spill into her, our bodies slick with sweat and trembling with aftershocks.

I collapse on top of her, my heart pounding against hers. But nothing has ever felt better than having her back in my arms where she belongs. I hold on to her for a moment longer before I roll off her, so I can dispose of the condom.

When I get back in bed, I pull her into my arms. Her skin is still flushed, her eyes glazed with satisfaction. She looks at me, a soft smile playing on her lips. But before she can say anything, I cut her off with a gentle kiss.

"I love you, Meredith," I whisper against her lips

She melts against me, her body fitting perfectly with mine. "I love you too, Romel."

We lie there, our limbs tangled and my fingers playing with her long, soft hair. "So, Boston?"

Her fingers trace invisible shapes on my chest. "One of my UCLA professors had a connection here, and they could get me in next semester if I do well in the interview tomorrow."

I kiss her forehead. "I'll be done with the season in early January unless we make it to the playoffs, so Kay and I could move here with you as soon as the season is up."

She twists her head so she can see me better, her pink lips parted in surprise. "You would move here?"

"Haven't you been paying attention? I'm going wherever you are. If you want to do grad school here in Boston, then Kay and I will be here too."

A mix of emotions flits across her face, but the most obvious is relief. I kiss her forehead. "I will follow you anywhere, Meredith."

"I love you," she whispers.

A smile fills my face as she relaxes against me and sleep finally pulls us under.

FIFTY

Meredith

Even though I interviewed well and got accepted into the Boston program, I decided to wait until the fall and go to a school in LA. I am not cut out for the cold Boston weather, and I never wanted to move that far away in the first place. Boston seemed ideal at first, but only because I was running away from my pain and heartache.

When Romel and I returned to LA, he made it clear things were going to be different. I believed him, but he proved it to me even more when he moved me into his room. He even brought up the idea of moving to a new house, but considering we hadn't even talked about the details of the future at that point, I thought buying a house together seemed a little too extreme for where we were in our relationship.

Besides, I didn't mind sharing the space Sydney once held. Her family was now mine and I felt a kinship with her.

It's been two months since we returned from Boston, and life is better than I ever could've expected. The Wolves didn't end up going to the playoffs, but it was still a decent season. As planned, Romel announced his retirement once the season was over. It was received how we all expected, with fans mourning the end of the Fierce Four, but sharing their love for Romel and best wishes for his future.

We've been getting into our new groove but trying not to change too much for Kaylee. Romel never told her that I quit in the first place. He told her I needed to help my dad for a while because he didn't have the heart to tell her I was gone. We were both grateful for that because she doesn't need any extra stress at her age.

Today, we're taking Kaylee back to the aquarium for our adventure day. My smile is practically glued to my face as Romel takes my hand while we walk around. He gives me a heated look and a flirty smile that brings out that dang dimple.

"You better stop whatever you're thinking," I whisper sharply.

He laughs.

"There are kids around," I hiss, but I can't stop my own smile from lifting my cheeks.

He pulls me into his arms while Kaylee has her face on the glass staring at the shark swimming by.

"You bring out the naughty in me, apparently," he says against my ear before nipping it.

"You're terrible." But my smile gives away how not terrible I find him. In fact, neither of us can stop smiling at each other.

Kaylee glances at us, and her little face lights up. "Is it time, Daddy?"

He chuckles as I arch a brow in question. Then he squats down to his daughter. "Do you think this is a good time?"

She looks around the space. There's a handful of people mingling around, but overall it's not very crowded today. She looks at her dad and nods.

Then he puts one knee on the ground and pulls a robin's egg blue box out of his pocket. My smile falls as shock fills my face.

"Oh my God," I whisper.

Romel looks up at me with so much love in his eyes, my heart feels like it could burst. "Meredith, you brought me back to life—both of us," he says, wrapping an arm around Kaylee while still holding out the ring with his other hand. "We would be honored if you'd officially become a member of our family. Will you marry me?"

Tears blur my eyes, and I nod my head like a damn lunatic. "Yes. Yes, yes, yes."

His smile is radiant as Kaylee starts jumping up and down excitedly. He takes the beautiful oval ring that's got to be at least three carats out of the box and slides it on my left ring finger. He wraps his hand around mine and brings it to his lips, kissing the ring as his dark gaze holds mine.

Kaylee grabs my other hand, pulling my attention from her dad—the man who's captured my heart. She pulls again, which is usually what she does when she wants to tell me a secret, so I squat down to be on her level. Romel does the same and takes the opportunity to wrap his arm around my back.

"What is it, KayBear?"

She almost looks bashful as she leans in to whisper— which isn't really whispering when you're four. "I call you Mommy now?"

When she pulls back so she can see my face, there's the faintest fear of rejection shining in her eyes. I wrap my arms around her and hug her tight as Romel says, "Yeah, baby girl. This is your mommy."

I twist my head to the side to catch the love in his eyes, and I hope he can see the same emotion in mine. He gave me everything I could ever want, and I love these two more than any words could express.

Romel

EPILOGUE

"Rome, Cross, get your shoes on! It's time to go!" Meredith shouts at our boys as she tosses her phone into her purse.

"Do you have everything you need for your sleepover, KayBear?" she asks Kaylee who's zipping up her backpack.

"Yep. All set, Mom."

It never gets old hearing her call Meredith her mom. Kaylee doesn't remember a time before Meredith, and that makes me happy and sad at the same time. She knows all about Sydney. Meredith has always insisted that we have pictures of Sydney available for Kaylee, who looks more and more like Syd every day.

Rome comes racing into the room followed by his little brother, Cross. At eight and six, they've hit that really fun age, but also have moments where they can't stand each other. Kaylee is the overprotective big sister who's always looking out for them and was thrilled when we brought Rome home from the hospital when she was six years old.

I put my hand out. "Woah, woah, slow down. Where are your shoes, Cross?"

"In my room."

"Go get 'em. We gotta go."

Kaylee is sleeping over at her best friend's house tonight after they go to the football game at her high school. Meredith is a wreck about it because she can't wrap her head around the fact Kay is already a freshman in high school. I teased her about it until she told me Kaylee would likely start dating in the next few years, which immediately wiped the smile from my face.

Yeah, no.

Cross runs out of the room, while Rome grabs his jacket. The boys are coming with Meredith and me to the Wolves game tonight. It's no surprise that they're huge football fans. After Meredith finished her degree and got her doctorate in physical therapy, she became a sports physical therapist for the Wolves where I'd joined the coaching staff. Nowadays, I work alongside my old coach Alison Fairbright, and I've helped take the team to three Super Bowls since my retirement as a player.

All in all, life is good. My kids are happy and healthy, and I'm married to the love of my life who never fails to make me smile.

The doorbell rings and Kaylee shouts, "I'll get it."

"No doubt that's Sabrina," Meredith says, walking up to me and kissing my cheek before she follows our daughter to the door.

I overhear her conversation with Sabrina's mom, but focus on getting the boys ready to go. We're already running a few minutes late. It gets infinitely harder to get out of the house on time when you have kids, but boys are a whole new adventure. Kaylee was too easy on me, I quickly found out. Rome and Cross seem to compete on who can be the most challenging on any given day.

Meredith waves as Kaylee gets in the car with Sabrina and her mom and walks back in looking excited but nervous.

"She'll be fine," I tell her for the fourteenth time.

"I know, I know. She's just so grown up. I can't get over it."

I drop a kiss to her head. "I know how you feel."

We look at each other, solidarity passing between us, and then Cross is running into the room with two different shoes on his feet, and the moment's passed.

When we finally get to the stadium, we're miraculously only five minutes late since traffic was light. The boys know the rules from how often they come to games, and tonight, Dom and Alayna are here with their three kids. Their twin boys, Ryder and Zeke, are a year older than Rome. We've dubbed them "The Three Amigos" because they've always been best friends. Their daughter, Talia, is a year younger than Cross, and I think Meredith and Alayna are both hoping they'll get married.

Dom's like me and insists his daughter will never date.

Rome and Cross run over to the first row seats where Dom and Alayna's kids are and all start talking with each other and pointing out their favorite players.

Dom walks over to me on the sidelines. "You know, if we were still playing, they'd say we were their favorites."

I smile. "I'm not so sure about that. Cross asked if I was any good. I told him I had four Super Bowl rings and he said that Singer, the new player we just recruited, has five, like four wasn't good enough."

Dom shakes his head. "Kids these days have no appreciation for how hard we worked to get those wins."

"I know!"

Just like we always said we would, the Fierce Four has stayed well connected, even as we all moved on from football. I was the first to retire, but Gabe followed suit two seasons later when he got a bad neck injury. The doctor told him he'd be risking his life if he kept playing football. He said it was the easiest decision he ever made. Ty kept playing for a few more years, but ended up being traded to another team that he didn't jibe with. He retired after one season there and moved back to LA with us. Dom retired the same year Ty got traded from the Wolves.

Football had been our lives, but once we all had families, our priorities shifted and it wasn't as hard to stop playing as we all had suspected it would be.

Of course, it might also help that we all live next door to each other.

After Meredith and I got engaged, we bought a new house. I insisted. I appreciated that she was okay with living in the house where I made memories with Sydney, but I wasn't comfortable with it any longer. Pictures were enough to hold the memories. I wanted a house where I could make new memories with Meredith. The house next to Gabe was up for sale, so we bought it and moved. When Dom found out, he offered the neighbors on either side an insane amount of money for their house. One took the offer immediately, and now Dom and Alayna live on the other side of Gabe and Danae. When Ty moved back to LA, he pulled a Dom and made a higher offer to our neighbors, who took the deal and ran.

And that's how the Fierce Four took over our neighborhood. Barbecues are a blast and super easy. Even better, our kids are all friends, and we rotate who takes them every so often so each couple gets alone time. It's the best setup I could have ever imagined.

Change isn't always bad—scary, maybe—but closing the chapter on one part of your life doesn't necessarily mean you're closing the book. It just means you move on to something that might be better. And in our case, it is.

"We'll take the kids tonight if you can take ours next week. It's my anniversary with Laney, and I want to take her out on the town for the night and then rechristen all the main spaces in our house."

I chuckle, but understand his sentiment because now that the offer is out there, I have plans to bend my wife over the kitchen table.

"Deal."

He pats me on the shoulder and then walks back to the stands. I focus on the game, but there's always a piece of me that's aware of Meredith. The medical staff stays out of the way, but they're still on the sidelines. It's another thing I get to share with my wife, and it's brought us closer in a lot of ways.

By the time the game is over, all I can think about is taking her home and fucking her in as many places as possible before we pass out. Realistically, I know I'll probably only get to fuck her in one of those places because our stamina isn't what it used to be when it comes to sex, but I'll take it.

Dom and Alayna leave with their brood and our boys, and Meredith and I hang back so we don't all arrive home at the same time. I want the boys to be fully distracted at the Smith house by the time Mere and I get home. She'll never let herself relax enough if she thinks there's a possibility of the boys coming back home to grab something.

The second we walk through the front door, my hands

are all over her. I push her against the closed door, wrap my hand in her hair, and tug her head back before I seal my mouth over hers. Her body melts against mine, and a fierce feeling of possession burns through my veins.

This is my wife. My beautiful, sexy wife, who's built a family with me that I'd only ever dreamed of having.

I unbutton her pants and don't bother pushing them down just yet. Instead, I slide my hand inside her panties until my fingers touch her pussy. She's not quite wet for me yet, but I know how to get her there. It's more work getting her ready for me since we had kids, but it's work I'll put in willingly every day of the week.

I trail kisses down her neck, feeling her pulse quicken under my lips. "You know what I'm going to do to you, Mere?" I murmur, my voice low and husky. Her breath hitches, and she shakes her head slightly, though she knows exactly where this is going.

"I'm going to lay you out on that kitchen table," I growl, nipping at her earlobe. "The one we picked out together. Remember how we christened it when we first moved in?" She nods, a soft moan escaping her lips as I slide my fingers deeper, finding her clit and circling it slowly.

"This time, I'm going to take my time," I continue, feeling her wetness build. "I'm going to taste you, Mere. I want you to get my face nice and wet with your arousal as you come on my tongue." I pull my hand out of her pants and she whimpers at the loss of contact. I smirk, loving how responsive she is.

Taking her hand, I lead her to the kitchen. The table is clear, ready for us. I turn to her, my eyes locked on to hers as I lift her up and set her down on the edge of the table. Her chest rises and falls rapidly, her breaths coming in short gasps. I can see the desire pooling in her eyes, and it fuels my own.

I hook my fingers into the waistband of her pants and panties, pulling them down and off in one smooth motion. She leans back on her elbows, watching me as I kneel before her. I run my hands up her thighs, feeling her tremble under my touch. Her scent is intoxicating, and I can't wait any longer.

I dive in, my tongue finding her clit with unerring precision. I swirl around it, feeling her jolt at the contact.

"Fuck, you taste amazing," I growl against her, the vibrations making her squirm.

I grip her thighs, holding her in place as I feast on her. She's soaking wet now, and I lap it up, savoring every drop.

Her moans fill the kitchen, echoing off the walls as I suck and lick her. I slide two fingers inside her, curling them up to hit that spot that drives her wild. Her hips buck against my face, her body tense with pleasure. I can feel her climax building, her inner walls clenching around my fingers.

"Come for me," I murmur, my breath hot against her. "Let me taste it." I pump my fingers faster, my tongue flicking her clit in quick, firm strokes. She cries out, her body convulsing as she comes hard. I don't let up, riding out her orgasm with her, drawing out every last wave of pleasure.

When she finally stills, I stand up, my cock rock hard and straining against my jeans. Her eyes are glazed, her cheeks flushed, and her lips parted. She looks thoroughly sated and so fucking beautiful.

"Taste yourself, Wife," I say, leaning down to kiss her. She moans into my mouth, her tongue tangling with mine. I can feel her hunger rising again, her body ready for more. I break the kiss, pull her up off the table, then spin her around and bend her over the edge. Her ass is perfect—round and firm—and I can't resist giving it a smack. She yelps, then moans, pushing back against me.

I push my jeans and boxers down and my cock springs free. I rub the head against her entrance, coating myself in her wetness as she pushes back again, eager and impatient.

"You want this cock?" I ask.

I tease her entrance with the tip, just barely pushing in before pulling back out. She whimpers, trying to push herself back onto me, but I hold her hips firmly, controlling the pace.

"Yes," she gasps, her voice hoarse with desire. "Please, Romel. Fuck me."

Her words send a surge of heat through me. I grip her hips tighter and thrust into her, filling her completely in one swift motion. She cries out, her body tensing around me. I groan, the sensation of her tight, wet heat enveloping me almost too much to bear.

"God, you feel incredible, Mere," I growl, pulling out slowly before slamming back into her. She moans, her fingers clutching at the edge of the table. I set a steady rhythm, my hips moving against her ass, our skin slapping together with each thrust.

I lean forward, my body covering hers as I reach around to cup her breasts. I pinch her nipples, rolling them between my fingers, feeling her pussy clench around me in response. She gasps, her back arching to press her breasts farther into my hands.

"Oh fuck, Romel. Don't stop," she cries, her pussy fluttering around my achingly hard cock.

I won't.

I can't.

I straighten up, gripping her hips again as I increase my pace. I can feel my orgasm building, the pleasure coiling tightly in my groin. But I want her to come again first. I want to feel her come undone around me.

I slide one hand around to her front, finding her clit again. I rub it in time with my thrusts, feeling her body tense and her breath hitch. She's close. So close.

"Come on, baby," I pant, my voice ragged. "Come for me again. Let me feel you."

She cries out, her body convulsing as her orgasm hits. Her inner walls clamp down on me, pulsing and drawing out my own release. I groan, my cock throbbing as I spill into her, my body shuddering with the intensity of my climax. I slow my thrusts, riding out the waves of pleasure with her until we're both spent, our bodies slick with sweat and our breaths ragged.

Leaning forward, my chest rests against her back while my cock is still buried deep inside her. I wrap my arms around her, holding her close as we both come down from our high. I can feel her heart pounding in sync with mine, our bodies connected in the most intimate way.

"I love you, Mere," I whisper, my lips brushing against her neck.

"I love you too, Romel," she says, her voice soft and breathy. I smile, pressing a gentle kiss to her shoulder before pulling out of her. She makes a soft sound of loss, and I chuckle, helping her stand up. Pulling out of her is my least favorite part too.

We clean up quickly, our bodies still humming with the afterglow of our lovemaking. As we make our way to the bedroom, I can't help but feel a deep sense of contentment. This is my life. My beautiful, sexy wife, our amazing kids, and a love that grows stronger with each passing day.

I pull Meredith into my arms as we climb into bed, her body fitting perfectly against mine like it always has. She rests her head on my chest, her fingers tracing lazy patterns on my skin. I can feel her breathing even out as she drifts off to sleep, a small smile playing on her lips.

I spent so many years protecting the boundary around my heart after Sydney died, but now I think that was because it was never meant to belong to anyone else besides Meredith. Every day I'm grateful that I figured it out in time —that I didn't lose her.

Because this life we've built together?

It was absolutely worth the risk.

Meredith

BONUS EPILOGUE

I've been staring at the three positive pregnancy tests for twenty minutes, my heart racing with a mix of excitement and nerves. Romel and I have talked about having kids, but it was always in that "someday" kind of way. We've only been married for eight months.

But as I sit here on the edge of the bathtub, I can't stop smiling. We're going to have a baby. Kaylee's going to be a big sister.

I need to find the perfect way to tell him. An idea hits me, and I grab my phone to order what I need.

For the next week, I have to act completely normal, which is harder than I expected. Every time Romel looks at me, I want to blurt out the news.

When the package I've been not-so-patiently waiting for finally arrives, I'm practically giddy with excitement.

After Kay goes to bed, I change into one of Romel's old Wolves practice jerseys that I sometimes sleep in, and grab the gift box.

When I walk downstairs, Romel's on the couch

watching game film. Some things never change, even though he's a coach now instead of a player.

"Hey," I say, getting his attention. "Can you pause that for a minute? I got you something."

He looks up with that smile that still makes my stomach swoop—that slight dimple of his on display. "What's the occasion?"

I don't miss the way his eyes heat as he sees my attire and his gaze scans down my body to my exposed legs. I hand him the box and sit next to him on the couch. "You'll see."

He pulls off the lid and moves aside the tissue paper. His brows furrow slightly as he lifts out the tiny Wolves jersey. When he holds it up, his eyes go wide as he reads the back.

BABY WATSON

#2

It might be our first child together, but Kay will always be first in my heart, so I thought having the number two on the jersey was more appropriate.

"Mere?" His voice cracks with emotion as his gaze drops to my stomach.

I grab his hand and place it over where our baby is growing. "Surprise, Daddy."

The joy that spreads across his face makes tears spring to my eyes. He pulls me into his lap so I'm straddling him and kisses me deeply. When he pulls back, there are tears in his eyes too.

"We're having a baby?"

I nod, unable to speak past the emotion clogging my throat.

"I love you so much," he says, his voice thick. "Both of you," he says, placing his hand over my stomach again.

"I love you too."

Sometimes love feels like an understatement for how much I feel for this man.

Romel cups my face, his thumbs brushing away the tears that escape down my cheeks. His touch is tender, reverent, and I can feel the love pouring out of him. I lean into his touch, my heart pounding with anticipation.

"You're the most incredible thing that's ever happened to me," he murmurs, his voice husky with emotion. "And now, this..." His hand slides down to rest on my stomach again, his eyes filled with wonder. "Thank you, Meredith, for giving me the future I thought I'd never have."

I smile, covering his hand with mine. "Ditto," I whisper.

His eyes darken with desire, and he leans in to capture my mouth in a searing kiss. It's a kiss filled with promise, with passion, and with a hunger that matches my own. I moan into his mouth, my body melting against his.

Romel's hands slide down to my thighs, gripping them firmly as he stands, lifting me with him. I wrap my legs around his waist, my arms around his neck, never breaking the kiss. He carries me upstairs to our bedroom, his mouth never leaving mine.

He lays me down gently on the bed, his body covering mine. I can feel his heart pounding against my chest, his breath hot on my skin. I tug at his shirt, wanting to feel his skin against mine. He breaks the kiss just long enough to pull his shirt off, then helps me out of his jersey.

His eyes roam over my body, taking in every inch of me. I feel beautiful under his gaze—desired and loved beyond measure. He leans down, his lips finding my neck, my collarbone, my breasts. I arch into his touch, a gasp escaping my lips as he takes one nipple into his mouth, his hand cupping the other breast.

Heat builds between my legs as the ache for him grows stronger. I reach for his belt, my fingers fumbling in my haste. He chuckles against my skin, but doesn't stop kissing down my body while I push his pants off. He kicks them away and then spreads my thighs, staring hotly at my pussy, which no doubt glistens with my arousal.

"Fuck, baby. So wet for me," he murmurs before he ducks his head and licks through my pussy, then swirls his talented tongue around my clit. My thighs tremble as he slides two fingers inside me, rubbing against that spot that never fails to make me see stars.

Romel's tongue continues its dance around my clit, his fingers pumping in and out of me with a rhythm that has my hips bucking against his mouth. I grip the sheets, my body tensing as he brings me closer to the edge. His fingers curl inside me and that's all it takes.

"Romel," I gasp, my body trembling as the orgasm rips through me. He doesn't stop, his mouth and fingers drawing out every last wave of pleasure until I'm a panting, shivering mess beneath him.

He finally lifts his head, his lips glistening with my arousal. The sight of him, his eyes dark with desire, sends another jolt of heat through me. He moves up my body, his cock hard and thick against my thigh. I reach down, wrapping my hand around him, marveling at the silkiness of his skin contrasting with the hardness beneath.

He groans, his hips thrusting into my touch. "Meredith," he murmurs, his voice a low growl. "I need to be inside you."

I guide him to my entrance, feeling the broad head of his cock push against me. He captures my mouth in a fierce kiss as he thrusts into me, filling me completely. I moan into his mouth, my legs wrapping around his hips to pull him deeper.

He begins to move, his hips pistoning against mine in a rhythm that has us both gasping. Each thrust is deep and powerful, hitting every sensitive spot inside me. I can feel another orgasm building, the tension coiling in my belly.

Romel breaks the kiss, his breath hot on my neck as he trails kisses down to my shoulder. He bites gently, his teeth grazing my skin as he continues to drive into me. The sensation is overwhelming and the mix of pleasure and pain sends me spiraling.

"You feel so good," he groans, his pace increasing. "You were made to take my cock."

His words send a thrill through me, and I meet his thrusts with my own, our bodies moving in sync. The sound of our flesh slapping together fills the room, mingling with our moans and gasps.

He reaches between us, his fingers finding my clit again and rubbing in tight circles that send me over the edge. I cry out, my body convulsing around him as the orgasm crashes through me.

"Fuck, Meredith," he grunts, his hips moving erratically as he chases his own release. He thrusts deep one last time, his cock pulsing inside me as he comes.

We stay like that for a moment, our bodies still joined, our breaths ragged. He finally rolls off me, pulling me into his arms. I rest my head on his chest, listening to the steady beat of his heart.

He kisses the top of my head, his arms tightening around me. "I love you so much, Mere."

I smile, tracing patterns on his chest with my fingers. "I love you, too."

We lie there in silence, basking in the afterglow of our

lovemaking. The future stretches out before us, filled with love, laughter, and the promise of a new life growing inside me.

I can't wait.

AFTERWORD

I promised myself I wouldn't cry writing this, but I'm already tearing up, so I think I'll probably be sobbing by the time I finish.

Where to begin?

This was the series that started it all. I've had these boys in my head since 2016, and while it's exciting to have all of their stories told, it's also a bit heartbreaking. I've held them close for so long, it's hard to accept that it's really done. This was the series that started my career. You can even see how my writing has developed from book 1 to book 8. It's been such an amazing journey and I feel blessed beyond measure to have found so many incredible readers who've fallen in love with my books.

I hope you'll stick with me for my next series. It's going to be a pucking good time

ABOUT THE AUTHOR

Cadence Keys is a bestselling steamy romance author. When she's not coming up with plots for her books, she's chasing her rambunctious toddlers around or cuddling with her husband. She loves writing heartfelt stories with relatable characters and a guaranteed happily ever after.

Learn more about her and her books on her website: www.cadencekeysauthor.com

facebook.com/cadencekeysauthor

x.com/cadencewrites

instagram.com/cadencekeysauthor

bookbub.com/profile/cadence-keys

goodreads.com/cadencekeysauthor

ALSO BY CADENCE KEYS

LA WOLVES FOOTBALL

In the Grasp

Across the Middle

Down by Contact

Taking the Handoff

LA WOLVES DEFENSE

Scorched Turf (author website exclusive novella)

Defending the Backfield

After the Snap

Closing the Distance

Protecting the Boundary

RAPTUROUS INTENT ROCKSTARS

Noble Intent

Forbidden Intent

Devoted Intent

Promised Intent

BREAKING THE RULES

Only a Kiss

Just for Tonight

About Last Night

CFU HOCKEY

Campus Crush

Campus Rival

MEADOWBROOK, MT

One Weekend in Montana